THE REDROCK QUARANTINE

Novels by Dennis Bowen

THE WATER DIAMONDS
Book 1: International Thriller Series

THE BLACKSTONE PERFECTION
Book 2: International Thriller Series

THE CRYSTAL SEDUCTION
Book 3: International Thriller Series

THE REDROCK QUARANTINE
Book 4: International Thriller Series

THE REDROCK QUARANTINE

Dennis Bowen

The Redrock Quarantine is a work of fiction. Names, characters, places, and incidents are the products of the author's imagination or are used fictitiously. Any resemblance to actual events, locales, or persons, living or dead, is entirely coincidental.

ISBN: 978-0-9960412-5-6

FIRST EDITION

www.DennisBowen.com

www.twitter.com/DBowenThrillers

www.facebook.com/DennisBowenThrillers

Book Interior Design by 52 Novels

ACKNOWLEDGMENTS

I extend my heartfelt thanks once again to the readers of my *International Thriller Series*. I have said previously that readers give writers a gift of immeasurable magnitude. It is just as true today. As with *The Water Diamonds, The Blackstone Perfection*, and *The Crystal Seduction*, those who offered suggestions and encouragement during the writing of *The Redrock Quarantine* deserve my appreciation.

For the fourth time, I wish to express my appreciation to my mentor, editorial consultant, and colleague, Laura Taylor. As in life, each successive endeavor—like writing a series of novels—is built on what came before. Her knowledge, skill, and consistency have helped make this series a source of great pride for me. Any errors or omissions in *The Redrock Quarantine*, I claim as my own.

Once more, I wish to express my gratitude to family, friends, and former colleagues whose presence in my life has made the International Thriller Series possible. Thank you.

—Dennis Bowen

CHAPTER 1

The unseasonably warm day peaked at eight degrees Celsius. Sitting across from each other, the man and woman felt the chill as the sun descended and cast shadows from the ancient fortress across the bay. The woman, who wore a red polka dot top, pulled the lapels of her parka tighter. The man observed. Her butterscotch-toned skin glowed in stark contrast to the pale-complected patrons of the harbor terrace restaurant.

She glanced into her guide book. "The fortress over there on that island is called *Suomenlinna*. The Finns built it to defend against the Russians."

"They may need it."

Onlookers made no effort to conceal their curiosity about the woman. Her appearance accentuated by waist-length, silken black hair set her apart, even among tourists.

"This is a beautiful place. I'm glad you've helped me to experience things like this."

He noticed a fleeting expression of sadness. Neither one of them would ever forget the cost of his insertion into her life. Her father. He reached across the table for her hand.

"Hekka, even after all the memory restorations, I don't remember my parents at all. But I do recall one of the lessons they taught me. Rather than grieve, perhaps we should consider ourselves fortunate to have had such wonderful people in our lives. Even when their presence is more brief than we'd like."

She nodded. "A good thought. I concede that I was most fortunate with respect to my father. But my mother …"

"Helsinki is our starting point. I'll do whatever it takes to help you. Until we find her or discover what happened …"

"You're here with me and for me. I love you, Mr. Crayle."

"I'm yours to the end, Mrs. Crayle."

"If my mother is dead …" Her voice broke. "… I need to know."

"We'll find out. We will solve your mystery as we solved mine."

"Father would have wanted this as much as I must have it." She changed the subject. "I believe Finland to be a good place, and my mother's people and their culture are good." She made a water-ladling motion. "The sauna with the rocks last night diffused our jetlag."

"I'm not sure about the blood-sucking cups. I'm glad we passed on that treatment."

Hekka sampled the Finnish fish stew. "I read about this in my travel guide. They call it *Kalamojakka*, Magus. It's wonderful."

He scooped some into his spoon and tried the mixture. A flock of seabirds taking flight caused him to jump.

"Those people of yours, Mr. Crayle, cost us our Christmas together."

"Lalumière, Pattie, and the rest are not my people. They never will be."

He tossed down a shot of vodka, then glanced at her.

"I'm not sure about this, but here goes." She felt the burn.

Crayle knew he needed to diffuse the serious topic. The alcohol helped.

"About Paris. Didn't you feel that starting Christmas Day atop the Eiffel Tower was special?" He remembered how she'd fought like a seasoned operative high in the Tower. He knew Hekka had been determined to protect him, whatever the cost. She'd sought an end to his demons so they could live in peace.

"It was to die for." She laughed, a rare occurrence.

He followed suit. "I believe we're safe now."

Feeling the effects of the customary vodka shots with every bite of food, she laughed again. "I wanted to see Santa Claus and his reindeer fly by."

He refilled their glasses as she forked a sausage into her mouth. "This is delicious, too."

"It's Rudolph."

She froze. "Reindeer meat?"

"Rudolph is terrific. I've learned enough of your Serrano culture to know that we must thank him for providing our sustenance."

They clinked glasses. "A toast to Rudolph," they chorused.

She pointed across the harbor. "Over there, where all those stalls are with white tops. On the jet, I read that it's called the *Kauppatori*—the shopping square. Take me there, Magus. I want to shop."

So intense was their focus, they didn't notice a group of young men attired in Adidas warm-up suits and approaching along the quay.

As if to alert him, Hekka pointed.

Crayle's head spun. His body tensed. Then, he exhaled. He shook his head. It was different now. He joined her for a final glimpse of the setting sun, a huge orange disk settling into the sea beyond the harbor's breakwater.

Hekka smiled her minimalist smile. "The sun is so bright and warm, it seems it would boil the sea."

The athletes passed by, but the last one, quite tall, pulled up behind Crayle. With the hint of a French accent, he whispered, "Do you remember me?"

Before Crayle could answer, the man slammed a ball onto their table.

Crayle recalled what he'd witnessed Christmas Eve atop France's Eiffel Tower. This ball, covered with a honeycomb material, was no ordinary rugby ball. It was Sylvain Lalumière's five megaton nuclear device. Made in China.

"Before you react, look at your wife's blouse."

Crayle turned his attention to the polka dot fabric. Something looked wrong—out of place. One of the red polka dots moved.

"She's not our target. You are. Come with me now, or …"

Crayle recognized a laser-sight dot from his days as a CIA operative. He knew he could take a bullet for her, but never the other way around.

"Now, Mr. Crayle."

A shocked Hekka Poppi Crayle followed her husband's gaze to the fabric that covered her breast. She knew what the mobile dot portended.

Crayle stood and departed with the tall man. He glanced back at Hekka. The dot vanished.

They approached a van. Crayle felt a pinch in his neck muscle. As cold fluid streaked its way into his heart, the face of the woman who'd seen him through battle after battle—and whom he loved with all of his being—blurred to black.

The unconscious Crayle felt nothing when the other young men tossed him into the van. He didn't hear Hekka scream.

The multitude of tourists and locals, all of whom had expected to experience the relative warmth of a fine mid-spring day in peace, snapped their heads toward the center of the uncharacteristic-for-Finland commotion.

CHAPTER 2

Hekka couldn't believe what had just happened. Her husband kidnapped before her eyes.

And her scream.

Uncharacteristic of her, it silenced the normal hustle and bustle of Helsinki harbor.

Her heart pounding, she struggled to catch her breath.

Someone noticed her distress. Practicing her own deep faith, the nun removed a black over-cloak and produced a widow's hat. She wrapped the distraught Hekka, and fit the hat onto the woman's head.

Hekka leapt to her feet, spinning, ready to defend. She grabbed for the Bowie knife beneath her parka.

An odor from the hat's veil penetrated her lungs. In seconds, she lost consciousness.

Passersby grabbed her as she keeled over.

"She just lost her husband," explained the sympathetic-appearing nun.

A car pulled up nearby. The driver lowered his window.

"Please, help her into the vehicle," instructed Pattie Norbrunn.

The good Samaritans did that, gave good wishes, and departed the scene, whispering in a *what just happened?* fashion.

The nun leaned into the window and French-kissed the driver. "You know where to take her, Jean-Marc. I'll meet you in the German port, Travemünde. It's just east of the border with Denmark. But first, I must check on someone here."

"Her mother?"

"I must verify her location based on my intel. And then I have a very important plane to catch."

"My father instructed me. The mother is backup. Mrs. Crayle protects us from Crayle, should he get loose, et cetera."

The young rogue spy, masquerading as a nun, produced an innocent, dimpled smile. "Your father—my Sylvain—has a very good plan."

"Father was specific with respect to Hekka Crayle. Do not kill her."

"Of course, Jean-Marc. But I do want her husband in the worst way, and that, I'm afraid, requires that she exit soon. Then I will bed him and …"

"My father was correct. You are the Black Widow of the CIA."

"I should be upset over that remark, but I kind of like it. Hmmm. Black Widow."

As the car departed, the nun reached into her burgundy-colored waist sash. She extracted her deadly compact—the one with the hidden blade she'd used to kill her husband. Flipping it open, she checked her makeup.

• • •

The uncommon commotion at the waterfront gained notice by the crowd of shoppers in the *Kauppatori*. Those on the promenade stopped dead in their tracks to gawk as well. Activity in Helsinki harbor was typically relegated to the Oystercatchers, who disturbed the peace with their plover-like piping while either taking flight or landing. White-bottomed, black-topped waterfowl with red legs and beaks seamed to be about all the excitement the staid Finnish capital and its inhabitants could manage.

None had noticed as the first two of the male athletes reached the van ahead of Crayle's captors. They'd extracted two high-end camcorders from the vehicle and had taken positions apart as if to provide angles to a film shoot.

A third man had pulled a banner and placed it on stands. It proclaimed they were of a production company—obviously low budget—filming a scene for an international espionage thriller titled *The Prescient Swastika*. Although the Finns had had enough of the Nazis many decades ago, they began an applause that initiated in staccato fashion near the Crayle's table and spread through the area, and across the water to the *Kauppatori* as a large tossed rock ripples a placid pond.

The onlookers, who'd just been manipulated by the two masterminds of the abduction, resolved the inherent tension in their minds. It was a movie scene rather than the double kidnapping of a pair of America's premier operatives dedicated to tracking and terminating international players who'd already utilized miniaturized nuclear devices. Who'd plotted to overthrow enduring, failing governments in two of the world's foremost countries—one democratic, one communist.

As the scene concluded, one of the photographers took a moment to wave as the other yanked him into the van.

• • •

With all the attention they had generated, it was a struggle to get the two vehicles away from the harbor and through downtown Helsinki. Since the sun had just set, lights flicked on around the city. The kidnap teams managed to move away and onto side streets. Fifteen minutes after the fact, the drivers waved goodbye to each other and split left and right. Separation was mandatory. Their tactics insured that, even if enemies of their cause freed, or by accident killed, either captive, the remaining hostage would still provide great value. Not nearly the value if both survived the transit to their separate destinations, but high value just the same.

Except for Pattie Norbrunn and Jean-Marc Desrochers, the participants had been drawn in to the operation by promises of a very large payday. It added a sweetener to the ideological connection to Illuminé, their ultra-secret society. And the videos they'd just taken as cover for their operation could later be used for extortion, ransom, or other nefarious deployment.

CHAPTER 3

It had taken eight hours for the men in the van to transport their male captive south from Finland. With all contingencies considered by their brilliant planning team, it was no surprise that the operation had gone smoothly. The target was now encapsulated in an environment they felt no one could breach.

The darkened chamber exhibited a red glow. It provided just enough light to make out bodies and faces, but not enough to overcome the dungeon-like feel of the cold, damp environment. The apparent leader broke the silence.

"Now that you have regained consciousness, welcome to *Rotfels*."

The man fastened to the operating table groaned. He tried to twist left, then right against the bright blue, woven leather restraints, but they were too tight. And he too weak.

"I, Otto, am your Aryan host. A gracious host, I might add, as long as you cooperate."

"Why did you grab me and bring me here?" the man, barely out of sedation slurred. "And who is that woman?" He glanced at a thirty-ish blonde who seemed to be sorting medical instruments on a stainless steel table.

"Allow me to introduce your physician, Herr Crayle. Frau Doktor Kraus."

The doctor smiled from the side of her mouth, then removed her wedding ring.

"How obtuse of me. Please forgive me. She's not really Kraus. But it tends to be more convenient, and less prejudicial, than her true surname. You would know of her great-grandfather from your history books. Fräulein Doktor Kaari Mengele."

The weakened captive could not respond. The other two smiled to each other at his heightened state of vulnerability.

"She will see to your every requirement. I have given orders that your biotic pathogen—which she has introduced—neither improve nor worsen while you are under our care. Should you affect an escape … and you cannot … a sensor would have your lungs displace oxygen with fluid. We call it I.P." He witnessed a puzzled look on Crayle's face. "No," he said as he laughed. "Not the Internet Protocol with which you are likely familiar. Induced Pneumonia. It is our latest success."

He nodded toward Mengele. "First, you experience a great deal of discomfort. After a brief period of agony, your brain will expire as dying cells are no longer replaced and, with it, your threat to our cause. I am afraid the body, slowly and painfully, will deplete last. But my explanation is inadequate. Kaari, please demonstrate for our guest."

The woman doctor pressed a button on a swastika-shaped remote control.

In less than three seconds, Crayle wracked with a coughing spasm. Then horrific screeching sounds as he gasped for oxygen.

She pressed another. The coughing and wheezing diminished.

"The *Rotfels*—Redrock—surrounding you is actually a container for the pathogen and is quite bomb and assault proof. The vault door at the far end of this room, likewise. We Germans invented this rock.

It is sprayed, but appears natural. As you can see, its surface is layered with a million rubies—hence the red hue." He let the notion of the tremendous store of value sink in.

The captive surveyed the rock surface some fifteen feet above his head.

"And don't think of air vents as a means of exit. Our design employs a thousand nano-vents, none of which even an ant could escape through."

Finally, Mengele spoke. "You are in a form of isolation, Herr Crayle. A Redrock Quarantine." Her mouth remained open in an *aren't I clever* configuration. "No one can descend to this level without our specific credentials."

"Come, Kaari. Remove most of the fluid from Herr Crayle's lungs, and give our guest a pill to quell his cough. That will allow him some much-needed sleep. You and I shall have a Schnapps. I made it myself."

• • •

After a few hours of working up human experiments and communicating by encrypted phones with others in their plot, the Aryan leader and his doctor assistant heard new moaning from the bed. Their captive was coming around. The Aryan waited a few moments longer to allow for the man to become lucid, then spoke to him slowly.

"We may need to move you, Herr Crayle."

"Why?"

"I am aware that you have been engaged fully with that Man In The Iron Mask fraud. Mitim I believe he is called. So you are likely not current on the state of affairs in my country. The fact on the ground, as you might say, is this. That horrible woman—the chancellor from before—is in charge of Germany once again."

"Merkel?" Crayle whispered.

"I am afraid so. But, no matter. She will be eliminated soon. To answer your primary question, that is why we have brought you here."

The captive's breathing improved by the minute, but it was still a struggle for him to speak. "The role that has been thrust on me, or that I've taken on—I'm not sure—is to stop people of your ilk from dismantling democratic systems and replacing them with autocratic or dictatorial rule. Certainly, I won't help you."

"Oh, I believe Herr Crayle that you shall." He turned to the woman. "Kaari, I believe you have other work requiring your attention." He left the last word hanging as if to communicate in code.

"*Jawohl.* I will be away forthwith, and on site in fifteen minutes. Not more than that. We will keep in touch, *ja*?"

"*Ja, Fräulein Doktor. Aufwiedersehen.*"

CHAPTER 4

Nearly 1,000 miles north of the *Rotfels* cavern, the smells of stone and sod penetrated the man's nostrils, causing him to feel even colder than he was. He sat on an uneven earthen floor, a small rug separating him from the dirt. He pulled his long legs up tight against his chest, as if to make a statement or to keep as warm as possible. A young woman entered the single living space through a cipher-protected, three-foot high, foot-and-a-half wide slate door. Though petite, she had to bend at the waist due to the low passageway to the living space inside.

"Where am I?" The man pronounced the words as if they were an accusation. "Where have you brought me?"

The words echoed in the stone environment. The woman, now on her knees and busy with what appeared to be an iron stove, gave no reply.

"You love me. Or, you profess to love me. Why do you do this?"

Still, the echoes held no answer.

The impatient man could demand answers, but knew this woman well. She operated on her own schedule, and it was fruitless to try to change her habits. Minutes later, she completed her work and turned to him.

"This is a safe house and, thus, you are safe. No one knows you are here. We must keep it that way."

"Turn on the lights. I can't see you."

"I wish I could. There are no lights in this place. There is no electricity."

The man produced a deep sigh. "Please tell me where I am."

"Your new digs have been around awhile. Five thousand years, to be exact."

"I doubt they had safe houses that long ago … I doubt they had spies."

"Yes. It was a simpler life."

For a moment, Lalumière longed for such simplicity.

"Actually, these ten houses were abandoned millennia ago."

Sensing that they might not be as safe as Pattie had inferred, he asked, "What was it that drove them away?"

"We're not sure on that, but it's a great question. But—and you must trust me on this—all records and science point to climate change."

The blending of sanity and insanity in her thoughts insinuated a headache right behind both of his eyes. He dropped the subject and felt the wall next to his CIA-provided Sleep Number bed. "These are flat stones stacked side-by-side, and one atop the other. Though the wind howls above the roof, none of it enters."

"That's right. Each extends a foot or so long and one to two inches thick. They built below ground so the severe Atlantic winds would pass over. Because of what has gone before, you and I must remain *below ground* so that the political winds can pass over. That was a euphemism, in case your English doesn't go that far."

"I know that word."

"Good. And then, when the time is right, we renew our march on Versailles."

He glanced upward. "This roof is not 5,000 years old."

"Actually, it's structural foam covered in turf. The original roofs of Skara Brae, and how they were constructed, have been lost."

"Where is the food? I am hungry."

"I must make a short trip, half-hour max. Stay here, my Mitim."

"I am no longer your Mitim. Or the Mitim of the French people. I am Louis the Nineteenth of France. Your father—the Prince of Monaco—and the new pope have proclaimed it."

"No disrespect, Louis. Back soon."

The diminutive spy crawled through an opening suitable for a medium-sized dog, re-engaged the cipher lock, and was gone.

"You didn't ask what *I* wanted," shouted Sylvain Lalumière in vain.

• • •

As she crawled into the open, a number of tourists began clicking their cameras and tablets as if Pattie Norbrunn were a creature ascending from the past.

She thrust her hands in front of her face, and switched to the local brogue. "No pictures, please." She placed her hand on a sign next to her. "House 7 is closed for preservation purposes. In Scotland, it is illegal to photograph workers at World Heritage sites. Violators are incarcerated on an island far north of here … with our country's nastiest criminals. It is best that you delete any you have of me."

Quickly, the tourists fought with their devices to perform the deletion as if a timer was in play. Their tour guide, however, just placed her hands on her hips and glared at Pattie. Seconds later, they were trooped back to their buses. That they represented the last bunch of the day brought calm to the resourceful spy. Scottish brogue. Not bad.

The stone footpath to her destination, a sizeable 17th Century mansion just over 300 yards distant, was narrow. The young spy proceeded with care. Something as simple as the twisting of an ankle could scotch her whole future. She pulled her coat tight around her and pressed ahead. The sea waves crashing at her back pronounced the fury of the late spring North Atlantic.

A sign outside the front entrance proclaimed the manor to be the Skaill House. She pushed through the unlocked front entrance and, once inside the main salon, selected a comfortable high-back chair and relaxed before a warm fire.

A voice came from behind. "I hope this hasn't been too discomforting, my darling daughter."

"Sylvain complains. He's wanting his castle, not this. This isn't France, and it isn't his kingdom."

"Soon you can leave his place. It will include a trek ever southward through the other Celtic lands. Recall from your studies that the Celts are enemies of the Anglo-Saxon English, or can be made to be. But that is for later in the game."

She nodded in agreement that she understood what he'd said, not necessarily what it meant. That her father would make conceptual statements from time to time was *de rigeur* with her. She knew it would become clear later.

"Because of his presumed royalty status, and his over ninety-percent favorability rating in France, rest assured that I have arranged for those who will help you dispose of him, should the time come."

"He's the one who gets us onto the real throne, Father. With me as the queen, he would become theoretically expendable."

"Theoretically? No, not theoretically. We must adhere to the plan."

Pattie Norbrunn knew she had to toss her father a bone. "How about this? Since his son would succeed him, I arrange for his son to precede him in death. Then, his grief-stricken father takes his own life. Poof! Daughter Pattie becomes the new owner and operator of the country known as France."

The Prince poked at the fire logs a few times, then turned. "You are brilliant. Two deaths after the coronation, and I am in power. From my little token principality to a major world leader."

Pattie sat back. Once again, her manipulations produced the desired effect. Once Sylvain and Jean-Marc had been deleted, then only her father would stand in her way.

For his part, he returned her trademark dimpled smile with a broad grin. He couldn't imagine a better daughter. He produced a whisky bottle. "Take this with you. Highland Park Distillery. Founded not far from here. 1798." He pushed it into a backpack replete with a meal he himself had prepared.

"So the first whisky bottle left the building about six years after Sylvain's aristocrat ancestors were beheaded. Perhaps I will leave that little factoid out. But thanks. He'll require some nerve-calming from time-to-time. I won't always be able to …"

Her father's glare terminated the dialog.

• • •

Pattie's trek back didn't involve any more encounters with tourists. It surprised her that they weren't in evidence twenty-four seven, this being a World Heritage Site and all.

She knocked on the slate portal.

Clunk, clunk.

The sound of Lalumière removing the ancient security pole inside didn't even penetrate. He swung open the door and, still on his knees, reached the backpack she held out.

"Be careful. There's glass inside," she admonished as she crawled in.

Curious, he plucked the Scotch and, ignoring the other contents, opened it and took a swig.

Had Pattie not resealed the door, his gasped "Ahhh!" would have resounded out across the landscape.

"The flavors are enhanced by the peating process. Since the peat contains heather plants, their aromas infiltrate the whisky. Aren't you impressed?"

"I would be impressed if you could name this aroma or the heathers."

Pattie took a sip. As if invoking a séance, she scanned above, smacked her lips, and wiggled her nose. "It's *Calluna Vulgaris* species. Otherwise known as Ling."

Lalumière turned. "Ling? Isn't that the name of Chin's daughter—the one he calls Black?"

"Scottish Ling, I believe, is not deadly. Chin's Black Daughter—who has mastered the ancient art known as *death touch*—is most deadly."

"Hmm. I like this."

"And I have more. Highland Park was founded by the Whisky Priest. The priest part was during the day, but at night he did moonshine. Don't you just love the notion of opposite values and personalities being resolved within one individual?" She extracted her often deadly compact from her purse and, utilizing her phone's flashlight app, gazed into its small mirror. For the moment, she felt as if all of her spy personas were resolved by the mirror—at least into one image.

"Chin and I met on the Scottish mainland. Several years ago, a whisky tour for the elite. It was on that occasion that I was educated in this sophisticated liquid." He took another pull on the bottle. "On the nose, I am sensing walnut, orange peel, and honey. Spiced honey. On the palate, this medium bodied liquor is modestly dry, and the herbed heather comes to the forefront. *En fin*, the finish is quite dry and again the essence of heather lingers. There. What do you think now?"

"I am duly impressed. Especially the part about the nose." She stroked his Gallic beak.

He pulled her arm down. "No, *I* am impressed."

"So who led you and the now Emperor Chin on this wonderful journey? I bet it was the Illuminé bishop. Did your host have a Croatian accent?"

"No. I could not place the accent until later. Then, Monegasque."

Her brow knitted a question mark.

"It was your father."

She made no comment, but instead retrieved the backpack she'd brought from the house, extracting a picnic basket replete with serving utensils, plates, and Stewart plaid napkins for two.

Lalumière chased each mouthful of food with the Highland Park. In short order, he was sound asleep.

• • •

"Wake up, my darling. It will be time to leave soon. To head south." Pattie had set her phone to produce a Marseillaise ring tone every three seconds.

Lalumière rubbed his eyes once, then turned toward the stone wall. "This Sleep Number bed is too comfortable to pass up. And please stop playing that song. France can wait. We shall leave later."

"You're right. I'll touch *Snooze* and update you on a bit of intel a Little Bird just told me."

"Little Bird? You talk to birds now. You are insane."

"*Mai non, mon Capitaine*. I've named my cell phone Little Bird. That way, a Little Bird can tell me stuff."

"Perhaps more than insane."

The snooze alarm sounded. Again the Marseillaise. Lalumière knew he must give up any semblance of peace and quiet until Pattie was finished. Chinese water torture had nothing on Yin—the way of women.

Before he could further expound, something seeped through the dark to assail his senses. He sat up, whiffing each delicate smell. Food.

"You had dinner earlier. This will be more substantial. For our trip."

"We are in darkness, you should know this. Half of the French dining experience is in the presentation."

"Let's try my flashlight app." She engaged the device, adjusting it to a candlelight glow. "Okay? First, I want you to check something out. This is cool stuff, Sylvain. You are thought to be dead after the Colosseum incident with the pope, the Crayle team, my father … oh, yes, and Doctors Rorschach and Rikki."

"And the Indian woman's paratroop brothers and Jack Sommers."

"Yeah. Them, too."

"Your news report verifies what I have felt since that catastrophe."

"According to the free Italian daily, *Metro*, a body washed up near Paris and DNA has been procured." She turned her phone to show a photo of a tall, full bearded, male body of similar height. "With all the facial and head hair à la Mitim—it implies that your alter ego is dead. It says that the ninety percent of France that are fans of yours have been devastated by the news."

"How could the dead man have my DNA?"

"You would think it a miracle if it weren't for my resourcefulness. That attribute is a must have for we spies. Anyways, I'm considering writing a book. One-Hundred-and-One Uses for the Homeless. What do you think?"

"How many times must I tell you that you are a crazy one. Eh?"

Pattie, obsessive about schedules and timing, reminded herself that they had precisely thirty minutes before having to depart their subterranean abode.

"Where am I truly? These stone walls. Is this not just another prison?"

"These are not prisons I bring you to. The French Château D'If, the Italian Forte di Exilles, the Spanish Montserrat, and now, Skara Brae. They are all safe havens in our journey. In our quest."

The girl-woman lit a candle that cast more shadows than light. Her attire was different. It was period, but the Frenchman didn't recognize it.

"Here's some supper. It will make you strong like this region's forebears. Now, eat your *tatties* and *veeps*."

He pushed the plate away. "I would kill for the French version of these potatoes and turnips."

Pattie shook her head. "The only way you are permitted to kill is with that." She motioned to a football-shaped object perched on a woven basket. It seemed to dance in the flicker. "Anything less than mass destruction is mine. And, since you killed all those people in Marseille, I've got some catching up to do."

Sylvain Lalumière retrieved the dish and forked the potato and turnip mixture into his mouth.

She uncovered another dish.

"What is this surprise?"

"It's delicious."

He peered at the large, round sausage, spices, and seasoning.

"Sheep's guts," she advised.

He dropped back into his bed. "I will not eat this."

"But, Sylvain, you are pent up with nerves. You need to relax. This food will help you."

"Ha," he scoffed. "I cannot move. I can barely breathe the polluted air in this place. I am …"

"Just over 1,230 klicks from Versailles. Roughly the same distance from Archangel due south to Moscow. I checked."

"What are these klicks?"

"Kilometers. We spies can be very brief. Anyways, that's roughly 766 …"

"… miles from my beloved France. And from my destiny. It is no wonder I am tense. I cannot be without tension."

She scooted across the floor on her knees. "Wanna bet?"

CHAPTER 5

Having dressed them both in silk thermals, appropriate outerwear, plus parkas and watch caps, Pattie Norbrunn led Sylvain Lalumière outside long after the last tour bus departed. Standing on House 7's turf rooftop, they peered at the beach below as the North Atlantic pounded the coast.

"There!" She pointed in the distance.

He shielded his eyes, scanning up the west-facing crescent of sand. "I see nothing. A few fishing boats bobbing at their moorings … wait! One of them is not a fishing vessel." His mouth fell open.

"It's ours, King Louis. Isn't it magnificent? Our first ship of state."

She handed him a pair of binoculars. "They're already set for your eyes. Take a look."

He did. "Oh, no. It can't be. That is no ship of state."

"You have to use your imagination."

"It's a fake."

"Not so, my Liege. I still have some pull. It's the one from the movie. They refurbished it, and—when not in the employ of we covert types—it services the tourists out of Key Largo, Florida."

"They?"

"Why the CIA, of course. And my new title in France is part of its name."

"Wait. Yes. I can make it out now. Oh, no. It can't be … but it is. It's the *African Queen*."

In her days of greater sanity, Pattie Norbrunn didn't giggle. She did now. She grabbed his arm and pulled him, dumbstruck, to a place where they could descend from the cliffs to the beach.

"We will attack the French government in Paris with this, this steam powered life raft. Impossible."

"In the movie, Mr. Allnut and Miss Sayer only had an old torpedo. And look what *they* accomplished."

"They sank a German gunboat …"

"Yes. The *Königin Luise*."

"I remember now. The Princess Louise."

"*They* had a torpedo. *We* have a mini-nuke capable of 5 megatons of destruction. All we need now is faith, like in the movie."

"Your German accent is perfect. Have you spied in that country, too?"

A "no comment" wouldn't have worked well at that point. She turned away and started down the slope to the sea like an excited little girl. "C'mon, Sylvain."

He quickly caught her, but trotted slowly so that she could keep up. As they drew near, he observed a makeshift floating dock that extended from the water's edge to the boat. He maintained his pace while she skipped along the metal floats like a child.

"C'mon, Sylvain. There is no time to stand and admire her. We have reservations tomorrow. We can't be late."

He stepped aboard and assisted her.

In minutes, the young woman had the ancient boiler up to operating pressure.

He hopped out to free the lines securing their craft. Due to the active surf, he almost wasn't able to leap back over the gunwales.

As soon as they reached the open sea of the North Atlantic, she showed him how to operate the boiler propulsion unit and sat him down next to the tiller. "Hold this as if you know where you're going." She plopped a weather-beaten captain's hat on his head. "The rudder is controlled by GPS. You'll be fine. I need to step into the cabin and change."

He scanned everywhere. "But there is no cabin. It is an open boat with only that ugly, loud, smelly, smoke-billowing contraption in the middle."

"Well, you don't have to look at it. When we pass the land mass on our left, look past it. You will be gazing into the famous Scapa Flow. The German High Seas Fleet was sequestered there at the end of World War I." She wanted to kick herself. In short order, she had mentioned the Germans twice. Sylvain didn't need to know about them. It was her own little side game. "Many of the ships were scuttled and are still at the bottom. So pilot the Queen with great care."

Dealing with a woman who was full of contradictions, innuendo, and enigma, he was ready to have some alone time. However brief. "Fine. I played the part of Mitim to perfection, and I will play this part as well. You can go change now."

"I do so love being dismissed by older men." She turned half away, then back. "While I'm gone, I need for you to be on watch for items."

"Items?"

"Yes. Items like other boats and anything that protrudes from the sea."

"Protrudes?"

She wore the look of a frustrated school teacher. "Such as islands and other land masses. And whales."

"Ah, I see. Then I will call you …"

"No. You will steer our fine craft so that it does not strike any of the *items*."

Without further dialog, she rounded the boiler and, out of sight, changed her garments to something a lot warmer, and a lot more tactical.

"What if we are stopped by the coast guard?" he called in her direction.

She stepped out in the open. "There."

"You are a nun again. How will that help?"

"I will promise to bless them if they allow us to continue."

"And if they are not Catholic?"

She just smiled her dimpled smile.

"I understand. You will kill them."

"You are a true cynic, my lovable husband. We have been cleared with them by Central Intelligence. If the authorities spot us, my nun's garb and this fine watercraft are the key. They will leave us alone."

"Whatever happens, happens." He moved down onto the deck. "I am cold. Bring your warmth to me."

She complied.

• • •

It wasn't long at all that Pattie was awakened by the sound of someone snoring. She tossed out a "Hey, they shoot sailors who fall asleep on watch" to keep the duty watch-stander fully alert. She knew she would catch little meaningful rest hollering at him every five minutes. As well, sound carried easily over the water and stealth beyond the chugging engine was as critical as ever.

Although hers was the twelve to four A.M. mid-watch, she threw in the towel and relieved a nodding Lalumière early. When he was fast asleep a few heartbeats later, she moved to the bow of the craft. She felt it was the best position for a lookout post. Besides, the boiler behind kept her back warm while the prow sides of the foredeck blocked head- and side-winds.

She'd carefully chosen a moonless period for their trip. Although the night was dark, she utilized her cell phone's flashlight mode and a CIA universal remote to program a course southward for the Minches—straits that would keep the Outer Hebrides islands between them and the unforgiving Atlantic. They would then proceed south past the Isle of Skye and into the Sea of Hebrides, ever closer to their next destination.

She imagined the people behind the lights along the shorelines to port and starboard and, to her, their simple, uninteresting lives. She further imagined her upcoming reign as Queen of all France where she would be kept aloof of such peasantry by her trusted courtesans. For a second, she wondered if that would make her sad.

• • •

At dawn, the *African Queen* pulled into a small boat basin next to a very large brown castle. While the two characters aboard stopped all manner of traffic with their new identities, they quickly tied up. Before any of the onlookers could reason as to what had just happened, or ask for autographs from the over-tall Humphrey Bogart and the petite version of Katherine Hepburn, the two were whisked into a surrey-style golf cart by a couple of non-descript locals and driven past a small gray stone building with HARBOUR OFFICES 1840 engraved above a white door framed in dark blue.

To the door's left, a lonely silver sedan sat parked facing outward as though hasty exfiltration would be both necessary and sufficient at quitting time. Beyond that, the two saw the spectacle of the ancient castle in apparent perfect condition. Without slowing, they zoomed past the castle gift shop and through the main portal. Heavy gates slammed behind them.

Pattie tipped the driver and jumped out, managing the full-length linen dress as if she had worn one all her life.

Lalumière exited more slowly. His attire appeared to be a mattress ticking shirt over white pants with a small, billed cap. Both appeared to have been through at least one world war.

He gaped at the surroundings. "I should have a castle like this one. With very high walls and a beautiful—and extensive—grass field, in multiple levels, inside. I could take up golf here."

She pulled on his arm. "Hurry up, Sylvain. I only have this for the weekend."

"A whole castle … for the weekend?"

"Daddy got it for me."

"It must be good to be the Prince of Monaco."

She smiled, tugging harder. "Come with me. There's someone I'd like you to meet."

She led him through a door and up a spiraling stairway with pie-slice-shaped steps. Then down a corridor within the walls, its stonework three feet from side to side. Lalumière felt the closeness—the confinement—and hurried along into what appeared to be a special room.

The Frenchman stopped. "There's a throne. And there is someone sitting in it. Hey, who are you?" He started for the throne. "You shall not usurp—" He stopped again as a narrow beam of outside light shone on the young man's face.

"Hello, Father. How do I look?" Jean-Marc tilted his chin upward. "Perhaps I could become the Prince of Wales. Charles was crowned here, you know. Nineteen-sixty-nine."

"Wales? Whales? I don't understand any of this. I do understand that we cannot be monarchs of anything in this place."

"Not so, I'm happy to say. When I attended graduate school at the Paris H.E.C., you told me especially to learn history. So, here it is. Edward I of England conquered Wales and placed castles in strategic places in order to control the Welsh. Once we have France sewn up, we may seek to free these people. Perhaps begin an empire like your hero, Napoléon."

Before he could react in a fatherly, omniscient manner, Lalumière caught the epiphany. "And the Scots, who were once enamored of and aligned with we French against the English, might join, too."

"It's brilliant, isn't it?" asked Pattie. "The Irish would come our way if we promised a united Emerald Isle and our centuries-old nemesis, the English, would be surrounded. *Ooh la la!*" She left out the inconvenient fact that she had primed his son with the idea by phone. And Jean-Marc, wanting to impress his father, played along to perfection.

As his father began to applaud, the latent French prince stood and affected a passable semblance of a royal bow. He held his palms aloft to achieve quiet. "I have missed you, Your Highness, but now I must take your leave."

Pattie threw him an admonishing scowl for his comical lapse into Shakespearean character.

"Why must you leave? We've only seen you for ten minutes."

"Because, Father, I have a date."

"A date. You are a prince. I must counsel you with respect to anyone you might date."

"You would approve. It's someone I met before. Do you remember my trip to Estonia and Poland? To discuss with interested parties the necessity to re-install monarchies across the region. I met her there."

"I knew it. I knew taking you to Amsterdam to see to your coming-of-age education could be a mistake. That's it, isn't it? A working girl. Estonian or Polish?"

Jean-Marc chuckled. "Neither. You should be proud. My date in approximately eight hours … is the new Queen of Sweden. We saw eye to eye, politically and otherwise, during that trip. I will pleasure her and see to a future alliance with her country."

"Whoa, cowboy," said Pattie. "When a man thinks he's that good, he seldom is."

"My son is correct. We require such alliances, and how they are obtained is immaterial."

"But—"

"Go safely, my Son."

The trio exchanged cheek-to-cheek *kisses of the air* and he was gone.

Pattie watched after him. It was bad enough that Lalumière's son was next-in-line in the mix. And now, the Queen of Sweden?

"He's a fine young man, don't you agree. I worried after the Paris affair. After his birth mother, Épiphanie, died so horribly. Do you remember it?"

"Do you mean when she and I and that Brazilian operative, Flori, grappled on the steel beam near the top of the Eiffel Tower? With rain and hail pummeling us, and lightning flashing like Armageddon, the whole time? And when the three of us plummeted what seemed like a hundred feet, crashing through the roof of the restaurant?"

Lalumière could see that she was worked up. Best to remain silent.

Then, she laughed. "Just answer me this. Why is it that women always end up doing the men's heavy lifting? Hmmm?"

"I don't know what you are talking about. But your reward will be to sit by my side as my queen. Is that not sufficient?"

She lifted on her tiptoes, gave him a big kiss, and molested him with her left hand. "What do you think?"

While the prospective King Louis XIX gave the Prince of Wales throne a try, Pattie began to devise a scheme whereby the young prince and his Swedish queen would cease to be impediments. A dimpled smile crept onto her face.

"I look good, yes?"

"Just fine. You look just fine."

No sooner had Jean-Marc departed, than a man dressed in vestments arrived. A fifty-ish man, he was quite polite. "I have been tasked by none other than the pope himself to assist you with your lodgings. He said we need to have you visually nonexistent as quickly as possible. Please, follow me."

He led them through more hallways and doors until the trio emerged on the parapets. "Please, you will absolutely love this. The Landmark Trust provided the renovations to the tower. It has made these rooms available—at the Monaco Prince's direct request, I might add—for the next few days. Don't worry a bit about any charges.

Pope Innocent declared to me that you are both honorable souls and your accommodations are, as the less religious say, comped."

The parapet ended at a castle tower that had been obviously reconfigured inside. Rather than mere arched holes, actual windows had been introduced. Inside through a door, the bishop provided them a quick tour of the facility's three floors. "I suggest you don't go up top onto the viewing platform. The locals and tourists notice things like that. You are here for privacy, I understand, and don't want to draw attention. Is that right?"

Pattie turned to Lalumière. "I'm exhausted. Please turn down the bed. I'll see the bishop out."

While he complied, she escorted the bishop out through the door and shut it behind her. A few minutes later, her husband stepped outside. "Since I can't see him, I assume the bishop is gone." He turned back through the door, but halted for her response.

"Yes. He is." She peered downward through a crenellation. Barely able to make out the top of the bishops hat as it sank in the bay below, she turned to face her lover.

"Oh, Sylvain. I need to climb down these steps to the bedroom deck you can see below." She indicated a stairway on the inward side of the wall, and a wooden deck with outdoor furniture. "The proprietor there is quite nice and runs a fabulous bed and breakfast called Victoria House. She'll bring dinner and our other meals so we don't have to go out."

"Like the bishop said, we need to remain incognito, my dear."

"Yes. Like the bishop said."

CHAPTER 6

On a shirtsleeve and shorts day in Southern California's Big Bear Valley, Phoebe Bransfield entered the Crayles' log cabin near the lakeside village called Fawnskin as she had done countless times before. Given that the residence possessed security protection, the door ajar caused her to slide her .45 caliber Glock 30 from its holster and assume the standardized FBI combat grip.

Inside, she found private investigator Lenny Lipschitz, sprawled on the floor with blood streaming from a head wound. She moved to clear the cabin and came face-to-face with someone she hadn't seen for several years. Her sister. "Oh."

Lenny moaned, "Jeez-Louise."

"Not Louise. Lenny, meet my sister, Mandy."

The woman with tightly curled dark brown hair, who stood a couple of inches shorter than Phoebe, nodded. She stepped over to him and handed him a small object from her purse.

He accepted the feminine pad to staunch the bleeding. He looked up. "We've already met."

Phoebe looked at her sister. "Can I tell him?"

"It's history. Sure."

"Delta Force, Lenny. Retired."

"I'm glad she's retired. Anyway, it's not what you think. I didn't make a move on her or anything."

"It's true. I stepped inside as he came out of the john. He said 'Alona?' right before I clocked him."

"Someone help me up."

Mandy reached down and yanked him to his feet. "Sorry. Bet you didn't know that Phoebe and I were Army brats. We boxed on military bases."

"I heard," Lenny shared, remembering his early encounter with the FBI Agent. He pointed at Phoebe. "She hit me, too."

"It's a family thing."

"Any more sisters?"

The women smiled. Without waiting for further discourse, Lenny staggered to the kitchen counter.

"I'm worried about Magus. I haven't heard a thing since he and Hekka made their refuel stop in Thule, Greenland." He checked his tablet computer. "Make that Bangor, Maine."

While piling cubes of ice into a tea towel for the P.I.'s head, Phoebe tossed a few words over her shoulder. "From all that's gone before, I think Mr. and Mrs. Crayle can take care of themselves."

"I'm still worried."

"It'll give you wrinkles." She smiled.

As if performing an inspection of her face, Lenny frowned. "Is that what happened?"

Phoebe's unseeing eyes stared at Lenny. One set of fingers massaged her Glock's receiver as they had many times before. She considered her first thought a bit too drastic. Her second thought, of using the ice pack as a weapon, lingered. She snapped out of her trance.

"They're tracking down her mother after all the years she's been missing. Let's give them a couple more days."

"You're right. It's just that I got used to being right there … in the action."

"Whatsamatter, Lenny? Honeymoon over already?"

"Ha. I wish. Five times today already. I thought about inducing a headache, but your sister took care of that."

Mandy had left the room and returned from the bathroom. "Here, P.I. Tylenol on steroids."

He tossed the pills in his mouth, then scooped water from a fish bowl, and flushed them down. "Seriously. About Magus and Hekka."

"Let's do this. Let's be ready to rock on a moment's notice. 'Go' bags, the whole smear. There's a 7X at the airstrip at our disposal. Jack's getting Neil's new 8X."

"Yeah. Hey, why didn't Jack tell me first about the new plane? I'm still his lieutenant."

"Look. What you are is a wreck. Go in on the waterbed and take a nap. Sis and I need to catch up. Here's how to relax. Think about it this way. Magus and Hekka'll be fine. Nothing could possibly go wrong."

CHAPTER 7

The knock came early the next day. And loud.

Phoebe had just arrived to spend more time with her sister. After checking out what appeared to be a delivery man on the cabin's television, she punched in the security code and opened the door.

"Courier, ma'am. Please sign here." He handed her a tablet and pen.

"Whose this from?"

"That's classified." He smiled. "Just kidding. It's from some company in Holland. Amsterdam. That's all I know."

She signed and closed the door on the man, who undoubtedly expected a tip. She heard the screeching of tires outside, but was too concerned with what might be inside to care.

"Lenny!" she hollered. "You've got mail. Fancy." Phoebe held up a four-inch square envelope. "Looks like an invite."

"Open it for me." He continued to prepare breakfast for the three of them.

"It's from Europe. Amsterdam."

He placed a red onion on the counter and stepped over to her. "Here." He slit the envelope with a butcher knife.

"Overkill, P.I."

He slid out a heavy card stock invitation and read. "It's from Wolfie's boss at the diamonds company. Condolences." He peeked into the envelope.

"Money?"

"No." He retrieved a folded paper. As he read it, a smile captured his countenance. "I'll be damned. They're offering me a job."

"You have got to be kidding." Phoebe shook her head.

"That wasn't nice."

"Let me break it down. You know something about diamonds? No. You're newly married. You're a member of the Crayle team." She expressed *well, duh* with a hand gesture and a facial expression.

"True. But wait a second. We have no idea what happened to Lalumière. Here's my three."

"Three what?"

"My dad said things always come in threes. It's nature, he said. Okay?"

She shrugged.

"One: Europe is Lalumière's stomping ground. Two: He probably needs to exchange cash for diamonds to buy a new bomb. Three: uh, …"

"I see who's behind this. Already Alona wants a long distance relationship."

The P.I. smirked.

"You're a newlywed, Lenny. You wouldn't want to be distracted by any of those gorgeous blonde hookers. Perhaps she should go along. She'd love Amsterdam."

"She can't. She's in a trial. Wait. I've got it. The third item is that I'm Jewish."

"So."

"The diamond business is a Jewish thing."

"If you add the film industry and Wall Street, that's another three."

"I guess. Whatdaya think?"

Eyes popping wide, Phoebe sucked in an excited breath. "Wait a minute, Lenny. You could fence the pound bag of diamonds that Magus confiscated in Kaohsiung. You'll need to run this by him. By Magus."

"Ha, ha, Phoebe my dear. *Rock and roll!*"

"Yeah Rock and Roll. Get your sorry ass home. Tell Alona the news."

Off guard by the prospects, Agent Bransfield was unable to avoid the intimate hug that came next. Before she could react and shoot the perpetrator, he'd yanked the front door nearly from its hinges—setting off the alarm—and sped off in his black Buick.

The flashing lights and sirens found their way onto Phoebe's last nerve as she—in manic frustration—punched and re-punched the wall-mounted security pad. Finally, the sensory blitzkrieg ceased.

Fortunate that the local sheriff was ticketing a tourist, Lenny exceeded the limit by a quantum heading for home. Arriving at their cabin, he rushed inside to find his new wife on the phone.

He panted and swayed and waved hands in front of her to indicate himself as the higher priority.

"I'll be happy to call you back, Your Honor. Please, just give me five minutes."

Click.

She pushed her pursed lips to one side, indicating her high degree of annoyance.

"Alona, I've got news!"

"It better be good, you little shrimp. Or the next news is going to be of the obituary variety."

In short, anxious breaths, he related his job offer. Then, he stepped back, a broad smile on his face and arms spread wide.

Alona appeared to ponder the relative benefits of quick death versus death preceded by torture. She drummed her fingers on her thigh for a moment before admonishing, "Here I've got a client whose ass I'm trying to save, and I'm talking to the judge on a crucial procedural issue. In comes Lenny like a new breed of Southern California tornado—"

"It's about the diamonds! The ones I told you about. I'm taking Wolfie's old broker job. We can fence them. Our share will be …"

Her face cleared of all expression. "We'll get a share. Oh, my."

"Actually, I'll get a share. You weren't with the team at the time we acquired them in Kaohsiung."

She held up her ring, then gestured to her lawyer diplomas on the wall. "Our share."

Before he could take on the attorney and wife before him, she jumped to her feet and started on his buttons.

"I know how this works." Her breathing approximated a locomotive accelerating to operating speed. "You'll go away with your friends, and I won't know how long it'll be before I get some again."

"You can come with me."

"I can't. I am with client."

Her phone chimed. Fortunately, she'd wedged the large iPhone 6 Plus between her cheek and shoulder, just in case. She touched in the security code with her tongue as she worked at Lenny's belt buckle and zipper.

"Oh, I'm sorry to hear that, Your Honor. Really sorry … yeah … bye."

She howled with such exuberance, the phone slipped and clunked to the floor. "There is a God," she trilled.

"What? What'd he say?"

She pulled a Lenny. "There's bad news and good news. The bad: my client hanged himself in his cell. The good: we're goin' to Amsterdam!"

CHAPTER 8

It had been some time since Jack Sommers had been at the Strategic Situations Office. That the offices were buried beneath the Civil War battlefield at Manassas, Virginia didn't bother him a bit. And that ingress and egress happened via a special porta potty elevator inside a walled-off potty section a short distance from the site's tourist information office didn't bother him, either.

He smiled. Even with his former boss dead, the ingress protocol remained in place. He'd ambled through the visitor's center, paid admission, then walked the fifty paces to the cinderblock surround. Through an opening, he'd stepped to the sixth, and last, porta potty which allowed him entrance via his proximity card. Inside, he'd pissed in the urinal and placed his palm hard against the wall mirror for a print scan. And, as always before, his hand left no residue on the mirror.

The potty's interior descended, with Jack safely strapped to the toilet seat, 312 feet into Neil Wohlford's former lair. The notion of rapid descent with a near full sewage bin right beneath his buttocks seemed like an accident waiting to happen.

No matter. He survived once again. Since retiring from the CIA, Jack had performed several off-the-books projects for Neil. He wondered how many of them had benefitted the ultra-secret Illuminé rather than the good old U.S. of A. Perhaps even the one that had gotten his ex-wife Marli shot and had led, in part, to their divorce. He didn't know and snapped out of his daydream. There was significant work to do.

What bothered him was threefold. The hallways of the covert facility were painted with what he deemed the brightest chartreuse in the galaxy. Second, the old office of his former double-agent boss was littered with French artifacts. And last, Neil Wohlford had never shared with him any of the other activities of the SSO. Now, at least temporarily, he found himself in charge. He observed in silence that shit rolling downhill had the same meaning for spies as it did for everyone else.

He knew that some serious surveillance was in order. First, check out his boss' old desk. He took a seat in the ornate gold and purple French replica chair and found it uncomfortable. A check of the drawers, all unlocked, revealed nothing. Empty. Then he remembered that the new United States president, Kimbel Stones, had had everything brought to him not long ago to help Crayle's team in Europe stop Sylvain Lalumière and Pattie Norbrunn from blowing up more cities and cruise liners.

He'd retrieve those items later. And it would give him an excuse to talk to the president. He smiled. No, all that remained on the desktop was one small, gold Louis XIV carriage. As he fetched it into his hand, the smooth top caused him to remember a past inconvenient arrival when he entered this same office to find Neil on top of Rorschach's boss, the good Doctor Monika Rikki. The two *in flagrante* atop Neil's desk. He hadn't meant to intrude on their private moment, but the scuffle he'd heard coming from inside the office when he'd arrived for his periodic in person meet with Neil seemed to call for intervention.

He'd noticed one other item when he'd scanned the room. A decanter and a crystal glass that sat on a wet bar in the corner of the room. He poured three fingers worth of his boss' top-of-the-line cognac. "Rémy Martin Louis XIII," he announced. "This is going to taste sweet." He returned to the desk.

The next sound was loud and terse.

Jack jumped.

The glass flipped from his hand. Desperate, he grabbed it out of the air and swung it at the descending liquid. His effort to rescue the pricey substance was in vain.

The sound blasted again.

"Oh. It's the frikkin' phone." He snatched the receiver from an archaic-looking French phone placed beside the desk. A friendly voice relaxed him.

"Phoebe. How'd you get this number?"

"Remember the phone Lenny found at Wohlford's place in Carcassonne?"

"Oh. So Lenny or Micmac found the number?"

"Excuse me. I'm the FBI Agent. I scoured the phone for intel and found Neil's direct number."

"I didn't mean it takes a guy …"

"Uh huh. Have you heard from Magus?"

"Nothing."

"This Finland place seems to be a black hole. First Hekka's mom, then these two. Whoever goes in doesn't come out."

"I've already tapped our resources, but it's too risky to put Magus and Hekka's pictures with it. The Illuminé would love to get ahold of him and, as we've learned the hard way, they have people everywhere. Say, you've got some time on the clock, how about the two of you track them down?"

"Micmac and I have been trying to make babies, but you're right. How about you?"

"I have to stay at Manassas awhile picking up on Neil's dealings. I'll send the jet."

"See that it contains pregnant lady supplies."

"I'll be damned. You've had success. Give my congratulations to that ex-Navy stud."

"Hey, what about me?"

"I can almost hear you saying 'Are we there yet?' " Jack covered the phone with his hand. "Ah!" he gasped. "I didn't meant it. Didn't mean it. Didn't mean it."

"Next time I see you, Jack ..."

"I can't wait. And when you head out to find our lost team members, don't forget to take along your favorite P.I. You'll need him for something."

"Good idea. We can use him as bait."

"*Ciao*, Phoebe."

Jack was worried. He felt sure something was going down with the Crayle's dropping off the map, but didn't have the slightest clue what. He wanted to go himself, but he had a great deal to learn right where he was. He dialed Phoebe back.

"Let me snoop a little more, then I'll meet you over there."

"Finland, right?"

"Yeah. Helsinki."

CHAPTER 9

Once again attired as a nun, Pattie Norbrunn had just seen to the refueling of the *African Queen* at its mooring in tiny Caernarfon harbor. She stood peering alternately at a side gate and at the timepiece embedded in the top of her cross.

After he'd tidied up the castle, Lalumière padded through the wooden-gated castle aperture and tossed their belongings aboard, followed by the tie-down rope. As soon as he'd hopped aboard, he helped her fire up the boiler, and slip the boat out into the late evening darkness.

When they'd settled down astride the tiller, she knew right away something was bothering him. Under the circumstances, she would have been surprised otherwise. "What is it, my love?"

"My failures are nagging me again. Paris. The Queen Mary 2. And being poisoned every time you see the need to move me to a *strategic* location, as you call them."

That he knew it was she making the strategic decisions made her smile inside. That he had emphasized the word, as if the necessity for a succession of Plan B's were on her, did not. She circumvented the notion. She became excited. "Poison?" She withdrew a tubular item from her pocket. "Look, Sylvain. I got this device from Science and Technology. You just rotate this upper part to how many days you need your patient to be out, and inject."

"How easily you confuse the word patient with the word victim."

"It would appear that I need to add a motivational chemical next time."

"I can do without a next time. We must get back to France. Then, I will be close to my goal. It will be better for me. Can you do something to increase the speed of this anachronism?"

"Our boat is slow, my dear Sylvain. We won't be arriving until dawn tomorrow. As before, we'll have to take turns standing watch during the night."

"It is going to be cold. It is May. When does warmth arrive to the British?"

She opened one of the three crates labeled as 12-year-old Scotch and withdrew a cloak for each of them. The two sat huddled together at the stern as the computer directed them out into the Irish Sea. With a full moon hidden behind the cover of clouds, its glow barely evinced the outline of the Welsh coast to their port as they turned to the south.

"Perhaps I should stand at the bow. Look royal. After all, I am king of France."

"That would be terrific, darling. But right now, the winds come from the east and, if you don't stoke that ..." She gestured from their fuel bin to the boiler. "... you will spend your royal days adrift on the North Atlantic."

Affecting an appropriate negative attitude, he performed as he'd been told.

Nodding her approval when he'd completed his task, Pattie yawned.

"One of us should get some sleep, my darling. In four hours, we shall swap, and every four hours—"

"We'll be there in eight. It's a grand idea. But let's just sit here close."

He lifted her onto his lap. When she pulled her arms in tight and raised up her legs, he felt like he held a helpless little girl—something he knew to be far from the case.

"Tell me about your childhood. I want to know more about you."

"The early days were more about my mother than me. I had to share her with her drugs … and her men."

"I am sorry. Don't continue if it's too painful."

"It's okay. I've never had someone I could talk to. My mother worked very hard to see that we had food, and that I possessed the very best clothes to wear to school. Each winter, she would take a day off and we would ice skate five kilometers—three miles—on the frozen canal. She'd bring a lunch of bread, cheese, and wine in a backpack."

She nestled even tighter to him.

The boat's computerized tiller moved from time-to-time with course corrections, but the movements seemed guided by a ghost.

Pattie's mood turned glum. "But it was what she did for him. She gave him, Neil Wohlford, my purity, for more money."

Lalumière had attended Catholic school as a young man, but in all that time, had never witnessed a nun crying. Now, Pattie, attired in her nun's habit, began to stream tears down her cheeks. Sobs followed.

He realized that, in the months he'd known her, he had never seen her cry. She'd always been so strong, so in control. He encircled her with his long arms.

Where she began to go wrong was now clear to him. And that she killed her own mother, justified. And that she'd closed the loop when she murdered Wohlford at his home in Carcassonne.

Perhaps recovery from her teenage trauma was not in the cards. But then, maybe it was. Maybe he had just witnessed the first step. He resolved that he would do his best. He would help her in any way he could.

• • •

Sylvain Lalumière awoke with a start. He'd tried his best to remain awake through the darkness, but had drifted off just after midnight. Ahead, he could see the lights of a town. And Pattie hustling about the deck. Preparing to make landfall.

She was digging in the third Scotch crate when she turned to him, holding two sets of garments in her hands. She marched to the stern lifting her arms high. "Here, my Captain. Put these on. The lights ahead will seem brighter as we approach, but you can maintain your modesty if you hurry."

He checked out the smile on her face, a far cry from the night before. "But these are costumes. It is May and not Halloween. And this one you hand me. It cannot possibly be my size."

"*Au contraire, mon ami.* It is precisely your size. Trust me on this. Put it on."

When Lalumière had finished, she affixed a tri-corner hat to his head, and quickly buffed its skull and crossbones medallion. "There. Jean Lafitte."

"I am not a pirate. I am King Louis. What is this farce?" They were near the port entrance now and he pointed to men standing on the dock. "They will laugh …"

He drew back. The men were dressed in pirate attire as well.

"Welcome to Penzance. It's pirate day and everyone is dressed up. Your disguise is perfect. No one will know you are the great, much vaunted Mitim, or Louis, or Napoléon, or even my Sylvain."

He acquiesced to his young, insane associate and lover. What else could he do? The good news—she'd recovered from her emotional breakdown just hours earlier.

Once the men lashed their boat to the dockside cleats, the fugitive pair carted the three 'Scotch' crates to a dolly and proceeded down the dock. Pattie, dressed as a bar-wench in similar period attire, led Lalumière to a nearby street, The Quay, and into a waiting cab. Other early risers, a fondness for this holiday treat putting smiles on their faces, waved.

"We're in an English province known as Cornwall," she said. "As we proceed away from the town center on the little hill over there …" She waved to their left. "… we'll head east down this frontage road.

The sunrise had begun its daily entrance ahead. Lalumière was taken by the beauty as it shed first light on a small coastal town in the distance, and on a conical island in the bay. "It is breathtaking, to say the least."

"There are beautiful sights here, too. The English get the same sun as the French. Did you know that?"

He blew out a breath. "I doubt that they would assist me. They would turn me over to that … that …"

"The French government? Well, consider this. The oldest of their regiments, the Coldstream Guards, restored the English monarchy in 1660. That's what we need, only in France. Maybe they would help."

"I need time to think. Driver. Let us out here."

He stopped.

"Take our supplies here. They'll keep them safe." She scribbled a note.

When the cab proceeded onward, Lalumière took in a deep breath. "Let's walk without speaking, taking in this new environment. Its sights. Its smells."

She understood. He needed to acclimate. Absorb.

After a ten-minute stroll, she halted and turned to their left. "There. That's our place. No more foreign castles, no dungeons, no underground abodes. It's a bed-and-breakfast."

He looked it over. "I can see the name. On the front." In vain, he battled a smile. "The Mount Royal."

"It's five-star all the way. I knew you'd like it. Let's cross the road here. But we're in England, so be sure to look the wrong way."

• • •

They ascended the driveway and entered the Victorian bed-and-breakfast through its east-side entrance and took note of the sole automobile parked outside. A Mercedes. Upscale clientele in small numbers was a good sign, Pattie decided.

Quickly met inside by an attentive, youngish man, they were shown upstairs to a large bedroom. "The bathroom is next door," the man advised. "Be sure to lock it when you are inside. There is no danger. It's just a courtesy." With that, the proprietor had taken his leave with a promise to reserve the window seat for their included breakfast the next morning.

Pattie latched the door, listening intently. Satisfied that no one would be listening at their keyhole as in the classic movies, she turned to Lalumière with her revelation. "It came to me, Sylvain. I've finally realized the truth."

"First, I am now Louis Nineteen—"

"You must say *We* are now Louis Nineteen. It's the royal plural."

"Of course, you are correct. Now, what do you mean by truth?"

"The biggest truth of all. The God truth."

"My little one. We shall have the finest doctors of the mind make the necessary repairs. You have been under excessive strain for too long." He smiled knowingly.

"It was that outfit—the habit. It's as if some manner of holiness was contained inside the fabric." She began to write in a notebook, one that had once resided on Montserrat. On Mother Superior's desk the day she was sent heavenward.

Lalumière peered over. "What do you write?"

"I will accept Jesus and salvation. It will make me the perfect Queen of France. I'm making a list of all the people …"

"… you've killed?"

"Yes. An inventory of sorts."

"And when do you present this inventory, and to whom?"

"St. Peter? The pope?"

"This is wonderful news, my dear. It means you've finished with the killing."

"Yes. Well, almost. There's one left." She smiled, embarrassed.

"You are right. Once you have removed Mr. Crayle, we shall be secure in our new status."

She nodded. But she'd forgotten Crayle.

"I need to use the head, as you refer to it." He unlocked and pivoted the door open.

Just then, as if on cue, in walked the new prince. Jean-Marc.

CHAPTER 10

The hidden chamber, one of many that belonged to the newly reformed Aryan Alliance, sported no windows and only a single door. Like so many other secret locations, it too was underground. There was no sense of time of day or weather or anything else. Certainly, there was no one to bear witness to the salacious activities there unless they were invited, or were the victim.

Although the room was large, it was not comfortable. Not in the least. That the walls and ceiling were covered in a thick padding, and that the floor was covered in a dense, multi-leveled carpet spoke more of a prison cell than a living space.

Hekka Crayle agonized, her hands bound and affixed to a hook overhead. Her clothing was still intact, but the man, by appearance the world's next embodiment of evil, stepped close and ran his fingers over her light-weight polka-dot blouse.

"Time to remove your clothing," were his only words.

Using a razor, he started a slit below her left shoulder blade, arcing it downward towards her spine.

Teeth clamped, lips pressed, she emitted no sound.

The Aryan halted his sexual exploration. He mulled over the current circumstance, and considered a more vicarious approach.

"Kaari?"

"*Ja, mein Herr.*"

"We will speak English. Don't you see that her clothes are damp from the rain? She might take cold. Please remove them. Carefully. Slowly. I will watch."

The tall blonde, whose figure approximated a stretched-thin hourglass, moved to the dangling woman. From a sheath on her side, the blonde removed an antique Hitler Youth Corps dagger. "That you've fastened her hands and suspended her from the hook used to maintain edible flesh makes my job easier." A furtive glance at him and she began to disrobe the young woman.

"Be careful, *mein schatz.* Our insurance policy must remain undamaged."

"She is not Aryan, but I feel strangely attracted. Her skin is flawless. Not dark, not light. It reminds me of the syrup that the Americans place on their ice cream."

"Butterscotch?"

"Delicious."

She stroked the suspended woman's back with her tongue.

"Take care. She is a warrior. With light skin and blonde hair, she would be one of us."

The blonde doctor diverted her eyes toward him without disengaging her prisoner. Not satisfied with the lack of reaction, she turned her face toward the man, leaning her head against her prize.

"I see that you are attracted as well."

"Mrs. Crayle is not to be molested, Kaari. By either of us or anyone else. Am I clear?"

"*Jawohl, mein Oberst. Ganz klar.*"

• • •

The man sat at a small, dark desk. As an indication of his demand for incessant precision, a knife-edge creased his spotless khaki uniform. Trying his best to absorb the papers in front of him, he lifted his head as the black figure passed by.

"Kaari. You are aware that the uniform of the day is the one I wear. Why do you insist to wear that tight black leather dress. It is much too short."

The blonde doctor, whose perfect curves pressed against their leather confines, smiled as she waved a silver cylinder at him. Without response, she stepped to another perfect figure. This one, wrists bound and suspended from an overhead hook, was naked.

She stepped within reach, then touched the flesh, its butterscotch coloring barely visible by the single desk lamp. As she stroked the long black hair, and again the flesh, she employed the now-vibrating cylinder.

"You must leave her alone," the man admonished. "She is our hostage."

"She is unconscious. I am the only one who feels."

CHAPTER 11

Finished with Mrs. Crayle, the Aryan had returned to the underground chamber known as *Rotfels*. He walked through the glowing red room to his other captive's side. Still, when he looked around, he concluded that there must be at least a million of the rubies. And that their incalculable wealth had been overestimated. Certainly, if all were placed on the market at once, the individual per carat price would plummet. His financier would therefore continue to seep them onto the marketplace.

At first, he was pleased by the magnitude of his intellect. Second, though, it saddened him that such a tactic was necessary, and that it protracted their scheduled Aryan resurgence by several years.

"I am sure you would like proof of life regarding your, how do you say, spouse, Herr Crayle. She's not far."

The captive moaned. "It's best that she's unharmed. For you."

The Aryan turned. "Come, Kaari. Help me place our guest onto the maglev transport."

The two pushed Crayle and his gurney through the open vault door to the modern-appearing vehicle on which he and the doctor had arrived. Its cigar-shaped gloss black surface was only interrupted by three evenly spaced, stainless-steel bands. It sat astride a single maglev rail that disappeared into a tunnel composed of the same reddish substance in the main chamber.

The man produced a remote control that matched all others Crayle had witnessed since his crash. Each was universal in function and universal in worldwide distribution, or so it seemed. The CIA remote. More difficult questions.

A push of two buttons caused an invisible door to lower toward them from the machine, turning into a ramp. They propelled the gurney aboard. With Crayle's head pointed toward the tunnel, he fitted an oxygen mask onto his head, one on his own, and handed one to the doctor.

The Aryan pressed the device once more, and a soft whir sounded. The aerodynamic car seemed to hover. "I understand you favor fast cars, Herr Crayle, but we will be taking this easy. In your present condition, fifty miles-per-hour should be fast enough. But that would take us more than an hour. Although maglev allows nearly 300 miles per hour in the open air, the tunnel's confinement would disallow that level of propulsion in this instance. We have developed an airlock system. Once past the initial lock, we shall accelerate to top speed. We reverse the process at the other end. I must advise you to keep your arms and legs inside."

Past the lock, the vehicle accelerated to speed with Germanic precision as they propelled into the vacuum portion of the tunnel. In a few seconds, the red glow from behind transitioned to darkness. Crayle understood the symbolism. In darkness, one cannot see the dangers ahead.

The seventy-five mile journey, including acceleration and deceleration, lasted just under twenty minutes. It terminated at a large, iron blast door.

Gurney in tow, the pair exited through the door into a waiting room. The floor was a polished granite while the rock walls were now charcoal dark, hewn to a near smoothness. At the center, four polished chrome tubes rose up and out of sight. At their center, connected to the tubes on all four corners, was an elevator like none Crayle had ever seen. Its sides and doors had been constructed of cut crystal. The waiting room lights caused it to glow.

The ride up was smooth. Lights placed in the shaft twinkled through the crystal causing a magical, yet eerie feel.

At the top, Fräulein Doktor Mengele wheeled the captive through a spring-loaded doorway into what appeared to be a kitchen. Stainless steel everywhere. Pots, pans, and tables were all engraved with swastikas signifying Hitler's Third Reich era. Crayle noted oaken blocks—likewise swastika-labeled—containing chef's knives, but realized he hadn't the strength or energy to use them.

"I know what you want to see most of all, but first, I have something else for you to cast your eyes upon. Kaari, you know where to take him. I will catch up." He exited through a nearby door.

"Come," she said to the trussed and beleaguered man on the gurney as she pushed him through a bar area onto a terrace. "It won't do to have you lying there peering up at the sky." She released straps securing Crayle. She pulled him up by his hands, swinging him to a sitting position.

She noticed a threatening look in his eyes. For a moment, she wondered whether their piercing blue would change when cooled to near absolute zero. She recalled her notorious ancestor's experiments.

Crayle struggled, snapping her out of her reverie.

She retrieved her swastika-shaped remote from her pocket. Furiously, she pressed buttons.

He grabbed at his chest. Phlegm and saliva spewed from his lips. "Stop!" he gagged. "Please!"

"There, there. I believe you comprehend this small, but remedial lesson. Let me dial down the lung fluids a bit so you can enjoy the view."

In seconds, Crayle's spasms subsided. He gave the doctor a quick glance, then surveilled the territory.

They were high in the German alps at the country's extreme south near Austria. He recognized it from photos he'd seen. He wasn't prepared for the dramatic beauty and its stark reality. Sharp craggy peaks guarded deep valleys.

"This is *Kehlsteinhaus*. You would know it as Eagle's Nest. Adolf Hitler once stood where you are. In those more orderly times, this was his view."

Clad only in a hospital gown, the stark chill of the afternoon air hit him. He wrapped himself in his arms.

Mengele whipped her hands to her mouth, as if surprised. "Oh. I should have thought."

Walking out onto the terrace, the Aryan swept his arm across the panorama. "So beautiful, is it not, Herr Crayle."

"It is good that you have arrived—" the doctor started.

The man held a vertical finger to his lips. "Our guest is in need of a blanket."

The doctor nodded, then disappeared inside.

Crayle tried to stand, but he lacked the strength for the move.

The man assisted, guiding him to within a few feet of a four-foot, gray safety fence. "Yes, the process inside your body diminishes strength, but produces no negative effect on brain power. You shall remain under our control and be useful. You will find we Germans quite efficient and attendant to details."

As he observed the vista and considered his dire circumstance, Crayle recalled a lesson he'd learned. A lesson learned from an operative he'd pulled to safety on a North Pacific island sandwiched between Siberia and Alaska. Against all possible odds, the man had infiltrated a foreign fortress, grabbed critical intelligence, and attempted an escape through an arctic blizzard. When Crayle had located him through the whiteout by means of an intermittent GPS signal, he lay face down in the powdered snow, near death.

Upon exfiltration by Crayle to a safe house, the operative had shared his survival secret through shivering lips. A mantra. "It's never this cold," the operative had whispered. Crayle's captor was correct about one thing. His own mind was working fine. He repeated the phrase aloud. "It's never this cold."

"What did you say, Herr Crayle?"

Crayle focused every cell to the center of his being. His martial arts *chi*. He summoned every viable cell to the task, and threw his shoulder into the man, knocking him backwards to the fence that skirted the deck's extent.

The man's arms flew into the air, waving as if to regain lost balance. Darkly humorous, his right arm approximated a Nazi stiff-arm salute.

Crayle landed on his side, sending needle-sharp pains through his shoulder and ribs. Nearing full depletion, he had energy for one final move. He kicked out with both feet, striking the off-balance man in both knees.

The Aryan toppled over the gray barrier.

Cries that lasted several seconds indicated a sheer and distant drop.

"What have you done?" exclaimed Mengele.

Having just returned, she dropped the blanket and grabbed for her remote.

Her breathing jumped.

Crayle knew he had to stop her, but had expended every ounce of energy. He lay motionless. If vulnerability had an extreme, he knew this was it.

She pressed MODE, then a second button, then another. Her lips clasped tight as she pressed Volume +.

The man on the deck gasped. Again and again. His condition deteriorated to racking coughs. It was clear. She controlled his pneumonia to the minutest level. And his body's reaction to the device, immediate.

"Yes. I am in control." With her chest still heaving, she continued. "He ..." She nodded toward the wall. "... can be replaced. Neither you ... nor I ... can."

As he fought to catch a breath, Crayle could hardly hear her, his coughs more frequent and severe. Out of control, his body flailed and bounced on the deck like a person being electrocuted.

Together, the two approximated a syncopated melody-harmony chorale that could have been misconstrued as a new music genre. But in mere seconds, she regained her mental balance.

"I will dial this down …" Which she did. "… only if you will behave."

She pressed buttons that both quieted and relaxed his body. His gasping for breath subsided.

"You will, won't you?"

More depleted than before this episode, he didn't respond.

She tapped her foot with impatience.

"*Stimmt?* I mean … correct?"

CHAPTER 12

A short time after the incident on the outside deck, it was the blonde doctor who removed a black Kevlar hood from Crayle's head. While he still felt fluids in his throat, he could breathe in short breaths without gasping. As weak as he'd ever been in his life, he managed to lift his head from his chest.

He found himself seated before a three-foot by five-foot desk, hands and feet bound by nautical rope. Across sat the Aryan—the same one he'd sent over the cliff shortly before—pointing a silenced Luger.

Impossible, Crayle assessed.

"The amazing stem cell. He and I are, or were, precisely alike."

Strange called for strange. Crayle acted as if the situation was not unusual. He bent over, his head touching his knees. His captor's weapon tracked him lower.

"There is no escape, Herr Crayle. We have our own human weapon. It is I. Are you surprised? I think, as do you, in systems methodological terms. We Aryans have our own Blackstone Strategy, renamed *Schwartzstein Kriegskunst*, for obvious reasons."

Crayle winced as he straightened. "*Schwartzstein* is easy. Blackstone. *Kriegs* is for war; *Kunst* for art. War Art. As in Sun Tzu. It's still my Blackstone Strategy."

They fixated on one another as if their two pairs of eyes would soon begin to lase.

"I see that, after all of the mind work performed by the Swiss psychiatrist Rorschach, you still recall your German." He allowed the implication of a former association to sink in.

"How about we skip the peripheral discourse and get to the point. Why am I here?"

"And you deserve an answer. I have utilized my own updated version of the vaunted Third Reich spy machine—the *Abwehr*—to obtain details of your planning, and have further filled in the blanks with the nuclear operations brought to us by the media. The town called Fasd in central Iran, Xinjiang and Beijing in China, Marseille in France, and the abortive attempt on New York City. Those tactical nuclear explosions, the absence of meaningful radiation, and the strategic political outcomes allowed me to assess your mind. Not just what you think, but *how* you think. Hmm, Herr Crayle?"

Crayle straightened, once again staring directly into his opponent's eyes. "If you try to implement a similar strategy based on those few puzzle pieces, you'll discover that the Devil is most definitely in the details. In short, you'll fail."

The Aryan considered for a moment that he might actually require the American's assistance, and then allowed his own ego to set that notion aside. "Your ultimate fate, I'm afraid, is unfortunate, really. It would be beneficial to our cause to possess a backup such as yourself. But reality says that you might provide a strategy leading me and my movement over a cliff. And should you escape—well, you would endanger our—"

Again, Crayle bent over his knees.

Again, the Aryan's weapon tracked him.

The prisoner grimaced. He cried out, as if expelling the pain in his legs.

"Truly, you and I are of the same cloth. I am, indeed, sorry."

Tilting his head up, Crayle watched as the pointed index finger pushed inside the trigger guard.

Now!

Just as the man squeezed, Crayle thrust himself left onto the desk.

He'd imparted a spinning momentum and twirled like a propeller. He rotated in the air, landing on his back.

At the precise moment, he thrust out with his bound feet, striking the man in the head.

The Luger fired.

Its bullet missed Crayle by an inch, and bore through a wall-hanging original portrait of Adolf Hitler.

The timed and aimed blow knocked the man to the floor where he lay unconscious.

Crayle slid from the table, landing on his feet. He heard a sound in the shadows. He glanced at a suspended figure.

His hands and feet still bound, he hopped to where Hekka hung, dangling from a meat hook.

Nearly losing his balance, he brushed against her.

As the body rotated with the touching, he saw the streams of dried makeup marring Hekka's familiar stoic expression.

He also noticed that they had positioned her so that only her toes touched the floor—a mild manner of torture. He stroked her cheek.

In slow motion, she opened her eyes. Filling her vision was the man she'd never expected to see again.

His height advantage matched his up-stretched hands to hers. Without a word, she began to tug at his manacles.

Now unfettered, he reached around her waist, lifting her, freeing her. He released his grasp once her feet touched the floor.

Due to the stress her legs had endured and the strength lost, she fell. In seconds, their hand and foot tethers lay disarrayed on the floor.

Crayle dropped to his knees.

She glanced up at him. "I'm fine. But … I need a bathroom."

In spite of the circumstances, the comment struck him as humorous. He chuckled, briefly. A groan from the Aryan brought him back to reality.

Walking to the fallen man, Crayle had to do something he didn't want her to see. He pried the Luger from the Aryan's docile hand, and pressed the sidearm under the man's sternum, pointed at his heart. He leaned onto his former captor, muffling the shot.

He straightened, and turned.

Her eyes were fixed on him. She knew what he'd done. She nodded. Life running her family's horse ranch had made her a master of the necessary.

And he'd remembered the spy tradecraft taught him years before: *Never allow an enemy a second chance.*

• • •

Kaari Mengele had stepped out to replace the weakened batteries in her vibrator. The gunshot, diminished in sound, had still caused the blonde to jump. She re-entered through the door.

To her surprise, she saw the man, Crayle, holding a smoking gun, and her colleague's uniform despoiled by the spatter of his own blood. The only exit was the one she'd just entered.

She turned to run. She stopped short. Her lips curled into a demonic grin as she spun around and raised her remote control.

In a furor, Crayle emptied the Luger's five remaining bullets into her. One of the shots exploded the remote, before penetrating her heart.

After the reverberations died down, the vibrating silver cylinder rolling across the stone floor made the only sound.

Crayle ran to Hekka, shoving the pistol into his waistband. He made a quick check for ricochet wounds, and found none.

Though the lighting was poor, Crayle scanned the room. On the far side against a wall sat a chair. On it, and folded perfectly, lay the remains of her clothes.

He raised her on a pair of painful, shaky legs, lifted her, and carried her trembling body to the chair.

Slowly, she dressed, still attempting to get her bearings.

She peered up at him. "Oh, God, Magus. I thought I'd never see you again. In my way, I prayed that you'd be safe." A couple of heartbeats passed. "If you'll wait a moment longer, I need to …" She motioned toward a bathroom.

Hour-like minutes transpired before Hekka returned. With all that had transpired since her capture, she was finally able to supply one of her minimalist smiles. "Once again you have surprised me with a unique experience, Magus. I am not ungrateful, but we should leave."

"First, I'm going to light this place up. No more holy sites for subsequent Hitlers."

Hekka, slowed by the treatment she'd received, helped him empty Nazi black file cabinets into a pile in the center of the room.

Having searched desk drawers with no luck, Crayle found a metal match box in the dead Aryan's pants pocket. He spread a bottle of the doctor's ether on the pile, and tossed in a lit match.

Hekka pushed several wooden chairs across the floor, tipping them into the conflagration.

By Boy Scout standards, they'd built a bonfire. However, surprise seemed to be their middle name. Hidden smoke sensors initiated a nano-suppression system as if a fog were rolling onto a coastal beach. The system also sent out a silent alarm.

Crayle pulled Hekka close. "At least we're together again … and alive. Quick, out the front door."

A screech of tires stopped them in their tracks. Then, another. Then, a third.

Crayle spun and withdrew the Luger from his waistband. "There's only one door!"

"I'm ready!"

He spun back. In an instant, she'd pulled together. They'd had many experiences. He recognized her resolve.

"There's a ventilation duct." She pointed to her right. "My Bowie."

Crayle ran to the table and grabbed the knife. They met at the wall duct.

Outside, a machinegun staccato of car doors slammed.

Crayle pried the vent cover while Hekka re-affixed her scabbard jungle style to her chest.

"They don't have the key code for the door." He referred to the noises of those outside as they attempted to violate the entry.

Pop!

The cover fell to the floor.

"You first!" He handed the knife to her. "You'll have to remove the cover at the other end!"

Without a word, she sheathed the knife and pushed into the opening. Her smaller size had become an advantage. Though the square cross-section was barely big enough, she pushed forward at surprising speed.

Crayle, still holding the Luger, realized he'd expended the magazine. He started to toss it on the floor, then realized the noise could signal the pursuers that they were unarmed. He stuffed it back into his waistband, and followed Hekka's path.

While she moved freely along the duct, Crayle's thicker body made for a snug fit. Arms extended, he pulled himself along by his fingers and pushed with his toes.

Light struck Hekka's eyes. Her captivity in the barely lit chamber below caused her eyes to snap shut. Applying sheer will, she pried them open.

Though the light filtered through a long-since cleaned grate, it signified hope. She plucked her Bowie and began work to free their path.

Below, Crayle, still in darkness, felt his body react. The ducting tapered. He was stuck just below her feet.

There was a crash below. The sound of the door being smashed in was blocked to her, but amplified tenfold to Crayle by the metal structure.

Uncontrollably, his heart rate accelerated. Heavy breathing followed. The residual fluids in his lungs initiated a panic response.

Hekka heard. Still weak, she applied all the energy she could muster, hoping to pry open the final grating.

Crayle's hands became drenched in sweat. Inside, he felt like his heart was on fire.

Hekka wanted to help, but kept her focus. The ten-inch knife had strength like her own. It didn't break. But the grating remained intransigent.

"I don't know whether to pry or pray," she gasped.

"Under the circumstances, Mrs. Crayle … you pry … I'll pray."

Her husband's remark caused her to smile only a bit. She redoubled her effort.

There! She had one side. She pressed her head against the grate. With every ounce of her strength and willpower employed against it, the rusted metal gave way.

She pulled herself out onto the ground at the rear of the building. Apparently, the Aryans had lost the notion of surrounding their prey. They'd only left guards out front, while the rest searched inside.

Hekka turned, reaching in to help the overcome Crayle.

Just out of reach.

A rail surrounded the opening. She grabbed it. Leaning in, their fingers touched. Further. Further. There.

At her ranch, she'd had to rein-in horses weighing several times her own weight. It helped. She moved him just enough that she could place her foot against the wall next to the opening and pull with all her might.

Crayle now received an onslaught of oxygen from the opening. In seconds, he rolled out of the vent and fell exhausted next to her.

They heard shouts from inside. The room, fogged with fire suppressant, caused a temporary disorientation of their pursuers.

Then, a rattling, as of metal striking metal.

Crayle grabbed his wife, pulling her to the ground.

Gunshots.

The bullets from the room below ricocheted a couple of times before buzzing past their heads.

With no cries from either of them, the leader knew the captives had exited the air duct. He yelled orders at the top of his lungs.

"Raus! Draussen!"

"Out! Outside!" the leader had screeched.

"Quick, Hekka! They've discovered our means of escape!"

He grasped her hand and, together, they disappeared uphill into the dense surround of trees.

CHAPTER 13

An hour before, the ostentatious tour guide with spiked blonde hair, Hollywood style sunglasses, blood-red pumps, and matching lipstick had caused other tourists and guides to take a second look. Her tour members toted duffels emblazoned with faux team emblems from a non-existent soccer club. Through a light drizzle, she marched her charges up the long single-lane roadway for what seemed like a half mile to the front of the Bavarian castle. Her brash exhortations in American English caused the continental Europeans and one Asian contingent to just shake their heads. And then there was the gum-smacking.

As anticipated, those leaving the site quickly put space between themselves and her group. Also as anticipated, they didn't have a chance to notice the individuals behind her nor the odd bulges here and there beneath their navy blue trench coats. That the over-garments were alike in color appeared like another gimmicky attempt by those across the pond to behave and dress unlike the rest of the world.

The guide, who happened to be the former wife of CIA spy Jack Sommers, clustered her people outside the fifteen foot high, arched, stone entrance. It sat centered in a four-story, red building, perhaps fifty feet wide, guarded on either extreme by ochre and gray towers. "Listen up. The other tourists are now out of earshot, if we speak softly." She stared at Lenny, then gestured at the hostage rescue team's leader.

"The intel supplied by Jack has brought us here." Micmac motioned ahead at the fairytale palace of King Ludwig. "As we trudged up the long driveway to the front gates moments ago, I observed that the only complaints came from Lenny. Since this operation does not call for complaints …" He glared at the P.I.

"Yeah, boss. I got it."

The former UDT man nodded affirmative, considering the issue resolved.

"Jack should've provided a vehicle," Lenny whined. "Clearly, we'll need one to storm this place. And we wouldn't have had to walk up that damned hill."

By now, the team scored high marks in ignoring the P.I.

Micmac stepped next to faux guide, Marli Sommers, and told the crew, "Excuse us a second. We'll be right back."

Before Lenny could react in fear of what might befall him, Micmac clasped Phoebe by the hand and slipped inside the castle entrance. Tossing off long coats concealing wedding attire, the two proceeded through the complex asking questions of the maintenance staff. An explanation that they were brand new honeymooners caused suspicions to drop and answers to come easily from the workers. The pair was allowed to move around on their own—seeking privacy in the world's most romantic castle.

• • •

Outside, Lenny couldn't keep quiet. He stepped over to Marli. "After the to-do in Malibu, how's come you let Jack sucker you into another operation. I mean, fool me once …"

Before Jack's ex-wife could take a swing, former Delta Force operative, Mandy, planted a stiff punch on the side of Lenny's jaw she hadn't already bruised. Down he went.

"Oh," she said. "Man down."

"Yes!" Marli exclaimed. "And look, he's gone quiescent."

The two high-fived.

• • •

Inside the castle walls, as they passed a sumptuous bedroom, Phoebe leaned her head against Micmac's shoulder and whispered out the side of her mouth. "You know, we don't know if Magus and Hekka's situation is desperate or anything." She nodded at the royal bed.

"Hold that thought," he said as he tugged her along.

Still ahead of Phoebe, he rounded a corner, then jumped back. He provided a *near-and-present* sitrep in a whisper. "There are a couple of guards—dressed as janitors—leaning on their mops. They're bored and tired. As soon as they see us … that changes."

"Suggestions?"

"You ever been drunk?"

"Only with you."

He frowned. "I've seen you."

"Well, that was because—"

"Shhhh!" He glanced back around the corner. "Crap! They heard us. Okay … we're faking it."

He stepped into the open, yanking her along. "C'mon, sweetie. Give me a kiss." He pulled her to him.

"Not 'til you promise me …" She staggered into the wall.

The guards slowed to a stop. One mumbled something to the other, and they pointed behind them toward a doorway with a warning sign across its opening.

Pretending to corral his obstinate significant other, Micmac caught a glimpse of the sign's wording.

Achtung!

Gefahr!

Eintritt Verboten!

Rotfels Quarantäne Unten!

Clasping her head next to his, he whispered, "It says that entry is forbidden due to a Redrock Quarantine, whatever that is. And it says it's down below."

"Don't you dare touch my boobs," she slurred. Then, in soft voice, "Everything below ground, so far, has been spy time. C'mon, stagger us over there."

The two, looking like the bride and groom atop a wedding cake *after* the reception, wobbled in the general direction of the sign.

"*Achtung*," advised one of the guards. He held up his mop as if to preclude the drunks further progress. The other man pointed at the sign.

Micmac shook his head in a semi-controlled fashion. "Kine Doytsh. Kine Doytsh. Speaken zee Engleesh?"

The men smiled. Then they laughed. They, too, shook their heads as the souses arrived at their station.

In his training, Micmac had learned the SEAL aspect of taking down sentries. With a flash of his right arm, he slashed a six-inch blade across the nearest man's throat.

The man grabbed at the wound as if to contain the spurting fluid.

The other man, as surprised as the first, flung his hand into his overalls pocket.

Too late.

Phoebe pulled a double-silenced Glock .45 from behind her wedding bouquet and fired once. The second man slammed onto the stone floor.

Micmac shoved the other one down and pulled at Phoebe's weapon. He needed to finish the job.

She pulled away. Her glance told him she understood his desire to save her from the ugly part. She fired once more.

While Micmac informed the others via cell phone, she pulled the two bodies with perfect between-the-eyes entry holes past the sign and into a stone vestibule. Out of sight.

• • •

Having found their way via a Vestige tracking chip that Micmac had placed in his pocket handkerchief, the rest of the team arrived. The team leader filled them in with the rest of Jack's intel. "I've got the original plans for Ludwig's castle. The keep, in case of siege, was deep underground. Check this out."

"There's a stairway down," Mandy observed.

The team was used to receiving intel in drips and drabs—only when needed. It precluded anyone from being captured and forced to supply everything that was known about an operation. No one complained. With one exception.

"Why weren't we told? How does Jack expect us—"

"*Lenny!*" Micmac prepared for a more drastic admonition, but Lenny shut up. The former UDT man returned to the last non-Lenny comment. "A spiral, Mandy. The steps are wedge-shaped. It's one of the medieval means of defense. No-one in armor could navigate up or down. It's been modernized for security. I've seen this before."

"And the satellite photos courtesy of NGA—that's National Geospatial Agency—that President Stones supplied confirm it's Magus they brought there?"

Micmac smiled. Lenny was back on point. "You bet. And since the castle is open to tours all year, this castle keep is the only place they could hold him."

"Alright. Listen up," the weapons specialist continued. "Open your duffels and extract your weapons. Leave the goggles in the bags."

They did.

"They're perfect for close quarters. Full automatic and less than six pounds. As you can see, the front and rear sights have been installed on the sound suppressors." He popped the barrel device off and on. "Simple. That's what makes the Russian weapons so effective."

"Boy, that's one ugly tommy gun," Lenny observed with disgust.

"That's not because I painstakingly assembled each and every one of them myself. They're Russian. They don't mind ugly."

Phoebe nudged him. "Let's finish this up, Mick. We've got work to do."

"A little more, and we're gone. The rounds are AP. They'll penetrate body armor and just about all else. They're also not the usual AK-47 7.62x39mm or AK-74 5.45x39mm ammo. They're 9mm. So don't plan on pilfering some downed tango's stuff to replenish your supply. It won't work in these. Use your ammo with discretion."

Phoebe frowned as if uncertain about Micmac's last comment. "I'll have to work on rippin' some perp a new asshole *with discretion*."

"Four twenty-round clips each. They've got a little heft, but the plastic mags minimize it."

Unable to remain silent for even short periods of time, Lenny glanced over at the FBI agent and threw in, "There's probably room in your bra. Just kidding." He smiled into Phoebe's laser-like glare. Quickly, he turned to the team leader. "This is rock and roll time, isn't it?"

Micmac grinned. "Okay, kids. Since I've got the helm, rock and roll!"

He led the team through a ten-foot passageway and turned, his finger across his lips for silence. He spoke just above a whisper. "Listen up. Ingress down the spiral will be one-at-a-time."

Lenny swiveled his head back and forth. "Doesn't look good from an attack perspective."

"Yeah, but check this out. Around the outside is a stone railing. I've created a new invention just for this task." He motioned them into a huddle.

Phoebe jerked back. "You have got to be kidding."

Micmac moved to an electrical box on the wall, quickly destroying its padlock with a can of liquid string—a mixture of C-4 with special, classified ingredients his mother had used in her Irish stew.

"Done," he pronounced when he'd finished inside the box. "Everyone. Weapons at the ready." He pressed his knife across two terminals.

Klunk!

The team peered down at the spiral stairway.

"Mandy and Marli. This is your post. Guard our sixes."

Micmac's machinations had caused the modern version of the ancient spiral stairway to reconfigure. Each pie-shaped step twisted to a 45-degree angle changing the structure into more of an approximation of an auger than a stairway.

Each donned night-vision goggles in anticipation of their turns. This was it.

Under his breath, the leader yelled, "Follow me!"

First in, Micmac slid round and round as his crew watched. Having produced a submachinegun from God knows where, he sprayed the walls as he slid down the slide.

The plethora of slugs hammering the walls produced a spray of ruby fragments, some of which embedded in his Kevlar.

So far, no return fire. He let out his breath.

Up above, Phoebe stepped to the side of the P.I. "Go ahead, Lenny. Pretend it's the E-ticket at Disneyland." She gave him a shove.

Although he was armed in similar fashion to the team leader, the fact that he fell head first produced a random spread of gunfire that caused Micmac to dive for cover. Slugs dinged off walls, the ceiling, the floor, the staircase, and everything else that didn't present a threat.

Phoebe waited a second, then followed. Unlike the two who preceded her, she sought actual targets before letting loose with her Glock. No luck. The chamber they'd invaded was empty.

Once Micmac assured himself that the room was clear, he stepped through the wide open vault door and located the rail transportation system. When the rear guard received his call, they re-joined the team. Their ingress down into the chamber evinced a release of tension. Micmac thought of his old fun-park days far from battle.

Phoebe stepped over to the red-glittered wall to investigate. "These are gemstones. Really." She spun on her heal to see a stainless steel table on rollers occupied solely by Doktor Mengele's tools of the trade. "Ah, a chisel." With the bladed tool and a heavy glass ashtray in hand, she returned to the wall.

"Phoebe!" Micmac yelled in a hushed voice. "Put that down. They went that way!" He pointed to where the rail system disappeared.

Just as she stepped over to him to have him repeat himself, the chisel flew from her hand, and snapped tight to one of the rails.

"It's maglev," Micmac deduced. "Wait." He set his weaponry a safe distance away, then moved closer. He heard what sounded like a whisper, and then it stopped. "Whoever is riding this …"

The chisel thumped to the ground.

"The magnetic power has been cut. They must've arrived at the other end." He grabbed the chisel and tossed it to Phoebe. "Wait. It's started again. Everyone, at the ready. Either they're coming back, or just returning the transport unit."

It was the latter. Micmac listened as the whisper grew louder and the empty car arrived at the station.

"I'm guessing on this, but there are probably only two ends to this line and, at the other one, we'll find Magus. Lenny?"

"Rock and roll!"

Following the same path that Crayle and his captors had taken not long before, the team took twenty minutes—and a number of concise conversations on what they might find—to reach the bowels of Eagle's Nest. Assuring that it, too, was empty, they carefully moved outside. They found neither cars nor enemies in the parking area.

"Hey!" came from the tree line.

The team crouched as low as they could, weapons at the ready.

"*Micmac! Phoebe! Lenny!*" shouted a grateful Magus Crayle.

"*Mandy! Marli!*" Hekka followed, waiving her arms.

"We're up here," they chorused. "The Aryans are gone."

Micmac stood first. Then, one-by-one, the rest. At least for the time being, all seven of Team Crayle were alive. They were safe. And at least one seemed to have retained a sense of humor. Marli. "Where's Jack? I'm gonna kill him."

CHAPTER 14

Just minutes after the rescuers had arrived, team members Micmac, Phoebe, Mandy, and Marli sat on lounge chairs, taking in the mountain vistas of South Bavaria and savoring welcome breaths of the cold, fresh air. Across from them on a wide futon, protected from the wind by a short stone wall, lay an exhausted Magus Crayle and his sleeping wife.

The calm aftermath was broken by Jack as he, having missed the entire battle, made an entrance. He took center stage. "Just in from my own battlefield."

"Which side, boss, the Blue or the Gray?" For once, an off-color comment emanated, not from Lenny, but from the former Navy man.

Jack smirked. "What does Phoebe see in you, anyway?"

"It was a news broadcast that did it. She thought they said SEAL Team Sex."

As with the P.I.'s lame jokes, this one drew restrained laughter.

"Alright. Listen up, once again. What we have here I call an SFU, my friends. A Situational Fuck-Up. Not to be confused with my lieutenant." He glanced around. "Where is Lenny, anyways?"

"He's off taking a leak, Jack."

"How do you know what he's doing?"

"I've got the watch. I'm required to know such things." Micmac tilted his chin to demonstrate his commitment to responsible behavior.

After a brief grimace, Jack continued. "Everyone's safe, and that's nothing to sneeze at. But that's the only good news. Pattie and the remaining Aryans are gone. The bomb's nowhere to be found. Lalumière, we can assume, is out there somewhere. His son, Jean-Marc? Who knows? On top of that, the Illuminé hierarchy of Monsieur Pope and Monsieur Elder are still in business."

"Quieter, please. Hekka needs some serious rest." Crayle lifted his eyebrows for emphasis.

Jack nodded and lowered his voice. "Having just arrived here at Eagle's Nest, I've come to a conclusion. Hekka is as much of a trouper as I've ever seen. Truth is, she can't go on. Her new groom here has been infected with a virus of some kind that can be enacted by remote control." He turned to Crayle. "Magus, I'm sending Hekka back to America to receive the treatment she needs and deserves. You're going with her. Are you up for that?"

"I'd like to fight with you on this …" He coughed up some phlegm. "… but this time you're one hundred percent correct. I'll get her back to whatever hospital you can arrange, and maybe they can eradicate this bug I have."

"My first thought was the triage unit we have at Manassas. However, I believe the chartreuse walls just might drive you nuts."

"What are you thinking?"

"The Quarry."

"You're kidding, Jack. I've got some serious history there. Besides, the Quarry hospital is three hundred feet underground, and filled with the tons of gravel that dropped through the ventilation system when Rorschach pressed the wrong button. Like the Manassas facility porta potty ingress, another one of Neil Wohlford's security features."

"Hear me out, Magus."

Crayle closed his eyes to calm the panting caused by the induced pneumonia. "Go."

"As you recall from our pitched battle at the Roman Colosseum last New Year's Eve, Rorschach—who appeared briefly—had not died from the flooding of his covert, subterranean hospital with the quarry gravel from above. Now how about this? Recently, I received intel informing me that he also didn't die in the flooding of the Colosseum caused, in full, by our save-the-day colleague, Lenny."

"Save-the-day? Lenny?" Micmac shook his head.

"Oxymoronic," Phoebe editorialized.

"Did I hear my name?" the P.I. called out as he strode across the deck.

Phoebe looked him over. "Oxymoron? I can see that. Your fly's undone."

With an uncharacteristic sense of decorum, Lenny stopped and turned away as he corrected his wardrobe malfunction.

Irrespective of Phoebe's comments and Lenny's antics, Jack maintained his focus. "At Lalumière's château? Lying blindfolded on the Frenchman's guillotine? Tossing Phoebe's weapon to her to take out our first triangle-jawed triplet, TJ? Did you forget?"

"You're right about that one." Crayle glanced wistfully at the Alpine peaks. "Not even a year ago."

"Back on point. Rorschach is cleaning out the hospital under The Quarry. The *company* can't afford to lose his research and that's where it was. The work is mostly completed and the place is fully staffed to handle any covert medical needs that stray onto our homeland soil. There is also a new, five-star virologist who can check you out. She's from Liberia where she helped put Ebola back in its box. Please, Magus, this is best."

Crayle mulled over the idea. "I agree. Let's all get ourselves to the airport and head back."

"Uh, there's one more thing." He allowed a collective uh-oh to pass, and continued. "With all the questions we have regarding the bomb and who went where, I'm keeping Phoebe and Micmac in Europe with me. And I won't let Lenny venture any farther than Amsterdam. I'll tap into him if I think he can help."

"In that case, Mandy and I—your permanently former wife—shall adjourn to Ludwig's lake for a swim."

"Can I come?" asked Lenny.

"Sure. You can watch our clothes."

"Whatever all of you are going to do, at least help me get Hekka to the jet. We'll have to retrace down below and take the A-train back to mad King Ludwig's place. The airport's not far from there. So you're all on your own while we recuperate. By then, you should have some actionable intel. Something operational that can help us put all of this mini-nuke crap to rest forever."

Jack chuckled at Crayle's reference to Duke Ellington's *Take The A-Train* big band tune. He'd once taken the Manhattan A-train to Harlem, himself. A quite different time and a quite different place. "You finding this a bit tedious, are you?"

Crayle grimaced. "I promised Hekka a honeymoon. No bullets. No explosions. No kidnaps. That kind of thing."

Phoebe smiled. "The guy's a romantic."

• • •

Besides the bodies and accoutrements of battle strewn along the way, the underground trip back to *Rotfels* proved uneventful. Crayle cradled his wife to protect her from the transporter ride, although moving her up the Micmac-reconfigured spiral stairway presented quite the struggle. The two parties said their goodbyes on the steps of the now vacant Ludwig castle, so Crayle and Hekka travelled alone. Transport to the awaiting Falcon 8X was smooth and uneventful.

As the crew helped Crayle get Hekka aboard, a frantic man ran across the tarmac waving a paper.

Crew members reached inside their leather flight jackets.

"*Die Ausweispapieren!*" he screamed over the jet noise. "*Die Ausweispapieren!*"

"Our clearance papers," advised Crayle. He reached down and received the papers.

The officer nodded, smiled, and turned back toward the flight tower at a steady pace.

The flight attendant sedated Hekka and strapped her to the bed while Crayle watched over her. The pilot accomplished a takeoff in the ensuing ten minutes.

• • •

Back in the castle, the remaining team members—minus swimmers Mandy, Marli, and Lenny—assembled in the former king's bedchamber. Worn out, they plopped onto the bed side-by-side. Eyes closed, Phoebe and Micmac snuggled together and quickly fell asleep.

Jack had one final thought before he followed their lead.

"Now, what would mad King Ludwig do?"

CHAPTER 15

Despite the cold he'd acquired while skinny dipping in the lake of Bavarian King Ludwig, Lenny Lipschitz finally felt he would accomplish something for the team completely on his own. His new employment in a third-floor flat on Amsterdam's infamous canal-street didn't impede his progress. What did impede his progress was a special ring on his special cell phone. He considered letting it go, but Jack never left messages, he just called, and called, and called.

"Will this be quick?" He winced, then cursed at his choice of a greeting.

"No, Lenny. What will be quick is your untimely demise once I get my hands on you."

"Sorry, boss."

There was a moment. "Me, too. I'm all wound up. I have a sitrep for you from this end, but it sounds like your deep into something. Care to share?"

Lenny certainly did not want to share. He was desperate for positive points and sure that a big, good surprise later beat the hell out of sharing today. "We attended Wofie's funeral this morning. I've determined that all funerals, whether for a legitimate brother or a bastard one, are a bummer."

"Is Alona okay?"

"She's bummed, too. She confiscated the black credit card you gave me, and went shopping. I'm expecting her back any minute, so let's get to your sitrep."

Before Jack could respond, there came a thump—thump—thump at the door that he could hear from his end.

Lenny couldn't believe his luck. His little white lie about expecting her back soon while she was out emptying the stores came true. Damn the luck. "Just a sec. It's Alona."

He wedged his cell between his cheek and shoulder, and pulled open the door just in time to catch a trio of shopping bags. Tossing a smile at his wife and turning to cross the room, he returned to his conversation. "Yo!"

"Next time, Lenny, we're getting a place with an elevator."

"This sucks. And to top it off, being on the second floor over here means you're two flights up instead of one. Something like that." He placed the bags on their small, off-white kitchen table and raised a finger to his lips. He mouthed, "Jack."

A very tired shopper found the energy to place her hands on her hips and purse her lips Phoebe style.

"Hi, Jack," she said.

Lenny waved her off. "Jack, it's me again. Let's hear what you have for me."

"Sorry you had to run back to Amsterdam after the recent op, but standing up Alona might have been worse than the Aryans. Long story short, we're done down here in southern Bavaria. Here's a recap. Tell me if I've left something out. The good news: we found Magus. The better news: he rescued Hekka. All of us are safe and sound—well, Hekka's kind of bunged up. Anyway, those two are on their way back to the States. I'm staying here with Micmac and Phoebe."

"Yeah, I know all that. And the bad news?"

"Everyone else that matters on the other side also survived. I've checked with the Germans, the French, and back at Langley. They've vanished."

"I don't suppose you found that final atomic bomb."

"No such luck. That mini-nuke is MIA, as well."

Lenny thought for a minute. He figured to have his great score completed before the end of the night. Congregating with the team might be a good idea. It would allow him to show off.

"Since we're done here, we can meet you someplace. I'm still a private investigator. You with your contacts and me with my P.I. skills can run these people down. Micmac and Phoebe can take 'em out. It's perfect."

"And Alona?"

"We'll have to see. She's still grieving for Wolfie. But listen. Nobody can find shops like her. She'll be cool wherever we alight. What do you say?"

"I take it by that last remark that she's not still in the room with you."

"Yeah. She rushed into the bathroom. Must've been the stairs. How'd you know?"

"If she heard that last remark about shopping, I would be experiencing a sonic rendition of your pain."

"Did I say something wrong?"

"I'll let that drop. I like your idea about a meet. Given our past with these clowns, I'm down to one place. I'm thinking Paris. Tomorrow. Noon. *Les Deux Magots*."

A smile crept onto the P.I.'s lips. "It's been awhile. How will I recognize you?"

A reddish tone crept onto the project manager's face, but he fought back an angered response. "Just ask for Mr. Hemingway."

Click!

• • •

Alona waltzed back into the living room, wrapped her head around Lenny's and affixed a category four kiss. She backed away to admire her lipstick tracks. "Jack wish us a happy honeymoon?"

"No. He wished us to meet him tomorrow at noon."

"Fabulous. He's coming here."

"Paris."

"I'd complain. But as miserable as I still feel, and the fact that Paris is the shopping capital of the entire world, I'm in." She closed in for another assault, but Lenny clutched her shoulders.

"Maybe you should stay here. I have a feeling that this whole mess is going to reassert itself, and that means it's going to get dangerous."

"Like bloody hell!"

"I completely understand where you're coming from, but I need you safe in case I live to need another meal. By the way ..." He nodded at the groceries. "... what's for dinner?"

• • •

The next day brought heavy rainfall to France's Île de France region and turned Parisians into indoor spectators. Automobile traffic stopped. Sidewalk traffic all but stopped. Only the most desperate of the locals hustled along, umbrellas aloft, staying at best damp, and hoping the gusts of heavy winds didn't turn them into real-life incarnations of Mary Poppins.

The restaurant on the west side of Place de Saint-Germaine-des-Prés, with its signature blue awnings, was packed with fugitives from the impromptu storm. The tall-paned, dark wood doors kept the beating rain outdoors, though the onslaught was apparent to those seated next to full view windows facing the street. Driven by spats of heavy wind, the rain pounded a relentless pattern on awnings that projected from under the restaurant's neon sign, making conversation all but impossible.

Those who'd managed themselves into the Parisian Left Bank *Les Deux Magots* observed the natural mayhem outside and pretended they wanted it to cease. So they could return to work. Someone pointed at an idiot across the street madly attempting to access an ATM. The man, obviously soaked to the skin, finally exhibited success. As he yanked a handful of bills from the machine's clutches, an even heavier gust arrived. Only the more desperate ran from the restaurant sanctuary to seek their good fortune.

In a way, the hapless man's disaster and subsequent melee drew attention away from the two men and one woman hunched over a small, window-side table.

"I realize that you both have gone to Amsterdam for the funeral of Lenny's brother, Wolfie. Now that it's over, I want you both to take some time off. For each other and to transport your brother's body back to the States."

"Thanks, boss." Lenny wasn't about to tell Jack about the one pound bag of flawless, one-carat gems he was attempting to fence in diamond city. "After his birth mother passed away, Wolfie moved to Holland and made it his home. He'd been accepted into the University of Leiden, but you know that. It's where he met Lalumière's son, Jean-Marc. You know that, too."

"Sure. Then he got the job as a broker buying and selling stones."

"Stones?" said Alona, proffering her third finger rock. "I don't mean to be sentimental, but my mother told me that carrots were good for you. I got the spelling wrong. These three carats are what keep Lenny healthy." She waved her ring finger for emphasis.

"As I said, you two should take some time off. I'm thinking, a whole week."

"A whole week," Alona croaked. "Gee, Lenny. We could … we could …"

Ever prepared to emit sarcasm, Lenny followed. "Did you give Magus and Hekka that much time? Or Phoebe and Micmac? We wouldn't want special treatment."

Jack stirred his coffee for the eleventh time, considering the special treatments Lenny might deserve. "Guys. We're sitting on a situation."

Alona elbowed her husband. "He's still sittin' on his ass. But go ahead."

"Recall that the new American president, Kimbel Stones—who participated in all of our marriages—is former NSA and is just to the right of the political center. On one hand, he doesn't want to prop up the socialist president of France. On the other, he feels compelled to prevent the deployment by Lalumière and Pattie of the final nuke and the subsequent slaughter of tens of thousands of innocents. It's a dilemma, but Stones is a first class problem solver. He and I talk every day right after he has his Intelligence Briefing. This issue is top-of-the-line important to him. I … hell … your country needs all of you 'til this threat is over."

Sotto voce, P.I. Lipschitz began the Star Spangled Banner.

"Shut up, Lenny." Alona's eyes engaged with Jack's. "Continue, please."

"I'm focusing on Lessons Learned, as we call them. A lot of time has passed, and we still haven't put this to bed. While you're doing all this relaxing in Amsterdam, I'm giving myself, and MI6, and France's DGSE—you met Charleroi in Paris after we thwarted the nuke threat on the Eiffel Tower—a few days to gather what we need. Then, we gotta go. I only hope we have that kind of time."

"So it's just the English and the French that can help. How about the Russians? If it's on the Internet, they know about it."

"I don't have anyone in the SVR. They play it close to the vest since they have more to fear from their own Kremlin than foreigners."

"How about the former *Komitet* folks?"

"The Committee? The KGB?"

Alona supplied a vigorous nod. "Little-known fact. My parents were Soviet Jews. They spoke Russian at home, lest they be recorded speaking Hebrew. If you could ferret someone out of your black book—former Mossad—who still has connections …"

"Are you saying you'd be willing to chase down, very discreetly of course, something there?"

"You bet. Ex-KGB still hate the Germans and would help the French in a heartbeat, just for spite."

"I support your heart on this, Alona, but you lack the training. There's more risk here than you can imagine."

"Training, schmaining. I'm betting there are closet Jews who are ex-KGB—they'll help."

"And she'll nag 'em until they do," Lenny asserted.

Jack knew when to capitulate. His options were few. "I'll check out resources from my side. In the meantime, think about taking it easy back in Big Bear, okay?"

"I can work best from Europe," Alona said. "A lot of folks remember the Holocaust. Lenny can go back if he wants. Just not for long. A gal can get awful horny in a week."

Jack could feel the P.I.'s pain as his wife's sex object, but he made no further comment. As he stirred his coffee remnants for the twelfth time, he considered the likely future to resemble a black hole. As you viewed it from a distance, you saw nothing. You stepped closer and closer, squinting, still not seeing. Until you crossed over its event horizon. At that point, it sucked you into its center, crushing you into its infinitely small, infinitely dense central mass. Its singularity.

CHAPTER 16

Another fabulous Southern California day in Big Bear Valley. May 5, *Cinco de Mayo*, and the skies were clear and very, very blue.

Magus Crayle took it upon himself to prepare breakfast. He intended that his new bride, Hekka Crayle, and former teammate, Lenny Lipschitz—who'd just happened back from Amsterdam for a visit—to be his "patrons" for a special meal. That is, if she were present.

He padded into the cabin's living room. The weave of the carbon fiber that comprised the tray would have been a conversation piece were it not for the camouflage Kevlar covering. He smiled at the certainty that this warm and wonderful cabin now belonged to him and, by that, to Hekka.

Lenny sat before a wall-length, floor-to-ceiling book shelf, his attention on a novel. "What if all this were real?" he mused.

"I've read that author. It's about spies and politics. How much could be real?"

"Hmmm. What'd you fix?"

"I prepared a nouveau Big Bear repast with eggs, herbs, red and green bell peppers, raw onions, Gruyère cheese, and bacon bits. Gruyère's used in Swiss fondue, French onion soup, and *croque-monsieur* sandwiches, in case you're not familiar with the name." Crayle waited.

"Actually, I wanted …" The diminutive P.I. glanced up at the silence.

Lips pursed, chef Crayle set down the tray. "Wait one, Lenny." After a quick retracement to the kitchen, he returned with a butcher knife, pretending to clean his nails. He glanced over his shoulder at a knife block. Not to select one as a backup, but to see how many more there were. "What was that, Lenny?"

"You're doing the pursed, protruding lips thing, just like Phoebe does."

"No. She does that. Then, she rubs her fingers up and down on her Glock's slide, imagining a ten-ring right between your eyes."

"At first, I thought it was a come-on."

"I'm sure it was. Like, come on … make my day."

"Hey, Mag. That was a good Clint Eastwood."

"Who's that?"

Lenny returned to his book. The repartee reminded him that Crayle had lost a greater deal of his life than even the team realized.

While Crayle pondered doing Phoebe a favor courtesy of the butcher knife, Lenny continued.

"I like this other author, too." He pulled a boxed-set from the shelf. "That's LT. She writes romances. *The Warrior Series*. A four-book set about warriors messing with women."

"They don't mess with them, Lenny. They love them."

"Ah. I see. *You've* been reading this shit. Getting ideas for Hekka? When you're alone?"

"You mean, when they've finished with her at the Quarry hospital. She suffered a great deal physically and mentally at the hands of the Aryans. It'll take a couple of weeks."

"Rorschach told you that?"

"Yes. Doctor Rorschach has a lot to gain by staying on my good side. I've agreed to help him restart his research as long as he sees that team members get triage, repairs, and rehabilitation wherever we happen to be."

"And you trust him?"

"Now I do." He drew the dull side of the knife across his throat. "He understands the consequences if he breaks that trust. As for Hekka, she'll be back in business soon and, when she's ready, we'll be headed out on a serious honeymoon."

"What about all the lunatics blowing stuff up? It's not like you to just give up."

"Jack's back at the CIA in the position vacated by Neil Wohlford. Out went the bad guy and in comes the good. He has all the backstory on this operation and all the assets he'll ever need. He told me the president weighed in, using the words *carte blanche*."

"Wow. Nice to have a friend in the highest place. But what about the Chinese guy? Didn't we learn that his number two, General Li, not only supplied all the nuclear stuff, but he also killed your dad during the Vietnam War? It's been less than a year, but I believe I know you. You're not one to let the important stuff slide."

"To be honest, I haven't ruled out violence in his case. But don't you see, Lenny? I can't leave Hekka for a revenge that even I consider selfish. She's been through far too much. Not for herself, but for me. Even you should see that."

"Even I, huh. You know, you're right." He shook his head as if an epiphany had exploded in his frontal lobe. "You're right. I lied to you up front. Last fall when all this began, I kept my dad's involvement in your stuff secret. That was selfish."

"If Alona hears you talking like that, she's going to double down."

Before Lenny could respond, the front door creaked open. Lenny reached inside his jacket for his Walther PPK, just in case.

It seemed that, throughout the Crayle experience, there had always been a succession of emergency gurneys in play. He recognized the medic rolling this one as the same man who'd brought him to the cabin for the first time—what was it, he asked himself. Last October ninth? Seven months ago? It all drifted into the background when the patient's eyes met his.

"Magus, I want a big kiss," she said. It sounded more like a formatted moan than a request.

"Hekka, you're supposed to be rehabilitating at the hospital. For weeks. What do you think you're doing?"

She drew in a deep breath, and then released it. "My mother used to talk that way to me. When I was young."

He knew he'd managed to step on a land mine. Besides the murder of his father and the missing Lalumière mini-nuke, the issue of her mother's continued sequestration in Finland remained unresolved.

"It's fabulous that you're here. I was just fixing some grub. How about *Omelette aux herbes à la Crayle*?" He fabricated a smile.

"With respect to your first question, I decided to rehab here with people who mean the world to me. After removing the tons of gravel and making repairs, that hospital is still cold and antiseptic."

"Well, duh," opined Lenny.

Still in serious pain, Hekka twisted her head in his direction. "Oh, hi, Lenny. I didn't see you there. Have you seen my Bowie?"

"Jeez-Louise. I was just kidding."

"Your delivery needs work."

Crayle jumped in. "I hate to break up another Lenny love fest, but how about that omelet?"

"Sure. How about the three of you extricate me from this metallic exoskeleton and position me at the table on the deck. Close to Lenny so I can kick him if he acts up."

"I'll be on my best behavior."

"We'll see if that's good enough."

He prepared a retort, which she quelled by raising her hand and pretending to thumb the blade of her 10-inch Bowie.

"Look, I'd love to stay, but Alona and I have a date back in Amsterdam. I'm out of here on the 10:20."

"It's *our* jet. Scheduling on demand," said Crayle. "There is no 10:20."

"No, that's when Alona scheduled it. She does all my travel planning now."

"All right. Rock and roll, P.I. The medic can help me get Hekka outside for some fresh air. Then he, too, can leave, and we'll have a modicum of peace around here."

"I almost forgot. Micmac wanted you to stop by his place this afternoon. Maybe when your lady here is taking a nap."

"I wonder what he wants."

Lenny was out the door before the question had been asked.

Hekka rocked her head back and forth. "I was a little tough on him, wasn't I?"

Before Crayle could answer, the medic cleared his throat and produced a questioning tilt of his head.

"Oh, sorry. You must have work to do. Here, help me get her outside."

The younger man wheeled her out the back door as Crayle held it open. "Perhaps I should stick around. She'll need some long rest periods on a very soft surface."

"We're good." Crayle glanced over at her. "We have a water bed. They've been used in hospitals for severely injured patients, but I suppose you know that. And I've carried her to bed before."

"Ah, a romantic. Then I'm out of here. Take care."

Like Lenny, he made a quick exit.

Seated, they moved in on their respective omelets, Crayle dug in while Hekka pushed her food around the plate.

"Yes, you were a little hard on the P.I. I thought for a moment you were channeling Phoebe."

"I'm a little worn out. Makes me snappish."

"Yes. Kidnapping and torture will do that. I'll see that you get a lot of rest—and want for nothing. How's that?"

"It's when I'm back in shape that I'll want for nothing, if you know what I mean."

Both smiled.

"Finally, we're together. Alone. It feels good."

"My dear husband, you don't know just how good it feels. I want this forever."

"As I mentioned to Lenny, we are out of this now. Lalumière and Pattie have the last bomb somewhere in Europe. I'm very sure that Chin won't give them any more. I hope Jack and his operatives find it and disarm it. In any event, I'm making this promise right now. We're done. Finished. No more. From now on, it's all about us. What do you say?"

At first, nothing. Then, for the first time in a long while, he could see her relax.

She closed her eyes.

"Us."

CHAPTER 17

A day later. The Ironwood plant in the back yard had started to green up and a gray squirrel sat on its haunches next to it, as if trying to remember where he'd stashed his pine nuts prior to the onset of winter. The Crayles were still in bed, their guests waiting patiently in the cabin's living room.

At about nine o'clock, Phoebe had stopped by for a visit and sat at the breakfast bar. Having just finished cleaning her Glock, she closed her eyes and, in the next few seconds, slid the components together, racked the slide, and dropped the hammer. Eyes still shut, the stabbed a full clip of 230 grain, .45 caliber Hydra-Shoks into the handle and racked the slide a final time.

Lenny had gotten the day wrong for his trip back to Amsterdam. It seemed Alona was enjoying the quiet. As a consequence, he just slept in the jet and retraced to Big Bear in the morning. Having seen the Phoebe MacKay show many times, the P.I. sat quietly and paid no attention. His mind was focused elsewhere.

"We need to party." Lenny hefted a gallon-sized, see-through jar.

"Is that all the vulgarity fines we have? I'd swear we'd have more by now."

"It was your swearing that helped us get *this* far. Besides, I tamped it down."

"You have half a jar. They're $5 bills, but …"

Lenny walked to a wall cabinet and popped open a door.

Phoebe's jaw dropped. "Wow, Lenny. The one you have is number six. Damn."

Lenny closed the door and gingerly approached her. Without a word, he unscrewed the lid.

Phoebe let out a gasp and withdrew her tactical billfold. "All I have is a fucking ten, Lenny."

"Just the right amount."

"Oh …" She thought. "… crap."

"Crap comes in under the wire. Let's have the ten, please."

"I need to call Jack for another advance." She stuffed the bill into the jar.

"Not to despair, my dear Phoebe. Don't forget about the pound of diamonds that belong to us. Magus has 'em well hidden."

"Not to sound unfriendly, but don't you have to be someplace? With respect to those very same diamonds?"

"No offense taken. Yeah, I need to get back to Amsterdam, fence the diamonds, and see to Alona's needs. I'm sure she's standing there right now checking her watch."

"Come on, Lenny. You make her sound like a sex-a-holic or something."

"Sex-a-holic? After the marriage, which I'm sure you remember, we went shopping for new furniture—to make her place ours."

"That makes sense. So what?"

"She buys a coffee table that's padded."

"Padded?"

"Any flat surface."

"I see. You need a ride down to Jack's airport?"

"Well, Magus is in the bedroom, standing watch over Hekka. Sure."

Lenny grabbed the spy novel and the boxed-set, explaining that the warrior romances were for his wife, and headed out. Just a bit of work in Amsterdam, and he and Alona would be back home. To a normal life.

They walked out to their respective rides, assuring that security was set behind them.

• • •

Thirty seconds after the two blood enemies departed, Crayle helped his wife out into the living room. Gently, he settled her on the sofa. He'd added a gel-foam pad for her comfort.

He glanced around the room. "No blood." He looked some more. "No bodies."

"I heard two car doors slam. I bet she took him to the airport. There's still time."

Before he could think of a response, she spoke again. "Come here, Mister Crayle."

He moved to the side of the sofa.

She gave the slightest of smiles, then pulled open her robe.

"You're …"

"Uh, huh. Naked."

"But you're in no condition to …"

"I need some loving, Mr. Crayle."

He sat up straight, pondering the possibilities. "Close your eyes."

CHAPTER 18

General Li, head of the armed forces of the new Imperial China, checked his watch. "Ah, May 7," he said to himself. He glanced over at the young woman next to him—his gift from the Emperor Chin.

Red daughter peered out the stone window opening at the day. She lowered her gaze to the city, and across the harbor to Kowloon. She'd viewed it from the platform on what was merely Victoria Peak. The fog-encrusted skyscrapers still hid the intrigues of the plotters and schemers below, but her new palatial residence made all that somehow distant.

Li lifted himself to a sitting position on the second most important bed in China. "Today's forecast, my dear?"

Red leaned into the opening as if to prognosticate. Out of sight, she manipulated her cell phone. "It will be another fantastic day. Wait." She leaned further. "Perhaps a little rain. We should stay inside and see if we can soften your new bed."

"My new bed is no longer new. Still, I see merit in your suggestion."

"Given your position, I believe it is your decision to make."

Propping his elbow on his knee, with his forehead resting on two fingers, he approximated a more robust—and far less muscular—version of *The Thinker*.

"I control the entirety of China's armed forces, yet I feel vulnerable. Part of me is intensely loyal to Chin. The other feels exposed. He is the supreme leader. Accountable to no one, Red. I am number two to the man, who has become one of the strongest men in the world, and I feel weak."

Red daughter stroked his neck with the backs of her fingers. "Let's think this through, as would Magus Crayle." She felt him bristle. Inside, she smiled. It was necessary to practice the manipulation of powerful men. In a non-threatening manner, of course. "I was present a few years ago while he developed the Blackstone Strategy. I heard many things."

"Then, let's try. But we must take care in mentioning Mr. Crayle. Chin believes the man walks on water. Or could. We must, over time, diminish him in some fashion … or see that he is killed. Sooner would be better than later. But, please continue."

"Our Chin developed wealth from the stock market. He earned no loyalty for that. But we must realize that the common people love him and will continue to do so, as long as he is their savior."

"Free market policies—that signaled the philosophical end to Karl Marx and led to individual and sovereign wealth—created a house of cards. It got away from Beijing. Citizens got a taste of the good life and demanded more. Democracy. Freedom. And when the Communists lost control, it all fell apart. The nuclear explosions in Xinjiang and Beijing confirmed that all control was lost."

"Their blaming of the Muslim foreigners had no effect since our people already opposed helping Iran gain nuclear weapons."

"Enter Chin—and I—to the rescue."

"As long as the common people do not know that you supplied all those weapons." She pressed with her thumbs.

"Oh! Easy … there … ah. You are right, my darling. It is no wonder the people are happy. And they will remain that way unless our secret is divulged."

"You have said it. No more mini-nukes. We have only the final one in Lalumière's hands to fear. Don't you believe it would be best to eliminate him?"

Li had been around a long time. And to survive in the People's Republic of China, one had to be able to read others. He caught Red's manipulation. Instead of admonishing her or worse, her conniving intellect brought a smile. She would become a most able assistant as well as his artful lover. "If we repossess the final bomb, we wouldn't need to kill him. Or that woman by his side, Norbrunn."

Red considered apprising Li of Pattie's multitude of identities, but thought better. Best to confer intel a bit at a time. "To your earlier point, the eyes of our people are on Chin." She thought a moment. "The daughters."

"What?"

"In the beginning, we were selected at age thirteen from orphanages and, secretly, from families with more than one female child."

"I remember the law. To control our population, Beijing permitted only one girl-child per family."

"We became Chin's daughters until age twenty. His way, his training, his thoughts … that was all we had. By the nature of our existence, we became loyal to the extreme."

"But he told me, the daughters are no more. He freed them. Freed you. We would have to track them down."

"The recent twenty-year-olds, Black and myself, are still here. The rest—I don't know."

Li couldn't bring himself to tell her what Chin had revealed in utmost secrecy. Before Chin's declaration of daughter emancipation, they had been led away on their twentieth birthdays and executed.

Red continued. "There are several of the current twelve on the island of Hainan. They guard the remnants of the old communist government."

General Li caught an inspiration. "A single bomb, one of the small nuclear devices could …"

"As Magus Crayle would have said, kill two birds with one stone."

"Two?"

"*Poof*, and the daughters and their threat to us is gone. Along with the remnants of the communist leadership. Hmm?" She placed a sensuous kiss on his neck.

"That is brilliant."

"And the radiation sponge covering the bomb would eliminate radioactive fallout. We could explain it as a huge gas explosion in the terra cotta mines of Hainan."

"Your scheme gathers relevance and momentum. In fact, it is brilliant. And it would destroy a third bird—the guardians of Chin's legacy, the clay warriors."

Her lips moved to his ear lobe. "It is *our* scheme," she whispered.

"It would take a miracle for us to pull that off. Forget it for now. Come here, Red."

• • •

New Beige had just rotated duty from Hainan Island, arriving at Hong Kong's Lantau International Airport. A quick trip up Victoria Peak by hardened SUV, and she finally relaxed. She'd taken a free moment to check out one of the many secret passages she'd already discovered in the palace.

Standing behind a wall panel, she'd just overheard Li and Red and their seditious plot. Truth be told, she'd developed a spiritual connection to her predecessor namesake, Beige—the girl Chin had executed in the Dragon Building's Training Room for a mere declarative statement. The plot of Li and Red, if carried to fruition, could be caused to evolve into her own vicarious revenge. In original Beige's memory, new Beige's lips were sealed. For now.

CHAPTER 19

Later in the day, General Li received a summons to a meeting with Chin Yao-wu in the Imperial Study of the palace. The windowless nature of the room disallowed the otherwise wondrous views afforded from the top of Hong Kong's Victoria Peak.

Li, prompt as usual, was greeted by a sullen Chin. With trepidation, he sat on a chair lesser by a magnitude than the new emperor's. He appraised the situation. Time to listen.

Blue daughter—like new Beige—on hiatus from assignment on Hainan Island, carted in the liquid refreshment. Chin referred to well-aged Scotch as mind-enabling. Li found it to be mind-numbing, but appreciated it just the same. Fifty-year-old, Blue informed, before exiting their presence.

The two clinked and sipped. When Chin was sure the young woman was gone and the door securely fastened, he spoke.

"We need to express our sovereignty, Li. During communist rule, the absence of Chinese hegemony in the region was the single-most prevalent source of citizen unrest. As you are well aware, protests against communism itself and the ruling elite were prohibited, but demonstrations against the Japanese, Taiwanese, and Vietnamese were allowed. We cannot make that same mistake. Our first move in this direction will be to secure the contested islands. I wish to hear your counsel, to make a determination of action, and then to achieve your commitment to that end."

"My troops can take the islands. The Vietnamese are quite busy with newfound wealth. They have taken note of our communist predecessors, who first swilled on the wealth production of capitalism and then allowed it to flounder. The Vietnamese government will pose no problem."

"We are no longer two countries under communism, so we are not required to cooperate with them. Aggression is an option."

Li smiled. He sipped his Scotch. He felt sure Chin had made up his own mind and was rendering mere professional courtesy with his inquiry. He sat back, smiling. "I've known you a while, Chin. You've thought this through quite thoroughly, as is your norm. Invasion is my thought … please tell me yours."

Chin appreciated Li's assessment of the situation. The general was a good number two. "I have a better idea. It could gain us not only the islands, but the north of Vietnam lost by those Tang Dynasty fools."

"Yes. In the 10th Century. What is your plan, Chin?"

CHAPTER 20

When Li returned to his apartments, he found Red lying in bed and clad in an eponymous negligee. His heart rate was already outpacing his mind's capacity to keep up with the possibilities. He was naked on top of her *in flagrante* in moments. Sampling every bit of her, he finished in short order.

"What I did … that was new for you?"

"Yes," she smiled and laid her head on the general's chest as its heaving lessened. "As Father's daughters, we were not allowed intercourse." She made a circle with one hand and poked a finger from the other through.

"Yet he allowed you and the others to pleasure me—and, I'm sure, other of his guests—orally. Why?"

"Only those senior enough to wear gold embellishments on our cheongsam dresses gave pleasure in that manner. The understudies were too inexperienced."

"So he didn't mind the potential legal hazard regarding underage girls?"

"To earn the gold, we had to do well in our studies, perform our tasks within the Dragon Building you visited in the Wan Chai, and be at least eighteen."

Li nodded both understanding and approval. "He kept Black Daughter exclusively for himself, didn't he?"

Red's jaw tensed. She rolled away.

"I am sorry to bring that up. I can see that you still hold being spurned deep inside."

He was right. The spurning transpired over several years and competed with her deep-rooted loyalty to Chin. She'd turned her anger and frustration toward Black. And that reality played right into Li's hands.

"I need your help, Red."

"I realize that Father gave me to you. Please don't be offended. It's perfect. I will be your most trusted warrior."

"And lover."

She sat up, turned, and sat astride him. As she leaned down, her silky black hair fell forward, obscuring her face, tickling his flesh. In secret, she'd viewed every bit of pornography she could find. And, in Chinese territories, porn was plentiful. Pressing her lips hard against his, she forced her tongue deep.

His body reacted.

She reached down and forged the connection. As she began to move, she pressed to his ear. "Anything you desire. Black has become Father's greatest ally. I will kill her if you command."

They both experienced an adrenalin surge.

He hadn't realized just how badly she wanted to do in 'sister' Ling. For a few seconds, he pondered how he would take advantage of that fact.

"Later, when I command it. I … we … need both of them for now." He felt his climax near. His panting interfered with his ability to speak. "You will … prepare … a commercial drone … to deliver a … very special … payload!"

"I am committed … intrigued. But now … I want *your* payload."

With an expulsion of all that was trapped inside, he complied.

• • •

Not too long afterward, Red realized that Li's project would require her to work outside the palace. As Chin's technology guru, she'd overseen the design and implementation of Intelligence Surveillance Reconnaissance, ISR, technologies. She didn't love the general. Not yet. But she greatly appreciated her position next to the second-most powerful man in all China. With Chin number one, and with no outside threats, she saw two possibilities for her future. Stay with Li and help him overcome Chin, or drive a wedge between the emperor and his favorite, Ling. Then, fill the void.

Before her transit became available, and while observing the beautiful Hong Kong environs, she took advantage of her private moment to reflect. And to scheme.

Despite his extreme personal wealth, Chin had recognized the role his daughters had played in his success and happiness, rewarding them with travel privileges. Missions. And though Black had captured his heart early on, she had failed in her December trip to Italy to retrieve Crayle. Red concluded that she needed a major success to add a few more arrows to her quiver. Her only dilemma at that point would be whether to fire, figuratively or literally, those arrows through Black's heart.

With the tram currently closed to civilians, and the road down Victoria Peak full of press and common people, Red travelled by one of Li's helicopters to his primary base of operations near Kowloon on the mainland. The soldiers recognized the young woman and her signature dress immediately. She was escorted, according to direct orders from the general, into a large hangar.

• • •

Red's instructions from Li were to become familiar with the new attack craft, and then to meet him at a specified secure location in nearby waters.

The room was austere. No place to hide microphones or cameras. Everything—walls, ceiling, and floor were painted a pearlescent white. The imperial color seemed inappropriate—she hoped it wasn't chosen by her general.

"*Ni hao!*" came a familiar Cantonese-accented voice from behind. "I am so glad to see you, I forgot that we are under orders to speak only English."

The surprise startled her. Prepared to spin and defend, she recognized the voice. The general's technologist. "Pleased to see you again, Gao. I am here to view the new aerial weapon. All I see is an empty room. That you are here to greet me tells me that I'm not in the wrong place."

"Ah, always the intelligent one. Yes, I am here to greet you." He drew close, and whispered, "The craft is so new and so secret, it cannot be displayed." He couldn't restrain a Cheshire cat grin, as he stepped to a wall switch. When he flipped it, the pearl white hue disappeared. All surfaces turned matte black. And there, in front and almost touching them, sat a giant four-cornered aircraft.

Gao stepped to a two-person ladder that had appeared against a wall and rolled it to where she stood. "Please, climb with me."

She proffered her hand, and he helped her to ascend alongside him.

"Magnificent, Red?" he baited her answer.

But Red couldn't speak. Multiple fuselages, four large rotors that would spin horizontally, and most significantly, no cabin or flight deck.

"It's a drone," he beamed.

"Oh, my," emanated from her blank stare.

"Come with me now. I will brief you on the flight characteristics, including its lift capacity. The general hasn't told me the mission yet, but I have some ideas." He whispered again.

Her eyes popped open. "But—"

He stopped her with a finger across her lips. "Do not speak of this. Are we clear?"

She nodded.

The briefing took all of thirty minutes—quite brief. He placed the room back into stealth mode, and led her outside to the landing pad.

Ever polite, her technological colleague pried open the helicopter door to ease her entry.

Red waved goodbye to Gao. She slid into the seat beside the pilot. She turned to authorize lift off. What she saw startled her.

The pilot responded by tilting her chin ever so slightly.

"Blue! What are you doing here?" Red demanded. "You are supposed to be standing guard over the remaining communist leaders in Hainan with the others. And what are you doing in the pilot's seat?"

The daughter dressed in blue twisted toward her foster sibling, and handed her a headset. "I received instruction in secret. By Father's direct order. It is my task to convey you to Macau. I shall do so forthwith."

Red winced at the upscale English being employed. What was going on? What *else* didn't she know?

Once they were up and headed west over the South China Sea, Blue broke in on the intercom. "I only have the minimum twenty hours, and I only passed the ground school test by Father's declaration, but I expect to deliver us in perfect condition."

Red's jaw dropped. She grabbed her seat harness straps with both hands and pulled tight. Then, a light turned on in her head. Of course. Blue had spent all her spare moments watching re-runs of the *Magnum, P.I.* series set in Hawaii. There had been a helicopter pilot—a Vietnam war veteran—who flew tourist flights like a pilot in combat. She held her breath as Blue took them down to sea level and skimmed the surface.

When they'd landed safely atop the destination casino in Macau, Red quickly bailed and ran beyond the idling propeller downdraft.

She turned to see Blue lift off, a brazen grin typical of most pilots adorning her face.

Bodyguards escorted Red straight to the penthouse suite. Her heart decelerated from a pound to a throb. As they neared a door with another two bodyguards, she felt able to transition from a near victim to a general's lover. It occurred to her that there were proper times for one's heart to race. And she smiled.

CHAPTER 21

The penthouse suite was far more elaborate than she had imagined. Done in a style honoring the oceans which defined the former Portuguese territory, the designers had taken it to the maximum. Red's university studies had included architecture. Classic, nouveau, retro, everything. She recognized the bold color touch of Zaha Hadid in every aspect of the great room. The softness and aquatic flow could be expected from the architect of the spectacular wave-shaped roof created for the London Olympic Games of 2012.

Red also recognized the 5'6", 200 pound frame of General Li from behind, as he gazed east. With the sun setting behind their casino, the skyscraper lights across the water flicked on here and there in Kowloon and in Honk Kong's Central District. If one looked far left, one could see the entrance to Guangdong Province. But she knew those lights were not his focus. Not by a long shot.

"It does you no good to stare at his palace. I can feel the vibe from here. It upsets you. Soon, you will leave me and head downstairs … to the gambling."

"They are planning a marriage."

"Except for Mr. Crayle."

He reached over and clamped his free hand on her wrist. "What?"

"Ah!" she cried out. "I can't tell you!"

He squeezed tighter.

She looked up at him, her brow knit tight, her jaw clamped, her eyes ready to plead. "I'm protecting you!" she gasped in pain.

Li loosened his grip. At first, he was amazed at her adeptness in turning the tables, and overjoyed in his choice of a woman. Then, reality struck. "Protect me how?"

"Do you believe that he would actually have sex with Black Daughter?"

Li shook his head. He pressed his hand to the window, clinked his drinking glass against it, and continued his stare. "No. To do so, Chin would have to despoil her. In reverence for his mother, and the rape that brought him to be, he would never—"

"He would and he will. Don't you see? By freeing all daughters, he sends a message: we are no longer indebted. He has pledged that we shall have whatever we wish."

"And what is it for you? What do you want?"

She moved up behind him, laying her head against his back.

"My daughter name is Red. I want a brand new, red Ferrari."

"You are below the average age for a Chinese owner."

"Which is?"

"Thirty-four."

"I've earned it."

"Pleasuring me was such an endeavor?"

Slyly, she smiled and reached around for his zipper.

He grasped her hands and admonished, "We must keep focus," he glanced down, "on the larger items of our agenda."

She withdrew her hands, noticing his body's quick reaction to her move. As she spoke, her smile evaporated. "You are number two, Li Ya-fei. If they marry, you drop to number three."

He reminded himself that Red was very young, yet precocious. He smiled. "As his wife, she becomes peripheral. She will care for the home, have children, and so on."

Red, now naked, stepped to where she could see his reflection in the glass, and he hers. She cupped one hand over her exposed breast, and pushed the other down across her belly. "You think so?"

The general gulped his Scotch and turned to face her. "Chin will not succumb to mere feminine wiles."

"Perhaps. But there's one more thing."

"What could there be?"

"She will become Empress."

Li's glass shattered on the stone floor.

CHAPTER 22

The jade tablet that Chin had received from the Elder had been installed on a protected pedestal in the center of his palace yard. For protection, its standard repose was lowered in a secure and very private chamber. He rose from his bed, and took a seat at his royal window. He glanced down at the empirical courtyard below.

The new emperor of China pressed a button on the remote control insinuated in his regal chair's right arm rest. The jade tablet engraved with his divine right to rule the empire rose on its pedestal to a height just above eye level. Any dignitaries allowed inside the palace walls would be required to cant their heads upward to view the left side, with its legitimate inscriptions. To the right, they would view the juxtaposed forgery legitimizing Chin Yao-wu as a pre-ordained emperor. He took a great degree of comfort that its existence had been promulgated to the Chinese public. They now revered him.

He viewed it for a full ten minutes, then lowered it back into its chamber. He returned from the window seat to his bed—one that had also belonged to his spiritual mentor, first emperor of China, Ch'in Xihuangdi.

Ling, lying on the bed fully clothed, set her tablet computer on the night stand and stood, facing him.

"I can no longer refer to you as Black Daughter. From now on it will be Ling. Or perhaps I shall use the name given you when you attended the university in California. They westernized your given name An-yee to Annie. I will call you Annie. What do you think?"

"Using such a name is very Western and means that we are close." She stepped to him and turned, facing away.

Chin stared at the back of her cheongsam. Staring back was the black zipper that contained her chastity. The implication, after all he'd been through, was too much. "You are twenty years old now … Annie. Like the others, you may have your freedom. You can go anywhere, do anything you choose. Do you understand the word, freedom?"

Still facing away, she responded with confidence. "The university taught me about freedom. Although I was young and required creative documentation to enter, I could hear and see what the other students did. And they invited me to parties, which I declined. I was careful not to drink with them or risk being slipped a drug." She peered at him over her shoulder. "My purity was key to our relationship. It is different now. I want to give myself to you. In every respect. Please do me the honor." She grasped the tab. "Let me show you what you have earned."

Before Chin could react, the huge doors burst open as if blown from their hinges. General Li stormed in. "Forgive me, Chin. Oh, I see you are pondering the requirements of your future wedding night. That is as it should be. Please excuse us, Black. I have an urgent matter demanding a decision at the highest level."

Chin still hadn't caught his breath. He glanced at Li, then at Black as she exited through the drapery. Still pure.

"It is the Aryans. They wish to take us up on our offer."

Chin really wanted just to sit there, exasperated. The call of his station in China's new politic, said otherwise. "I'm sorry. To which offer do you refer?"

"The bombs, of course. Don't you recall. We had decided to end employment of the mini-nuclear devices towards our strategic political goals. Since we had achieved those goals, the bombs could cause us severe grief with the world community should they be further employed, and should their origin trace back to us. The hard fact is that the Aryans want them and have huge stashes of cash or equivalents in their Swiss vaults."

"Why do we need cash? We have a whole country's treasury. We own China, and through our possession of the American and European bonds, we own them, too. Why, Li?"

"Through the research of my technical guru, Gao, I have discovered that the communist leadership, having run into strained times, played the stock market with our country's financial resources. And having loaned trillions to a bankrupt America, we shall never see a penny. Europe is even worse. In short, we are somewhat desperate. I urge you to consider and to authorize this deal."

It was too much. In the span of a few paltry seconds, the general had dismantled Chin's dream. They were broke. He hung his head, then glanced up at Li.

"No one must know. About the bombs. Or about our financial condition. Do you understand that, my friend?"

Li, ready for a long back-and-forth give-and-take, couldn't believe his ears. He knew from experience that he had made the sale and needed to pack up his virtual valise. Further dialog could only change Chin's mind. He bowed deeply to signify the emperor's wisdom on this issue. He departed the royal apartments sporting a quite large smile.

• • •

General Li stormed into his own apartments like someone staging a one-man assault. "Red! Chin has bitten. We must brief new Beige and send her on her mission. This is fantastic!"

"Congratulations are in order, my darling. I will fetch her immediately."

"Not just yet. There's something else."

Red had turned for the door. She stopped. She twisted her head, eyeing him with raised brow.

"You have all the skills of my trusted technologist Gao. The two of you have worked well together. But, sadly, he had become a liability. Should Chin, or one who is loyal to him, cause Gao to loosen his lips, the fortress we plan for ourselves could become a house of cards."

"He has been with you forever. He would be loyal. I'm sure of it."

"But there is a small chance, one too dangerous to take. It is time you prove to me that you will do anything I ask, and do it in any manner I specify. Do you accept this challenge?"

She stepped back and gave careful thought. Was this a test? She didn't know. What she did know was that she must give the correct response. "Anything. I said anything." She held her breath.

Li looked at her in surprise. He considered the momentous situation at hand, then found the words he needed. "Good. Very good." At this moment, Li felt the need for a clear conscience. "I want you to seduce him. In that way, you will demonstrate his disloyalty. At that time, you will evince justice."

"So that we are clear. You want me to take him to bed, and then you want me to kill him."

In another circumstance, Li would have smiled broadly at Red's commitment to him. But Gao had been like a son. He closed his eyes, wondering what manner of narcissism could drive a man to even consider such an act. He thought of Shakespeare's Macbeth. What manner of man?

He broke through that train of thought. "We now have something of far greater import to discuss, Red. Far greater."

She began to breathe easier.

CHAPTER 23

General Li glanced around the room, then spoke in a hushed tone. "The Nazis of the 1940's were close to having an atomic device. World domination was within their reach."

Red—far too young to have even learned of the Nazis—wondered where Li was going.

Li continued. "We can supply the bombs. The mini-nukes. The Aryans are a scientific people, and they will appreciate the radiation sponge technology."

"Have they not observed the recent five nuclear explosions?"

"Most assuredly. And they have, without doubt, observed the absence of radiation and calculated the tactical and strategic benefits of such weaponry."

"How can we be sure that they won't conquer Europe, then use them against us?"

"An excellent question. They will ask for more than they require in Europe, and then attempt to reverse engineer our radiation sponge."

"For areas they don't wish to control, they might want the fallout—to wipe out the inhabitants and make the land unlivable. Could China fall into that category?"

"Ah, that's what I love about you, and why I shall make wonderful love to you, as usual, at precisely 8 p.m. We have thirteen minutes to continue our plotting, and you know how this excites me."

"Yes, my General."

"We must string out delivery so that they only use the devices tactically. They will need the supply chain for more weapons and won't risk destroying it. And since there will be no more devices detonated in our country, the world will focus its attention on Europe."

"The Aryans must not attack nuclear nations. That would invite reprisals."

She could see the excitement expressing itself in the general's apparel.

"How many minutes, Red?"

"Seven."

"Quick! The rest of it!"

"Yes. They will do what they always wanted: destroy Paris. Then, because of Mussolini's failures: Rome."

Her breathing accelerated to match his. "Three minutes!" She began to disrobe.

He tore at his uniform buttons. "They will take out religion—their nemesis—with a Rome bombing. Two birds with one stone."

"Properly timed," she said as she panted, "they will take out the pope."

"Severely damaging Chin's powerful Illuminé friends."

Li shrugged his pants off—his physical control overtaking his mental.

They fell to the dense, lush carpeting. Red went to work.

"I can see a timer in my mind's eye … four … three …"

Red pounded atop him.

"Two … one!"

Their outcries approximated a nuclear explosion in miniature.

In a special room not far from Li's quarters, the sounds emanated from headphones. The cacophony would have caused anyone else to yank the phones from his head and toss them aside to dissipate the pain. That is, if Red hadn't paid him a visit earlier. No one would find the security man's body. The secret space wasn't even on the architect's drawings.

The pounding of the two lovers continued unabated, Red's vertical moves crashing into Li's. Their plot, and their sex, climaxed as one.

• • •

On the third day following Li and Red daughter's meeting of the minds, the operation, already drawn in broad strokes in Li's mind, was set in motion. Two days later, it transitioned to Europe. From the general's point of view, they needed to move quickly before an unknowing Chin could throw a monkey wrench into the plan.

CHAPTER 24

The sun was busy setting on the western landscape of Bavaria. Eighty miles northwest of Eagle's Nest and the catastrophe for the Aryans that had occurred there, the co-conspirators sat in an upstairs room, meeting for the first time. As workers arrived to initiate the weekend, the cacophony of brotherhood reverberated up the stairway. From the lederhosen-bedecked oompah band, strains of the prosaic toasting and drinking songs, *Ein Prosit der Gemütlichkeit* and *In München Steht Ein Hofbräuhaus*, punched through the heavy wooden flooring from below. It caused the pair to speak much louder than they would have preferred.

This was, indeed, the hall of the happy when it came to letting down one's hair. Hundreds filled the place. They drank and sang until the doors closed for the night.

Otto von Prem, upwards of six feet tall and sporting just over 200 pounds of toned muscle, raised his one-liter glass of golden, fresh beer and toasted the woman who'd just arrived.

"*Ein Prosit, mein Liebchen*. A toast."

Pattie Norbrunn, not a shade over 5'3" and just north of 100 pounds, lofted her own liter of dark beer. Together, they bounced the bottoms of the heavy glass steins hard on the oaken table, then clashed them together. The splash of liquid from one glass to the other was tradition. Without taking their eyes off one-another, they drank the toast.

"*Ausgezeichnet!*" the Prussian aristocrat exhorted as his deep blue eyes penetrated hers of artificial blue. "Magnificent! With your blonde hair, stunning blue eyes, and the body I imagine under your south German attire—*Dirndl* it is called—you are representative of Aryan perfection."

The young woman, who'd entered moments before and had taken the appropriate seat next to him, smiled her dimpled smile. From the years she'd spent in southern Germany in her late teens, she not only knew about the *Dirndl*, but also how to take advantage of its accentuation of one's feminine charms. And while a man stared, she could scope him out in search of other vulnerabilities.

"I stand but 1.6 meters. My height might be considered perfection in miniature. True perfection would be taller, like the doctor, Kaari. *Stimmt?*"

"Yes, you are correct. It is unfortunate what happened to the doctor. There are not many with her talents … or her bloodline. She will be missed. But hear this well, *mein Schatz*. Perfection is not merely a look. It pervades. Every cell takes part." Seated at the end of the table with her to his right, he leaned over and kissed her forehead.

Pattie had done her homework. She'd reviewed photos of the man's wife and daughter. She knew about their tragic accident on a rain-slicked autobahn. "I remind you of your daughter, don't I?"

"Please, another subject." That a Turkish immigrant had struck and killed his loved ones was too difficult a reminiscence.

She tilted her chin only slightly. "The bomb, then. We shall discuss the bomb."

"Ah, yes. I am in need of your nuclear device. You almost caused me to forget."

"Trouble is, Otto, I have a use for my bomb."

He leaned back, as if to construct a line of logic she couldn't deny.

She smiled. "But I can connect you to someone with a supply of them. An endless supply. What do you think of that?" She reached her foot under the table to provide a first distraction. Then she reached him with her hand.

Otto seemed to like the idea very much.

"Come on, my darling. We are quite alone here. Make me happy. Then we will talk."

• • •

Three days later, Otto von Prem travelled to the Caribbean island called Barbados to meet with Imperial China's top military man. Pattie set up the encounter, assuring both parties that she would be present to perform introductions. And that she would see the arrangement to fruition, whatever that required.

Normally rock steady, the Prussian aristocrat's nerves were a bit on edge having been tested by the drive-on-the-left nature of the former British territory. Upon being shown into a sumptuous suite, reflective of his own normal, the nerves dialed down noticeably.

"General Li." They shook hands. "I've heard much positive about you." Otto managed a genuine-appearing smile. He witnessed Li's skin tone. Similar to that of the non-Aryan Turk who'd taken his loved ones.

"Ah, Herr von Prem. Likewise, I know of you." He nodded at Pattie.

Prem appeared nervous for a second. "Please introduce the beautiful lady who accompanies you."

"My number one, Red, is taking care of business in Hong Kong. I have borrowed this one from Emperor Chin. She is called Beige."

"A lovely name. She is quite pretty." Von Prem discerned a certain intelligence about her. He'd never slept with a non-Aryan until

Pattie. He considered that perhaps the characterization *inferior* was too harsh for those with cosmetic imperfections.

"I've been informed, Herr von Prem, that you may wish to construct a new Germany and, in the process, to blow things up. Certainly, what I have at my disposal could be applied to pre-construction projects. A sort of clearing the way?"

Prem inferred immediately that Chin was no fool. He would not be sucked into any plots or schemes. He would keep his skin *out* of the game. To him, this meeting represented a business transaction.

Li continued. "For instance, if a project required, say, five million tons of TNT, it would be far more practical to use one of my compact devices the size of, oh, say, a rugby ball. Wouldn't you agree?" He followed the rhetorical with, "And for that convenience, one should be expected to pay …" He turned to Beige.

"Twenty million in Euros. Twenty-four million in the preferred U.S. Dollars."

The Prussian winced at the dig. Surely Li realized the Aryan goal would include a retreat from the Euro to a new German currency reinforced by substantial ruby reserves. "We will, if you agree, General, conduct all transactions in the American dollar. It is the least weak of the world's currencies. Until we have back our Deutsch Marks, of course."

"And until the new Imperial China floats the Yuan."

"I concede that your currency is the strongest, Li. And by your comment, I presume that such floating might occur in the near future." He nodded approval. "Perhaps this begins a long economic relationship. Of mutual benefit."

"At some point, you may have something we need." Lips closed, the general smiled. "I propose a toast."

"Excellent. We Prussians do that frequently."

• • •

A short time later, Pattie, Beige, and von Prem arrived at Sandy Lane. While one would expect to find rich and famous patrons, the

Prussian chose it for the reputed discretion of its staff. The luxury resort, positioned on the west side of the island away from the crashing Atlantic ocean, provided the white sandy beaches and shallow, warm turquoise waters for which the Caribbean Sea was famous.

The three gathered poolside, utilizing a nearby two-story waterfall to cover their conversation.

"Thank you, Pattie, for everything. At this point, I'm sure you want to meet in private with the general. I will see to Miss Beige."

"She's young enough that I should chaperone. Appropriate, my dear Otto?"

Beige interrupted. "I'm eighteen. I can chaperone myself." She caught her indiscretion. "But thank you for your consideration, Ms. Norbrunn."

Three items came to Pattie's mind. One, she did not like being dismissed. Two, she wasn't sure about eighteen, although Asians could be a difficult tell. And three, for reasons tactical and sensual, she wanted to stay and play.

In less than five minutes, the trio entered the Prussian's sumptuous and quite large lodgings. The two women toured and inspected the facility—both for security and just plain curiosity.

Their host selected a classical station on the room's stereo system, but kept the sound level moderate. He wished to establish a mood.

Beige, caught out of a comfort zone she'd enjoyed for several years in Hong Kong, stepped to the bar and poured first two, then three glasses of Scotch from a crystal decanter. She turned. Her smile for the occasion disappeared. She dropped the two glasses she carried for her guests. There, standing before them, Pattie disrobed. She caught both onlookers by surprise, affecting them both.

Von Prem, used to being in control, was not.

Naked, Pattie stepped to Beige, reaching for her buttons.

• • •

Two hours had passed. Von Prem and Beige were fast asleep. Pattie stepped out onto the balcony and punched Li's speed-dial number on her cell phone.

"So, how many?" he asked over the single-use phone Pattie had supplied him. "And where for delivery?"

"He needs five. It's good to keep him hungry. Let's give him two. Delivery to occur in a small Swiss town in northeastern Switzerland. Gossau. From there, he can easily move the devices north into Bavaria."

"Funds?"

"Also in Switzerland."

"I need you there. To oversee and ensure delivery, and to see to the money transfer, and then the deposit into the specified account."

A few seconds passed. Li disliked delays. It meant the other party was considering options.

"Ms. Lalumière?"

"Sorry. I was checking on the logistics. I had to locate the village on my tablet. Yes. There it is. Fly into Zurich. Ensure the deposit of good Aryan funds into the account as I specified. Receive the bombs. Hand over Swiss account number to you. Train east to Gossau. Deliver the bombs. Are you coming or is someone else bringing the product?"

"You will be informed when that decision is made. However, I want this transaction concluded as soon as possible. Do you understand?"

"Once you get Chin's okay, we can get it done. I'm with you on the hurry part, by the way. I have some other things to accomplish." She smiled to herself. She could almost feel Li bristle when she suggested the need for Chin's approval.

CHAPTER 25

Another sunny day in Barbados. The winds—severe as they accosted the eastern coast, but mild trade winds as they crossed to the west—kept the air sweet, balmy, and fresh. International spy Pattie Norbrunn looked like a delicacy in her black bikini. The only embellishments were gold fleur-de-lis, kept small by virtue of the paucity of material.

Having dismissed Beige back to Li, she and the leader of the new Aryan movement, Otto von Prem, had spent the night together. She had, once again, made herself unforgettable. They took breakfast in the room the next morning, opting for European fare.

They both sat naked, unashamed, with pillows propping them up for their repast. Pattie had convinced the much more formal aristocrat to try something new and exciting. "Food," he had said. "Exciting," he had said. Between bites, she showed him what she meant.

Once they had finished in all senses of the word, he leaned back onto the pillows, and pulled her against his side.

In turn, she laid her head against his chest.

"I understand that you are a superior assassin."

The young woman said nothing. She reached for the Luger she'd placed on a night stand. "An '08." She popped the clip, assured herself that it was full, and returned it to its operational position.

"You seem comfortable with it."

"My grandmother acquired it during the Second World War."

"I hope she wasn't too severe with its owner. Hmmm?"

"Like her mother before her, she was a spy, Herr von Prem. A Dutch spy." She emphasized nationality to remind the Prussian that his beloved forebears, the Nazis, had invaded her birth land.

For a second, he stared. "I've read that the Dutch had the second-best whores. Many spies used that façade to acquire intelligence, and to assassinate." He lowered his monocle. "Excuse me. I must use the men's room."

He stood. His 6'1" height and perfect Aryan physique had already made an impression on her.

Being a detail type, she knew all about the man. In order to display his extensive knowledge of spy tradecraft, he'd left the firearm accessible to her, with cartridges, but had removed the firing pin. She suspected it gave him confidence that someone—she in this instance—might expose themselves by accessing a weapon of convenience. Then, he would pull his SIG-Sauer 10mm from under his pillow.

When he returned, the Luger was back in her hand. He'd already assured himself that, had she intentions to kill him, his mental superiority would win out.

As expected, she pointed it at his head. Unlike the typical assassin, she smiled. She drew her dimples deep. She fired.

Had Pattie not turned the barrel left at the last second, the Prussian would've been dead. As it was, he reeled from the blast that had singed his ear lobe. Burned gunpowder darkened his flesh.

Façade shredded, the fear of death seized him by the throat. He gasped.

She placed the smoking gun before him.

He lunged for it, pointed, and yanked the trigger. Nothing.

"You'll need these." She lifted an ashtray cover to reveal the remaining cartridges from the clip. A soaking in cigarette ash and Schnapps rendered them unusable. "I know more about you and your habits than your mother."

His face resembled the soup in the ashtray. Ashen skin and beads of sweat. He knew there was no need to access his own weapon. He also realized that the smartest man in the room was this woman.

"Now," she said, sounding like a business executive. "You want what I have. Scratch that. You need what I have."

"Please." He raised his hands in surrender, then moved from the bed to a deep red, high back chair. "Your position affords you an unobstructed sight line to all manners of entry, should the sound isolation of the room have failed."

Pattie observed his move as a corroborating sign of capitulation. "I put you in the Rock and Roll Suite. Sound proof. Anything else?"

"We shouldn't have lost the war. Our leader lost his mind. Like your previous president. He—"

"Save the ideology for another time. Bedtime, perhaps." She smiled. Additional sex would have to wait. Still, how his demise might befall him would be left to her imagination. "You want my bombs."

"I … we require the devices. Our—"

"Stop!" From under the covers, she produced his 10mm. "Cut to the chase."

"Twenty-four million U.S. Dollars was the agreed-upon price."

"Remember the Swiss, Colonel? And their francs? I want those. Same amount, different currency. *Verstehen Sie*?"

"I do understand. But that's more expensive. The Swiss Franc has moved ever upward, and the Dollar in the other direction. One franc equals 1.2 Dollars now."

His plaintive plea fell on deaf ears. "That's the deal. Swiss bank. Swiss Franc."

The Prussian was clearly perplexed. There existed no Dollar tree to produce the money, only the Nazi rubies embedded in the *Rotfels* caverns. And fencing that could expose not only him, but also the entirety of the Aryan Alliance.

"If you'd like to think it over, I have a nine-o'clock with German royalty. They have access to my amount." She started to rise.

He raised his hands in surrender. "It will be as you say."

She handed a slip of paper with a long number and a bank name. "Memorize it. Wrong bank … or wrong number, and we're done."

He did, and then he watched her as he dressed.

She retrieved the paper, dropped it into the ashtray, and covered it. She pointed the SIG at him and motioned him toward the door.

As he moved, he noticed her placing the ashtray atop his desk candle. He started back.

"*Halt!*" She assumed a combat stance. "*Schtop!*"

The sound-proofing muffled the ashtray explosion.

"I'll postpone my royal meeting. Once. You have twenty-four hours. Remember that, like all the other citizens of Europe, the German people are finished with the democracy crap. It's you or the royals. Oh, and the royals are all gathering next week. What's that place? *Neuschwanstein*. Celebrating their re-ascendance in mad King Ludwig's palace."

"We must have your bombs. With them, we can destroy democracy, and the royals."

"I need you to replace the democracy with an emperor."

For the first time in a while, he smiled, his lips curling at one end. "Would a kaiser do?"

"It will have to be a peaceful kaiser. I need for you to make an entire people very happy."

"I can make my people—"

"No."

Non-plussed, he shrugged. "Who then?"

"My people. The French."

• • •

Having agreed to take a commercial airliner rather than risk each other's private transport, it took the two conspirators just under an hour to pack, travel to the airport, and lift off for their destination, southern Germany. Pattie had suggested that, to defend against surveillance, she enter the terminal first, followed by him twenty minutes later. He agreed.

It was a fact of life under current circumstances—and the paranoia that kept spies alive—that caused her to tote her sole remaining mini-nuke wherever she went. She knew it was safe from Otto since he needed more than one, and would scotch that possibility if he absconded with hers.

A security officer ordered the young woman carrying a football to deflate it. When she protested, he threatened confiscation. She made enough of a fuss that he sequestered the both of them in a secondary inspection room.

Sometimes in the Caribbean, rules become non-rules, and non-rules become rules. She imagined the man arriving home with a brand new, confiscated rugby ball for his son. The unfortunate fact: her paranoia forced her to transport her ball wherever she travelled. And, she couldn't deflate a five-megaton nuclear device.

Her mind vectored into resourceful mode. What would the officer like to have even more than a new rugby ball?

When she exited the special room, she blended in with the regular foot traffic immediately. The customs officer lay quiet and tucked away beneath a stainless steel inspection table. He was not as happy as he'd intended, but no longer posed a threat.

Once on her flight out, she placed the device in the overhead bin. When she turned to see a flight attendant smiling at her, Pattie said, "You got it. For someone special."

The Aryan arrived minutes later and took a seat, separated from hers by an empty one they'd purchased.

Another several hours of Pattie stealing everything emotional from the normally iron-cast Prussian and she felt fully in command.

When she leaned over to advise him that it was time to ready for their descent and landing, she at first feared that he'd really been sent to heaven. The sound sleeper soon roused, and they safely touched down just prior to dusk.

Munich was a fine place during the day, but even nicer as the lights came on. A couple of hours later, they reached Neuschwanstein. It was her first time.

"Perhaps you would reconsider, Otto. We could live in luxury and ecstasy in this castle. What do you think?"

"What I believe is that your betrothal to the new French king is somewhat of a sticky wicket—as the Brits say—in that regard. Besides, should I become Kaiser, as planned, I won't be needing any castles. And all the action shall migrate to Berlin and that is where I shall reside."

"I could handle Berlin."

"Are you familiar with the term, butterfly? The Japanese use it to indicate someone who flits from man to man."

"The real story is that you want Kaari. Too bad Magus Crayle filled her full of holes."

The Prussian only smiled.

Her father had warned her about the stem cell experiments of the Aryans. The notion that there might be Mengele clones gave her pause as they descended into the bowels of Neuschwanstein known to the Aryans as *Rotfels*. They noted that the spiral staircase had been repaired and the large, red-glowing chamber had been refitted from an interrogation chamber into a sumptuous bedroom.

"The bed is huge, Otto. I like big." She leaped, spinning in the air, and landed.

Foomp.

"It's fabulous!"

Having been somewhat out of practice before meeting Pattie, the otherwise sophisticated man now became naked in under thirty seconds.

Before he could join her, she jumped up, grabbed her suitcase and ran with it into the bathroom, throwing behind her, "You gotta see what I have for you."

He moved to an armless chair at a desk not far from the bed, not sure what to think, and took a seat. His life had centered around everything being in order, or approaching order. With her, life seemed to be spontaneous. He pondered his own future, unsure of just who governed it.

CHAPTER 26

"How do you like it?" Pattie spread her arms and circled the Prussian.

"We do not wear black leather and Nazi arm-bands anymore."

"So here we are. Deep down inside a hill. Does your Aryan Alliance own what's above, or do you just rent this space?"

"We are beneath the castle of our infamous King Ludwig, which is owned by the people of Germany. The quarters here are adequate—and quite private."

She glanced around. "Adequate? It appears your decorator was operating with the Nazi gold hoard." She picked up a life-size, solid gold bust of Hitler.

"Yes. I will concede a surfeit of gold objects."

"And art." She examined a piece that caught her eye. "Van Gogh?"

"Compliments of the late Field Marshall Göring."

"So will you become the next mad King Ludwig—or someone else?"

He laughed. "We've tried kings and presidents. To no avail."

"You'll need allies. Sovereign allies. How about the French?"

This time, a heavier laugh. "The French are an insane people. Always a thorn. Are you aware that it was they, not us, who perpetrated the First World War? Before that, in 1870, they attacked my beloved ancestral homeland, Prussia, with what they called their Grande Armée. Our militia forces defeated it in less than a year."

"This time, why not remove the thorn?"

"I believe you have a proposition."

"A proposition would be *let's screw*. What I have is a proposal. I can deliver the French."

This time, no laugh. "You are as crazy as they come."

"Perhaps. But I am also Queen of France."

"I should shoot you myself." He turned to summon security.

"I have royal blood."

He stopped.

"In a private ceremony, a man has been named King Louis XIX. And I, his queen. The whole affair was sanctified by the new pope, Innocent, and a true, royal personage you would recognize in a heartbeat." She pecked at her cell phone, then handed it to him. "The video was taken at Rome's Colosseum under less-than-ideal conditions. But you can make out the pope, Sylvain and myself, and our gold crowns."

He pointed into his mouth. "I have gold crowns, but they don't make me a king. Still, I recognize you, the pope, and a man that fits the Mitim lore. But this other man. That's …"

"Hmmm?"

He drew a quick breath. "The Prince of Monaco!"

"Daddy."

The man massaged his temples. The bulk of information brought to mind a large dose of ice cream pressed up against the palate. Too much in too little time. Similar pains streaked through his brain. "We have money in that country."

"I'm sure you do." She removed pins holding her hair. "Any other questions?"

"I suppose this new Louis is the lunatic the French call Mitim. Am I correct?"

"*Das stimmt* … yes, you are."

He replayed the video. The man who'd spent his entire manhood always in control now seemed lost.

"You can't pass this up. The people of France have been dumped into a trough by successive governments, each worse than the one before. They are ripe to return to the perceived glory days and fantasy monarchy. We have a fail safe plan for formal accession—blessed by the church. At the highest level."

She moved behind him as he pondered. Massaging his rock-hard neck muscles, she slid his chair back two feet. When she moved in front of him again, she was naked. She perched on his desk. "I could lay back, and let *you* service *me*. But you wouldn't like that role."

Once again, he realized that he was clearly out of his league.

"Here." She climbed onto his lap, face-to-face. She smiled. Dimples always worked.

Their sounds reverberated within the chamber for the next fifteen minutes. In the end, she felt the ultimate power of total ownership.

• • •

They had relocated to the bed and had barely drifted off, when voices echoed within the room. Loud voices. Pattie sat up, searching frantically for her weapon. Von Prem calmed her with a touch of his hand.

"It is alright, my dear. I have prepared a little skit—a minstrel show—so you may experience what happened here two weeks ago with our primary threat. Please watch as I play the lead role."

A man strode into the room, dressed in a black uniform replete with death's head insignias, and looking exactly like the man next to Pattie. She calmed only slightly as she observed others join him, ostensibly for her benefit.

"Bring in the captive," the von Prem lookalike ordered.

Two men dressed in brown uniforms half dragged, half carried a fully depleted Magus Crayle, dropping him at the feet of a beautiful blonde woman. Pattie couldn't believe her eyes. The captive appeared really to be her nemesis. Was he an actor, too, or was he real? And the woman? Mengele? No, they had to be mere actors.

Crayle appeared as if he'd been run over several times by a steam roller trying to mold him into a roadway. His clothing looked more like red with black highlights than their usual black. This man seemed within a centimeter of death.

"We will quarantine Herr Crayle here amongst the red rocks. With the insinuation of the fluids to both lungs and the appropriate bacterial pathogen, he will be unable to cause further trouble. Under control, we can easily lower his oxygen saturation and initiate brain damage, if we choose."

Pattie slid her hand beneath the covers.

"Lest we forget, he's brilliant. Think carefully before you destroy that."

"There are many who are brilliant," said von Prem

"We're talking top five. Don't underestimate him. China, formerly governed by firmly entrenched leaders with absolute power and authority, is now an empire—it's leaders in exile. With a new emperor. By means of this man's Blackstone Strategy. What would you give for him to develop one for you? For your conquest? Hmmm?"

The von Prem character turned to his Doctor Mengele counterpart. "Kaari, be very careful. Double your monitoring of the subject. Death cannot be an option. Not until I say it is. *Klar?*"

"Clear."

"Bring him around."

Slapping him several times, the brown shirts did.

"Make him docile. Conscious, but immobile."

With several body punches, they did.

The pace of Pattie's heart stepped up a notch with each action, with each sentence.

"Place the tubes and infuse the fluids … into his lungs."

The victim racked and heaved, just as had happened before as Mengele manipulated a remote control.

Von Prem noticed activity beside him. He turned to his bedmate. "This excites you as it does me." He turned back to his actors. "You are *fertig*. Finished. Leave us."

All sounds from the troupe disappeared, as they disappeared. Those sounds were replaced by the two frolicking sadists with Pattie's gasping dominant.

When they'd finished, von Prem prepared a couple of cigarettes. He offered her a choice, indicating that neither was drugged. He took a long drag, puffing out three perfect smoke rings. "And when you are installed as queen, what will you tell the masses?"

"They will never have to elect a government again."

"And when they are hungry?"

"Lassen sie Scheisse essen."

Uncharacteristically, he laughed until his stomach ached. "Very good, Marie."

"You guessed the Antoinette bit."

"With all due respect."

She grabbed the cigarette from his hand and stuffed both of them into an ash tray. Turning back to him, she reached under the covers. "Ever fuck a queen?"

CHAPTER 27

When the desire is high enough, and the money good, sometimes things move much faster than anticipated. A day after *Rotfels*, Pattie and Otto heard from Li and made their way into Switzerland. Later that same day, Pattie pecked Otto's cheek goodbye, and hopped onto an unmarked Principality of Monaco jet for the ride out. She'd chosen the transportation both for its sumptuous comfort and for the secure communications necessary for her next call.

"*C'est la Verité, Papa!*" Pattie Norbrunn sounded like the little girl from so long ago. "I have added another success!"

"You met with the Aryan, but you've been out of contact for days. I worried for you. He is dangerous in the extreme. You must discuss these, uh, operations of yours before—"

"Ah, but you must have the proper security clearance for my little ops."

"I am your father and Prince of Monaco. I need nothing else."

"Okay, I'll grant you that. Then there's this Need-To-Know thing."

The Elder blew a grenade-sized puff of air through his lips.

"Oh. It's the love thing. And the caring thing, huh? I struggle with those notions. There wasn't much of that sort of thing in my home environment what with the sex-for-sale and all. My bad. I'll do better."

He gave a silent nod. He believed her. "Then tell me of your travels."

She knew that mention of her extra-curricular activities in the *Rotfels* cavern would be a non-starter. She skipped it. "We landed in Zurich, checked the bank balance on my smart phone, truffles and café-au-lait at Sprüngli, half-hour train east to Gossau."

"And ..."

"It went just as General Li and I planned. The bombs showed up. Otto and I handed them over to one of his associates named Herr Rein at a factory-sized bakery called Jowa Bäckerei, and that was that."

"With you, *that* is never *that*. What else?"

"I almost forgot. You'll like this part. I switched Swiss Franc payment for the dollars. Same millions, different currency. We made some money on the arbitrage."

The Elder considered using the profits for therapy for his errant daughter. Or perhaps a protective squad for her crown prince half-brother. "So the Aryans have their five bombs and you have moved the money from our Swiss account to a safer place."

"That's it."

"All of it?"

"Well ..."

"The rest, please."

"When I chatted with Otto, I got the idea that he'd not only wipe out German aristocracy and democracy, but somehow take out Paris and the French. That would be bad for us. So I switched the bombs."

"You what!" The man of absolute calm couldn't believe what he'd just heard.

"Yeah. It's better that way. They'll just think they're duds. Perhaps Chinese knock-offs instead of the real thing. Besides ... now I have three."

CHAPTER 28

The two tall men stood next to a four-foot stone pedestal bearing a brass insert. Etched words proclaimed it to be the triangulation result of an ordnance survey. They glanced about, searching for cannons pointed their way.

While the surf pounded against the rocky coast below, they looked west at a group of volcanic outcroppings and the aged light house that had warned many a sailor of the dangers there. Lalumière wondered for a moment about the absence of his Pattie for nearly two weeks.

"Why have you driven us here? Why through the narrow roadways southeast of that Penzance town? Roads so narrow, that flowers along the road brushed both sides of our German car? So narrow, that the British man you asked for directions at—what was it …"

"The Old Post Office."

"… referred to them as horse trails? Why?"

"It's because you are upset. You are beyond your nerves. It is best that we talk, and here no one can surveille us. The crashing surf is too noisy, and the birds, and times are so bad that there are only a handful of tourists. That's why."

Lalumière knew his son was right. He needed to talk. It would clear his mind. With a clear mind, he would be able to act.

"You don't know where she is, do you?"

"I don't. It grieves me, Jean-Marc."

"I understand. Wait. Perhaps her father knows. You are on excellent terms with the Elder. And he approved of your marriage to her. We can contact him." The young man extracted his cell phone.

"When he spoke at the Colosseum encounter, his eyes burned into mine."

Jean-Marc stopped. "But this Pattie Norbrunn—your Sandrine, with all her aliases—is his daughter. Surely, he wants her to reign as queen of France."

Sylvain Lalumière sighed. His son sported a graduate school education and had helped enormously to further his father's goal. However, he'd not yet mastered the connivances embodied in such an effort. "I believe his motives are less loving and more selfish than you can see. As queen, she'll be second to me in terms of power. Should I die …"

"I see. But as your son, I am *Dauphin*–uh, Crown Prince—and will succeed you."

His son's use of the present tense caused a smile. The young man accepted the monarchic restoration as a *fait accompli*. With the pope in the loop—and a founding member of the reconstituted Illuminé—the Parisian clergy had no choice but to accept. "You've witnessed Sandrine in various manners. At first as the Dutch whore, Angel, and in other incarnations. But I've seen her in action."

"What does that mean?"

"I've seen her kill. Execute. My jailer at the Bastille. The boatman who ferried us to the Château D'If. The jailer there. I propose that she's the most facile assassin ever." Lalumière didn't believe he needed to complete the picture. "There's a bench over by the gift shop." He led the way.

Holding his chin in his palm, Jean-Marc walked slowly to the tall white columns guarding the store and peered into a window, translucent, of handmade glass. "I see. Because of her ancestry, she possesses the Mata Hari bed and dead gene. And now that she's helped you become king, you're afraid that you may be next."

"And, after me …"

"Oh. I see." The son turned, observing his father with care. "The queen may require an accident."

"Jean-Marc!" the older man cried. Then, in a tone so soft his son could hardly hear, "I can't. Don't you see. I love her."

Lalumière brushed a few leaves from the bench and sat. He dropped his face into his hands.

Moments passed.

"In that case, we must be careful and not provide opportunities. But from what I've seen, she loves you, as well. We probably worry about nothing. Uh, look. I still have to be fitted for the public coronation we have planned in two weeks. I can worry about that. And you, Father. Don't fret—we'll be fine." He stepped over to a door and inside. He purchased two bottles labeled CORNISH SCRUMPY – STRONG FARM CIDER. It seemed right for the occasion. He paid and stepped back outside.

Only when the door had clunked shut behind did he emit a gasp. It hit him like ice cold water in the face. It was high time he stepped up and behaved like the Crown Prince. By fate alone, it had fallen on him to see to the queen's demise and to that end—hers—he would bring the new monarchy its first victory.

Before the crowning would be best. A broad smile reformed his lips. He would take her to bed one last time … and do it there.

CHAPTER 29

The fifty-three-year-old man stood pale, tall, and thin as he ambled first through arched stone hallways and through the manicured gardens. Beyond were the flowers, the grass fields, and the trees through which he'd strolled so many times. This time as he wandered, it was different. No armed guards. No doctors or nurses looking after him. Watching for the slightest mental misstep as reason enough to place him back in high security.

He breathed the fresh air with its floral aromas for the final time, and stepped inside for his final doctor visit. He knocked three times, as always, and was greeted with '*Entrée*' as he'd been each time before.

"Please, *Monsieur*. Take a seat."

The thin man sat carefully into the eighteenth century guest chair, hoping not to run afoul of the authorities by breaking it. He stared across a desk at the doctor in the most unthreatening demeanor he could manage, considering his oversized triangle-shaped jaw, and piercing charcoal eyes.

The doctor blinked at the sight of the man's frightening appearance. He allowed that this man, in death, would still be scary.

"I have checked your papers and they all seem to be in order. Because there are so many patients at the Saint Paul de Mausole asylum—eh, hospital—I have to remind myself that each has his own particular backstory. I see that you were brought to this location because you did not fit in with the others at Charenton. I have personal knowledge of that facility and can tell you that only a very few belong in a place where the Marquis de Sade himself was held. Some believe that his ghost still haunts the place. In any event, it seems they selected this place just outside of Saint Rémy de Provence because … hmmm … because your first name happens to be Rémy. Sometimes I wonder just whose brains are functioning properly. But you have done well, *n'est pas*?"

The patient nodded imperceptibly. The doctors at Charenton had decided he would respond to a better environment. In fact, he'd returned to his room and had beaten his hands bloody with outrage. As a young man, he'd worshipped the marquis and had wished to be just like him. That attitude had landed him in the French Foreign Legion.

The doctor looked over the papers. He noted that Rémy Jacquard had impregnated a Caucasian woman in North Africa, who had given birth to triplet boys. His first thought was to suggest that his patient be reunited with them—it could do him good to be with family. Oh. That would not be possible. All three had been killed in separate, violent incidents. Very well. On with the process.

"It has been a long journey, Monsieur Jacquard. You have reached the end of this long and arduous road, and, due to your fine record at this institution, may now begin anew."

"I want your tie."

The doctor smirked before continuing his dialog. "You have been granted this particular release date based on your own request. Apparently," He checked his papers. "it is the birthday of your triplet sons. I trust you will utilize the day to properly grieve for their early departure from this world."

"I want your tie."

"We have been associated these past fourteen years, you may have whatever of mine you want."

"I want your tie."

The doctor's eyebrows raised. He removed his school tie. *Pas de problème,* he thought. He had several.

Jacquard took it in his right hand, and flipped it around the doctor's neck, catching it with his left.

Frightened, the doctor tried to pull away.

Jacquard was the stronger. He'd exercised and built himself up for the duration of his sentence.

As he pulled the man's head against his own cheek, he said, "We must kiss the air. In the French tradition."

He felt as well as heard the other man's breathing calm.

Cheek-to-cheek, they each made the kissing sound.

The doctor, wanting this over and the hideous appearing Jacquard gone, proffered the other cheek.

Again, the kiss of the air.

Jacquard pulled back with a smile. His next move was lightning quick for a man of fifty-three.

He swapped tie ends in his hands, snapping them tight.

Then, tighter.

Now without oxygen, the panicked psychiatrist tore at his patient's arms.

Unphased, Jacquard tied the tie tight. He stood and walked around behind the flailing doctor.

"I learned the knot in the Foreign Legion. You will find it impossible to defeat."

He snatched a pointer the doctor used for flip chart instruction from the desk, running it through the tie behind the doctor's head. He pushed the head forward with one hand while twisting with the other.

The doctor fell forward, his head banging on the desk.

Dead.

Jacquard stepped to the huge fireplace, removed the screen, and hefted the smallish doctor on top of the gas logs. He replaced the screen.

He fetched a remote control from the hearth and stood back, leaning against the desktop edge as he pressed the symbol for heat.

The logs came to life. Blue and yellow flames lapped at the doctor's clothing, as if searching for purchase.

At that moment, his mind switched back to the day the good doctor had informed him that the last of his triplet sons, Thierry, had been killed. On that day, he'd decided to depart his otherwise pastoral existence. On that day, he'd decided to exact revenge.

He pulled files from the ten steel cabinets—always unlocked during working hours—and piled them from the fireplace to the desk. Next, he hoisted the doctor's personal supply of laughing gas and twisted the knob for a slow leak.

He smiled at the sound. The mixture would take several minutes to fill the room.

After checking his coat pocket for the requisite exit papers, he twisted the lock and pulled the door shut. It took a mere twenty strides to exit the building. The sounds of his shoes echoing on the tiled floor brought another smile. Two smiles in fourteen years.

• • •

Ten minutes later, he walked without a care in the world save the revenge he needed to enact. A loud whoosh sounded from behind.

He stopped, produced a sardonic grin, and continued on.

The conflagration behind him and the cries of fear and anguish produced all the pleasure he required for the moment.

In twenty-five minutes, he arrived in Saint Rémy, hijacked a car, and left its owner's body in a safe location. He was outbound. The Marseille airport was a mere sixty miles southeast. An hour on the A7. He might still be insane, but he knew about Magus Crayle. He knew how his sons had died. He knew where he needed to go.

CHAPTER 30

It had been a long time, but Magus Crayle finally had a moment to himself. Like most May days in the Big Bear Valley, this one called for shorts, a t-shirt, and sandals. It seemed long ago, but it was a mere seventeen days, since he and Hekka had been kidnapped in Helsinki. Two-and-a-half weeks.

Already a mile east of his cabin, he'd just passed the white-domed observatory on the lake's north shore. A moderate breeze scooped the water here and there, a perfect day for the boaters. He observed that the wind and motor sailors, plus the jet ski crowd, all seemed to be able to share the lake in peace. If he could bring opposing factions from the rest of the world here, would they make the same observations? Or would they break out into fights?

Crayle withdrew a silver object from his pocket. He checked the battery on the Rorschach recorder. Still good. It had been a long time—too long. He began yet another internal dialog.

"Hi, Doctor. It's Magus Crayle. But by now you know my voice. We had a mess in Germany, took down some bad folks, and seem to be none the worse for wear. Hekka is up the hill now and recovering well. We are anticipating a long-awaited honeymoon to nowhere in particular. Let me correct my last. To nowhere that has nuclear bombs or empire-seeking narcissists. To a place with no Pattie Norbrunns or Lalumières of any kind.

"We've finally settled on one. We're going to the ultra-peaceful Caribbean. Rest assured that I will keep my part of our bargain. When I return, I will drop down to the refurbished Quarry hospital, descend the 300 feet to your mind lab, and continue where we left off. There is an additional condition, though. None of my current memories are to be disturbed. I will supply Hekka with a list of questions and she will test me each day. If I miss any of the questions, she will head your way with that ten-inch Bowie knife that she keeps razor sharp.

"Oh, yes. The new project. Let's see if we can learn something from those Neil Wohlford memories you have in your archive. I know that, in theory, they must be restored to the person from whom taken, but at least we can look at the images they produce on your computer. It might give us something for Jack and his team so they can track down Pattie and Sylvain, and take them out. Well, thanks for the conversation. A little one-sided, but this recorder was your idea. I'd say goodbye, but I'll use one of your Swiss phrases instead. *Auf wiedershauen.*"

Crayle smiled and replaced the device in his pocket. His walk had taken him to the water's edge side of the Serrano Campground. He stopped and looked past it and up the mountain. There, among the pines, he and Hekka had outsmarted and outrun a hit team lead by TJ2. Jerome. There, high on the hill, he and Hekka had made camp for the night. They'd made their own heat. The smile faded. The next day they had returned to her ranch house and found her father murdered by the same TJ2.

The killers had traced Crayle there via a Vestige transmitter planted under his own skin. That's when they had killed her father. Crayle was certain that her father hadn't talked. TJ2 and his crew had been able to pick up the Vestige track from there that led them to their quarry in the hills.

It was the brutality of his enemies that formed a knot in his stomach. The desire to kill every one of them competed directly with his promise to Hekka. But he'd decided. He'd set his own compulsion for revenge aside, as he'd just transmitted to the doctor. They were going on vacation. They were going to be happy. Forever.

CHAPTER 31

It took Crayle an hour to complete his walk alongside Big Bear Lake. Even after the emotional drop from remembering the grisly murder of Hekka's father, he felt well in the physical sense. After entering the back door code, he walked in to hear a squeal that had to have come from Hekka.

He reached behind, under his shirt, for his pistol.

He heard someone else.

As he peaked around the doorway, he saw them.

She and Phoebe sat playing video games on their tablet computers, ignoring the world news of various catastrophes emanating from the flat screen on the wall.

"I hate to break up the party, but are you staying for dinner, Agent Bransfield?"

"I'm thinking of hyphenating my name so that you'll at least get part of it right. How about Phoebe Bransfield-MacKay?"

"I'll just call you by your first name. You can't change that."

"Well, legally, I could … wait … oh, Micmac wants to see you. He didn't say why, but I bet it's to save you from having our delight stop your heart every time something goes in our favor with these stupid games."

"Then I'll hop in the Cobra, and leave you to your games. I will, with your permission, drag that sorry SEAL son-of-a-gun back here for dinner. Five o'clock okay?"

There was no response. Only another squeal. He started to ask Phoebe if her 911 was in his way, but knew that, for the games' durations, he was a non-entity.

He entered the kitchen, and reached for a fresh cinnamon roll for his trip.

"It'll ruin your appetite. 'Bye."

With a smirk, he entered the code on the thermostat and descended into the tunnel to the garage. He tossed off the parachute cover and punched the garage door button.

"Terrific," he said to himself. "Phoebe's parked her Porsche so I could get out. Thank you, Phoebe."

The Cobra slid out onto North Shore Drive heading west through the little town called Fawnskin, then south along the west end of the lake. He spent the entire ten-minute ride munching on the roll and trying to guess what Mr. UDT wanted.

• • •

Magus Crayle pulled into Micmac's driveway. He stopped. The former Navy Underwater Demolitions Technician stood on a window washer's scaffold, swiping away what was probably Windex.

Crayle parked the red Cobra and ambled to the front of the cabin. "Didn't you ever hear of a long pole?"

Micmac spotted his friend and comrade and, as if to show off, raised the CIA's infamous universal remote control and engaged the motors. Gently, the scaffold touched ground. He nodded at his nearest neighbor, who'd observed the whole operation and just stood there scratching his head.

"Another toy," Crayle sighed.

"You know that thing about keeping up with the Joneses? Well, screw that. Let them try and keep up with me."

Crayle glanced at the neighbor.

"That's right," Micmac said as he scrambled off the device. "His name is Jones."

"One of your UDT associates?"

"Hell, no. Witness protection relocation." He slapped himself on the side of his head. "It's supposed to be a secret."

"Let's agree to keep Mr. Jones' little secret. How about a beer?"

As the men moved inside, they saw Jones leave his place next door and head down the road in a pickup truck with steel frames on both sides. He was still shaking his head.

The two men enjoyed a local craft brew and talked about old times. From two comfortable wicker chairs that Micmac had made himself, they watched the darkness approach over the lake. The lack of activity before them and the few maple leaves that blew across their vista made a statement about the value of peace and quiet. Conversation gave way to a light sleep as both dozed off. The world and its tendency to chaos and violence faded away.

• • •

Outside and out of view, there were nine in all. Dressed in various colors and textures of recreational clothing, they appeared like the residents and tourists of the Big Bear Valley. Except for the machine guns.

At the onset of dusk, the sun moved behind the mountains to the rear of Micmac's east-facing property. With just enough light left to allow unaided sighting, the men moved to the front window.

Unknown to them, the former UDT man and current unconventional spy had implemented both motion and pressure sensors throughout the property. And, for such occasions, had weapons stores accessible to each room.

The first two men planted small explosive packs on the glass; they stuck flak squares over each to force the explosions inward.

One of the men pressed a special code on his cell phone.

Frump! Frump!

The large window exploded into the cabin.

With orders to obliterate the inhabitants, the assault team raced up to it, raising AK47's.

An alarm sounded, and lights flashed on and off in the cabin.

Micmac ran to a central safe room, waving for Crayle to follow. Once the door was secure, they settled into sumptuous recliners and studied the scene.

Instead of an old flintlock above the fireplace, the weapons expert had placed one of his M134 mini-guns on display. A couple of clicks on his remote control, and the 4,000 rounds-per-minute weapon swiveled out, and began a left-to-right journey.

"My electronic machete," Micmac shouted above the weapon's hum.

Instantaneous results.

Five men eviscerated on the first pass.

The four remaining crouched under the window sill—beneath the field of fire.

Safe.

Grateful to be alive.

Micmac grinned. And clicked.

The assailants appeared startled as the window washing scaffold jerked into motion. Upward.

Their heads spun in unison toward where they'd last seen the UDT man.

Panning now right-to-left, the modern Gatling gun whirred.

Like those before, the final four were blasted half way across the front yard.

MacKay waited several minutes, then punched buttons on his cell phone. "Hi, Jones Glass and Door?"

• • •

The event at Mick MacKay's cabin, and the subsequent nine bodies, drew both local sheriffs, the county coroner, the nearest FBI resource, and an ATF agent taking a break at what he perceived to be a tranquil lake resort. They offered Micmac everything from a safe house to protective custody to incarceration for possession of a profusely automatic weapon.

Magus Crayle and friend sat at the dining table, listening to each one of the law enforcement minions argue for his version of what should be done. Finally, Crayle tapped his phone, which rested beside his hand. "May I make a call?"

"Not yet," the sheriff answered. "We're not quite sure if charges will be filed, or what those charges might be."

"I'm not calling a lawyer, I'm calling the president."

That drew a round of guffaws and hollers as if it were the best joke of the day.

"Seriously," followed Crayle.

It was the FBI agent's turn. "Be my guest, sir. I'm sure you have him on speed dial."

They laughed again.

Crayle punched his speed dial code and set the phone on speaker.

"President Stones … oh, hi, Magus. Haven't heard from you for a bit. Heard about the Carib—"

Crayle pressed Mute. He saw that Micmac was about to bust his gut, so he tried to close down the episode quickly. "Are we done here?"

"I think I have the cause of death," said the coroner.

"Since Stones is my boss's boss's et cetera boss, I'm good," added the FBI man.

Fascinated with the remote, the ATF agent was repositioning the mini-gun flat against the fireplace, but took the time to toss, "Ditto," over his shoulder.

That left the sheriff.

Micmac glanced down at the table in an unintimidating manner. "You want to buck the trend, Sheriff?"

Within the next half hour, all scions of justice, along with all nine corpses, departed.

"Well, Micmac, I suppose I should head home. I'll provide Phoebe a sitrep and let her know that you're all right."

"Don't do that. Give me an hour and you won't be able to tell that I've been doing anything other than snoozing off all day."

"Just know this. If she finds out, and you weren't the one who told her …"

"I'll give her a call. She can let Hekka know that you're okay."

"Deal. So unless you want some help, I'm outta here."

"You sound like Lenny, only he wouldn't have offered to help."

"Easy now. He has helped us more than a few times."

"So, get yourself gone. I've got a bit of tidying up to do."

With that, Magus was back on the road home. A reluctant Micmac dialed his new bride and provided a concise sitrep.

"We can't stay out of this, can we?" was Phoebe's response.

"They're dead. Really, really dead. I believe this is the end of them. Honest."

"I'm coming home."

"It's okay here. Jones just showed up with the replacement glass for the front window. Give me a couple of hours. Keep the love birds safe. Okay?"

"Two hours … Go!" She hung up.

CHAPTER 32

The ride home in the dark of night proved uneventful. After Crayle parked in the garage and navigated the covert tunnel to the cabin, he stepped into the living room, ready to explain how he felt that no one was in any further danger. It was something he wanted to believe with all his heart.

"It would seem that we're done with the surprises," he started, but got no further. There, next to Hekka and Phoebe, sat Lenny. Crayle took the available seat in the bean bag chair.

"What in the world are you doing here? You went back to Amsterdam. To sell our diamonds." His voice raised at the end as if he were re-explaining the mission to a dense P.I.

At first, no answer. Then, an enigmatic, "I need to let my mind wander, Magus." Lenny picked up his fishing gear and headed out the back door for the dock. "Later."

"Wait up." Phoebe sprang out of the loveseat and followed him.

"Now there's an unlikely pairing," Crayle said to himself. As he had just freed himself from the bean-bag chair, he heard a loud clump from the iron door knocker.

"Hekka, I need to explain. I'll only be a minute."

"It can wait. I'm tired." She ambled into the bedroom, closing the door behind.

He wheeled toward the door and glimpsed the latest intruder into his life through the security spyglass.

He jumped back.

He looked again.

With a perplexed shake of his head, he opened the door.

"Hello, Mr. Crayle."

Dumbfounded, he stared.

"Mr. Crayle?" the young woman queried with her perfect, rounded lips.

"Ling!"

The 20-year-old, wearing an alluring black cocktail dress that would have stood out anywhere, brushed past him into the room.

He glanced left, then right at her two companions. Dressed in typical Big Bear Valley attire, their shaved heads save for six-inch top knots gave them away as two of Chin Yao-wu's eunuchs.

Without a word, they stepped to each side of the entry, performed an inelegant about face, and stood guard.

Crayle shut the door, still shaking his head.

Ling settled into a corner wing chair. Her posture—knees together, feet together, arms resting on her lap—belied her youth. Whether or not Chin was worthy of the title Emperor, she appeared as a perfect young empress would appear. Regal.

"What …"

"Father, I mean Emperor Chin, said he wished me to look *all grown up*. He wanted you to see me in a new light."

"Stunning is the operative word. And please call me Magus. As you did in China. In private."

She smiled at that. She remembered well every encounter with this man over the past four years. "I'm here on business. Like me, you were a different person at the time you plotted the overthrow of our government."

"Ah, yes. The Blackstone Strategy."

"I realize that you may still not remember everything. We became close."

His memories of his strategic planning trip to China had been long ago restored.

"I had secretly read a book in English titled Seduction. I tried to seduce you." She blushed. "We made out, as you called it. No sex or anything. We just kissed."

"I didn't realize you were …"

"Sixteen?"

A similar flush overcame him. He nodded.

"Business, Magus."

He took a seat opposite her. "What does Chin want?"

She acknowledged his quick and accurate assessment with a smile. "Do you remember when Iraq was invaded? The war ended quickly. But no one knew what to do next. He wants … he needs a master strategy to rule our country."

"Why me? He has the general. He has Li."

"Li commands the armed forces. As you know, we have contained the former communist leaders on the island called Hainan. But the second and third tier leaders—those not killed by the Beijing detonation—are still in place. They require leadership. Direction. Years ago, Emperor Chin Yao-wu perfected a stock market strategy. And with the market moving ever higher, he couldn't lose. The only question was how much he would win. He likened it to rigged sports matches, or to American elections."

"With due respect, you're saying that General Li would wish to impose a rigid martial law style of control if left unhampered, and Chin wants a more civil approach."

"It's as he said previously. He requires a Sun Tzu-Lao Tzu combination."

"And he's looking in my direction."

"He knew you would understand immediately. He requires genius and wisdom, at the highest level."

"Sun Tzu is known as the master military strategist of all time. Lao Tzu produced the philosophy of life: *Tao Te Ching*, and is still regarded as the Old Master. Many say that he was mentor to the great Confucius. I believe Chin is setting the bar a little high."

"He has faith in you. Complete faith. Without you, China will fall into chaos. He is convinced." Unlike her, she pleaded. "Please, Magus. *Please*."

Crayle studied her before rising and stepping to the window. The lake before him experienced a late spring calm. There was just enough breeze to produce the calming sparkle—from cross-shore lights and a full moon—that he had once labeled as *The Water Diamonds*. They had belonged to him, at first. He now shared them with Hekka.

"We have heard of your loss. That you have left behind perhaps a portion of your heart. Chin sends his condolences. He has considered that, perhaps, new employment in the field of your expertise might take your mind to another place. One less painful."

His loss? He ducked into the bedroom. Hekka lay fast asleep on the water bed. When he returned, he passed Ling and walked to the picture window. All of a sudden, he wasn't sure of anything.

There Lenny and Phoebe sat next to each other on the dock. Without conflict, chatting like old friends. None of the expressive hand gestures deploying the middle finger he'd come to expect. He almost smiled.

"The compensation will be of your choosing. Anything you want. Chin will even conclude manufacture of the mini-nukes—as you termed them—should you so desire."

She had him, and he knew it. No more deaths by the tens of thousands. No more Xinjiangs, Beijings, Marseilles, or the close calls in New York and Paris. But Hekka would never forgive him if he severed his ties to Big Bear. And, by extension, to the United States of America.

"Give me a few minutes. I'll write down my conditions and terms." He turned away from her.

She closed the distance, stepped around him, and kissed him. "I'm twenty now," she whispered.

He stepped back to arm's length. "And I'm married now. Wait here a second." He entered the bedroom and closed the door. When he reached the bedside, he saw that Hekka slept deeply. Choices existed. Each one sucked. He bent close, feeling Hekka's warm, relaxed breath against his cheek. He pressed a gentle kiss to her forehead.

CHAPTER 33

With their flight across the Pacific Ocean behind them, Crayle and Ling were transported by helicopter to the landing pad of the new palace atop Hong Kong's Victoria Peak. She had seen that he slept well—he didn't even remember lifting off not far from his home. Still rubbing his eyes, he followed her into the labyrinth, attempting to observe and remember the slightest details. For later.

Ling led her charge into a room of suitable palatial stature and seated them in elaborate Ch'in-period chairs of China's first emperor. Chin approached them with a glass in each hand. Each contained a three-finger pour of well-aged Scotch.

"Might we bypass the pleasantries, Mr. Crayle?"

"Fair enough. How can you assure me of no more bombs, Chin? I've already provided a post-coup strategy, so you no longer need me."

"I've learned a great deal from you. Your notion of transference of knowledge from one space to another has finally struck home."

"It's the essence of systems thinking. Go on."

"Yes. So, I've transferred my extensive understanding of the stock market—in which I excelled—to the reality of being emperor." Making statements he felt were profound pleased Chin. He smiled.

"Let me guess. The market showed you where a particular investment strategy would succeed. You employed it and did well. But time changes. You had to become aware of the changes and make adjustments … or you'd lose everything. And you needed intel and counsel from experts to evolve your strategy. You realized you could not only avoid disaster, but improve your position by staying ahead of the changes. Just by deploying a dynamic strategy."

"And the approach—what you termed the Systems Approach—allows me to do just that. On a grander scale, of course."

"I'm the only expert in this manner of strategic problem solving, aren't I?"

"You are the only one, Mr. Crayle, with the required skills and whom I trust. As long as you see to my needs, in this respect, there will be no more bombs."

"Thanks for giving me a choice."

"I believe it to be a fair exchange."

"You don't even need the bombs. I feel I'm getting nothing."

"There would be no more bombs going to Europe. No need for your team to chase them down. You could allow the situation in France to play out." He conveniently left out the new German component.

"What about my life back in Big Bear? What about Hekka? I'd have to correspond on your issues and changes via computer … or phone. Are you okay with that?"

"Well, in a word, no. You see, I need assurances that you are quite safe. To that end, you will have apartments—sumptuous, mind you—in this palace. All your needs will be satisfied. All of them." He took another sip. "There, I believe everything has been decided. Another Scotch?"

Crayle stood and turned to leave. Chin's huge eunuchs moved together to block the doorway.

The American spy and strategist retook his seat. "Yes, I'll have another."

"Excellent choice. Enough of that for now. We shall revert to small talk, resolve your marital problem, and then break until tomorrow. I want to discuss with you a mission statement for the direction of my country, to which we shall adhere whenever specific issues arise. After you have had time to rest, you will join me in a formal dinner at six P.M. Proper attire has been provided in your new quarters. I hope you find the items suitable."

Chin refilled their glasses.

The small talk suggested that Crayle's "Indian Woman" was not suitable for him. Chin offered to enlist Ling, whom he knew Crayle trusted, to find an appropriate mate. Perhaps one of the educated and martial arts-trained former daughters would be best. Chin had then viewed the incoming light through his Scotch glass. "Perhaps an eighteen-year-old," he'd offered.

The eunuchs escorted the American strategist and spy to the west wing of the palace. They pulled open the heavy wooden door with ease, and then locked it when they had seen Crayle inside.

He spoke, mainly to himself, but also to Rorschach as he reconnoitered. "The living room is approximately fifteen feet by twenty feet. Mirrors, paintings, chairs, all surrounded in gold. One of the paintings over a fireplace hearth—also gold—is a likeness of Chin in his emperor's attire. It probably indicates that he is watching me …" Crayle gave a mild bow toward the portrait. "… and listening." He walked through the nearest doorway into the bedroom. "The bedroom has a king bed, and a gold frame, and there are windows, umph, that don't open. However, I do have a decent view of Macau."

• • •

After an hour's time, Chin felt he had pondered his situation long enough. As full of himself as he'd become, he knew when he needed assistance. "Blue. Have the general report here to me immediately.

Tell him there is no crisis, but, with respect to our future sovereignty, I believe I have a pathway forward."

Blue caught the urgency in Chin's tone and had Li sitting in front of the emperor in ten minutes.

"I've brought someone in for you to meet."

A man entered through Chin's draped doorway.

"Oh!" Clutching his drink with both hands, Li stood.

"I predicted your reaction. Mr. Crayle has agreed to provide another one of his fail-proof strategies."

What Crayle might receive in return remained unsaid, and Li caught the oversight.

The American strategist bowed, an act acknowledged with a nod by the other two men.

"Please, Mr. Crayle," said Chin. "Have a drink with us." He turned to Li. "It would interrupt our flow to summon Blue for this purpose. If you will, pour three fingers for our colleague."

Li felt a sense of outrage burning inside, but he maintained his cool. He needed to hear and process every word.

Crayle took an honorary sip, and spoke.

"General, I've been away for some time and otherwise occupied. Please correct me if I have any of the facts wrong." He turned his head slightly to supply the question mark.

Li nodded affirmation.

"You currently possess the remnants of the Chinese Communist Party leadership, quarantined on Hainan Island."

"Yes. They are of no threat."

"But they may be of use."

"How?"

"Suppose there were several explosions killing them all and rendering them unrecognizable."

"Who would do such a thing?"

"Once you have provoked the Vietnamese, blame of such an attack could be laid on them."

Li's eyes opened wide. His consideration of Crayle as a threat could wait until another time. The notion was brilliant. It was his miracle. "I see! We would be justified to retaliate!"

"And strategic use of your radiation-free, tactical nuclear devices—or threat thereof—could drive them to submission."

The general stood and paced the chamber.

"Do you see?" said Chin. "Mr. Crayle has provided another brilliant solution."

"Perhaps we could have him on retainer." Li cast a serious glance at Crayle.

"I accept the compliment. With the north of Vietnam and the islands, you would have returned to China nearly all of its former extent."

The *nearly* portion of the comment stopped the two Chinese in their tracks.

"And you could lay your dramatic success before your people." Crayle let that set in for a few heartbeats. Then, "Well, gentlemen, I must leave you to ponder the possibilities. In the meantime, I'd like to see Hong Kong again, and Chin has arranged a tour."

Black daughter stepped in from the shadows and the two exited through the room's huge gold doors.

"Yes, Li. Mr. Crayle has a way with words."

"What did he mean by *nearly*?"

Chin smiled. "If we want Taiwan in order to complete the reconstruction of our once imperial country, we will require his services again."

Magus Crayle's brief dialog dramatically changed the mood in the room. Neither Chin nor Li saw Magus Crayle as an immediate threat. Without further discourse, each man extrapolated what a lingering relationship with the American could do for his own ambitions.

CHAPTER 34

A soft knock came at his door. Groggy from a much-needed nap, Magus Crayle pushed himself up, and onto the side of the bed. As soon as his feet hit the floor, he jerked them up. Apparently the heated marble wasn't for bare feet. And the knock, not the heavy thump from one of the eunuchs. He poked his feet into slippers, padded to the door, and creaked it open.

"Good afternoon, Mr. Crayle. I wanted to give you time to prepare for dinner."

He watched as former Black daughter, Ling An-yee, passed him on her way to a red lacquered, antique armoire across from his bed.

"I can dress myself, you know." He reconsidered. "I *could* dress myself."

She took a seat at a small period desk next to the armoire. "You will dress yourself. However, these clothes are not like any you have worn before. I will supervise."

Not quite awake, Crayle had difficulty imagining the import of dressing properly. It was clear, though, that Ling was *teaching him to fish*, rather than *giving him a fish*. The philosophy lesson indicated that Chin planned many more such dinners, which boded well for Crayle's longevity.

Within the half-hour, he looked like he'd just stepped out of a kung-fu movie, albeit one of high class. Ling nodded final approval and marched him what seemed like a quarter mile to the dining hall.

The table of creamy white jade extended perhaps twenty feet long by four feet wide by four inches thick, six ornate chairs on each side. A map with small scenes in several places had been carved quite artistically into its surface. Crayle noticed a simple homestead at the west end of the Yangtze River. He knew at once that the story told was of Chin.

His eyes were drawn next to a large circle in the table's center with the emperor's emblem, and a grand chair at the far end. There, looking like the spitting image of China's first emperor, Ch'in Xihuangdi, sat Chin.

"Please, Mr. Crayle, be seated anywhere you like, although I recommend sitting close to me, perhaps to my right, so we will not be required to shout. Ling, please take a seat to my left." He gestured with the appropriate arm demonstrating a grace unfamiliar to Crayle.

The American moved along the right side of the table and saw to Ling's seating.

"A gentleman. I approve."

Crayle sat himself to Chin's right as appropriate for a right-hand-man. Chin nodded his recognition of that protocol.

"After all that my wife endured in Europe because of your grand scheme, I should be home with her. She's not well. I left without even saying goodbye. She didn't deserve that. And your men have taken my phone so I can't call her and explain just how important things had to be for me to run off like I have."

"It's alright. Ling will find you another."

Crayle couldn't believe the pompousness of Chin's last statement. Then it occurred to him that, given the man's early history—and how he dealt with it—he might not understand the nature of love at all.

"The bombs, Mr. Crayle?"

Crayle couldn't let the issue of Hekka slide. "There must be an arrangement where I can be with her, and help you at the same time. I just haven't thought of it yet."

"I have thought … and I have decided that away from here, you would be of no use to me. Partially implemented strategies don't work, you said before. And a strategist must watch over implementations of even the finest of his strategies to see that they are executed to perfection, you said. Is my characterization accurate?"

"You heard me well, Chin."

"Oh, I almost forgot. Tomorrow there will be a special event. You must attend in period costume, as you are now."

"I wondered why there was Sun Tzu replica attire in my wardrobe." He forced a smile.

"I will not spoil your surprise by telling you. And, I'm afraid I must make final preparations this evening. I shall bid you adieu until tomorrow." Chin rose first—unusual for an emperor—as a sincere sign of respect.

Once again, Crayle was escorted back and locked in his room.

• • •

There were no late night visits from Ling or anyone else. The master strategist was left to heat tea with a tea service in his bathroom, sip it, and ponder his situation. His first thoughts went to Hekka, but without a phone and her voice, he was truly alone. To escape the feelings, he began thinking of Chin's dilemma. He drifted off.

• • •

It was late morning before the soft knock came again. Clad in her black cheongsam with gold embellishments, Ling walked in and proceeded to supervise dressing of the Americanized Sun Tzu for the second time. She led the fully regaled Crayle down a hall and then outside.

At first, he found the shoulder to floor conical-shaped gown a challenge. As long as he stayed a couple of feet from walls, chairs, and tables, he was okay. It was the more narrow doorways that he had to push the garment through.

The first impression upon stepping outside was that the dinner table from the night before had somehow been moved outside to the center of the courtyard. The same chairs adorned the sides with four daughters sitting two across from two others. Chin sat in his seat of honor at one end and, this time on his left, sat General Li.

Crayle scanned. His eyes searched everywhere. No Ling. He crossed the pebbled yard and retook his seat to Chin's right, across from Li.

"Please say hello to my daughters, Mr. Crayle. They are delighted to meet you."

The young women bowed their heads almost to the table.

Crayle returned the bow, not as deep, and replied, "*Ni hao*."

Accompanied with a few giggles, they returned his Chinese greeting.

His gaze returned to the general. It was met with a glare. "Good morning, Li. How are you today?"

"The general is fine," said Chin. "Please, gentlemen. Before you is a cordial found in the country of our colleague, Monsieur Lalumière. *Pastis*, it is called. You can drink it straight, or add a little of the Nordic water. No more than a few drops."

The men tried the drink and immediately noticed an overwhelming taste of licorice. Both added water. They observed the normal Pastis phenomenon in which it turned from clear to translucent in the presence of the additive.

"Shades of gray, gentlemen. Like all of life's mysteries."

Crayle noticed that Chin seemed to be turning into—or was at least influenced by—ancient philosopher, Lao Tzu. It worried him that the man's new role might be going to his head.

At that moment, Chin rose. He lifted his arms indicating that the other guests should follow. They stood. He waved his right arm.

What happened next surprised everyone. Period-dressed guards, perhaps thirty of them, stepped from doorways into the courtyard and took positions close to the walls. Dressed in gold, they looked like an Imperial guard from the past or a period video game come to life. Alternately, they carried spears and halberds. Not wanting to have a hole punched in him or his head lopped off, Crayle put himself on alert.

Then a flood of press corps streamed into the space, taking pre-arranged positions to one side.

Something was about to happen. Of that Crayle was certain. Something momentous.

A stream of musicians entered, setting the mood by playing songs from the Chinese opera. Sounds enigmatic at best reflected and refracted off walls and crevices.

It was crazy.

It made no sense.

The musicians formed a two-line column leading to the palace's main door. On cue, they spread their lines apart three paces.

Crayle the strategist didn't know what to think. But the spy inside caused all muscles to tense.

It hit him. His head spun to the end of the table away from Chin. An empty chair. He heard doors creak open.

His head spun back.

There she was. "My God," he said under his breath. "Absolutely beautiful."

He was right. Ling An-yee stepped forward in the most ostentatious outfit he'd ever seen. Yellow, green, blue, white, red, and black. All of the daughter colors. He glanced at Chin, who couldn't take his eyes off her. Back to Ling as she made her way to the end of the twenty-foot ramp.

Chin leaned over so that only Crayle could hear him. "It is important that someone of import escort her to this table. I believe it is appropriate that you be the one. Please cross the yard and lead her to her seat of honor. The handmaidens shall follow at either side.

His eyes shot back to the far end of the table. At the empty chair.

"Yes, Mr. Crayle. Ling is to be my new bride. Empress of all China."

The seasoned CIA operative and strategist was too dumbfounded to drop his jaw at the sight. After gathering his wits, he moved to her, bowed, stepped to her side, and turned to face back to the emperor. He raised his left elbow toward her, keeping his forearm horizontal, and his hand palm down. Had it not been for the design of his robe, he could have stood closer to her. He understood that detail to have been of Chin's design.

With a grace attributed only to royalty, Ling placed her right arm on his, and they strolled to the muted beat of a drum across the thirty feet to the table. At that point, she bowed to Li, then finally to her new husband. "This ceremony constitutes a change," Ling asserted. "I shall bring the Yin to our unity, and I shall bring children."

The American spy couldn't take his eyes off her. He barely heard the words coming from the man next to him.

"Mr. Crayle," Chin spoke softly. "In your world …" He paused to compose himself. "… she has no father to give her away. The only one she knows is the substitute she is about to wed. Would you please do us the honor?"

Crayle felt like he was watching a tennis match. His eyes shot back to Chin. The man's eyes were wet. Tough as nails, until this. Then he glanced over at Li. That man was far from joyful about what transpired. He glared at his hands as they fumbled with one another. Crayle could tell that the situation reminded the general of a checkers match when one of the pieces became crowned, and much more powerful.

All in all, Ling had been correct. There'd been a change, alright.

CHAPTER 35

Chin was pleased with himself, but was finished with the merriment of his grand wedding reception. He whispered to Crayle, and they left for one of the palace safe rooms. The press had already been dismissed. They raced off to populate their rendition of social media. Each needed to be first to apprise all of China of the great news and to show off their fabulous pictures. Of course, they knew that the information would be shared—by subscribers—to the rest of the world within seconds.

"I can see you are happy for me, Mr. Crayle, but I also know you've been confined in my new abode since your arrival. If you would like to leave the palace to visit your old Hong Kong haunts from your stay here just a few years ago, now is a good time. You will recall that it was something I allowed last time when Ling and the soldiers brought you here after our … mmm … disagreement in Vancouver."

"I am truly sorry that I and my team destroyed your new castle-residence there. With your vast fortune, I suspect that you could rebuild it, if you chose."

"You destroyed it because I was inside, isn't that more accurate?"

"The assault was about the new bomb you were providing Lalumière. I needed to remove it from the playing field. With him dead, the problem goes away. With you dead, same result."

"According to our deal, the problem goes away period. There will be no more such devices."

"Yes. With the possible exception of the Vietnamese-claimed islands, is General Li on board with that?"

"Of course. He is *my* general, after all."

Crayle rubbed his forehead as if to wipe away a severe headache. "If I don't immerse myself in your work …"

"All you will do is dote on your Hekka. I respect that love—in the Western sense—is involved. I'll send for her, if you approve."

"I need to talk with her first. Nine o'clock tonight will be fine. It should be noon at the cabin."

Chin sat back. "I'm afraid I've been putting off a bit of bad news."

"Hekka? Something's happened to her?" Crayle demanded.

"Relax. The news is not about her. It is more my problem than yours. The Elder, whom I understand you met in Rome, seeks your presence immediately." That the Elder had commanded Crayle's presence Chin felt to be a slight. Still, he needed to accede to the demand and have his strategist back at the earliest possible date.

"I'll bet he wants me to strategize his conquest of the entire planet. Or is it just Europe?"

"He didn't specify, and I wouldn't expect a man of his stature to do that. I must comply. It will only be for a few days and you can use your travel time to consider my strategic plan for China going forward. We will require a new code name since, as you are quite aware, Blackstone has been used."

Crayle noticed that Chin's use of the language was evolving. He was starting to sound as elegant as the Elder in Rome. He concluded it to be a trait of royalty. Careful to exclude any mention of his quarantine there, he posed his suggestion. "How about Redrock?"

"Hmmm. Not bad. The Redrock Strategy. Hmmm. Yes. I do like that."

Crayle let slide that he'd spent tortuous time beneath Mad King Ludwig's castle in the eponymous cavern the Aryan had called *Rotfels*. "Alright. Redrock Strategy it is. I understand that you must accede to the Elder's request, and I'll go along if …"

"Very well. If I am going to entrust you with the future of China—and myself—I may as well trust you to converse with your Hekka. Due to the time differences, you will have to make your call from my private jet enroute to Monaco. I shall see that your comms, as you term them, are enabled. Do we have a deal?"

"You're sounding like an American, Chin." Crayle neglected to add that he was thinking of a used-car salesman.

"Ling will see you to the airport in thirty minutes."

Crayle stood and bowed. "I'll pack a few things and meet her in her chambers."

Chin's jaw tensed ever so slightly. Then relaxed into a minimal smile. "I shall instruct her to acquire you at your … chambers."

As before, the eunuchs escorted the American strategist back to his room. He packed what was basically a boogie-bag and a handful of European currency.

• • •

At precisely thirty minutes after Chin had made his promise, a soft knock came at the door. To Crayle's surprise, it croaked open to reveal the new empress of all China wearing blue jeans and a halter top. Unlike the standard Chinese woman, Ling demonstrated noticeable cleavage. She carried a black trench coat over one arm. "How do you like the look. I'm going for the California Girl image." She twirled with the lightness of a ballerina.

"It looks leftover from college. What do you say to that?"

"I say, *Go Trojans!*"

"I'm not sure you filled out your outfit then like you do now. Anyway, let's get on the road. I need to finish this little mission back to Europe and return. In order to preserve all that you now have, I've got work to do."

"Father has decided that the more than one billion Chinese for whom I am empress will not discover that fact until you have returned safely."

"You'll have to lose the Father nomenclature. You'd best check protocol for the correct honorific. I'd help, but I don't have experience with this either."

She slipped into the trench coat, took his arm, and proceeded to the royal helicopter. A short ride later she saw him onto Chin's Dassault Falcon 7X and away. He'd played coy, but she wondered just how much of her he'd noticed. Her gaze lingered as the jet lifted into the Hong Kong sky, headed west.

• • •

Chin's taking of an empress had been much less formal than the one anticipated by Lalumière in France. The new king would require the most ornate ceremony possible. He would spend money his starving nation didn't have, and the people would cheer and clap with delight. Chin reasoned that, when a people needs something real bad, oftentimes they get what they asked for.

For him, though, the addition of Ling had called for a much smaller ceremony. To that end, his guards had sequestered the departing press corps and deprived them of any and all communication devices. To be sure, his Red daughter—master of all things technical—had enveloped the palace with a Wi-Fi shield, just in case.

Now, with Crayle headed off to Monaco to meet with the Elder, he faced the biggest challenge of his life. He'd forbidden himself sex with any woman due to the rape of his mother that brought him to life. He was faced with a task more fearsome than any stock market situation, or any other battle. Yet Ling had been special since the first day she was brought to him. From a thirteen-year-old to a twenty-year-old, he'd watched her grow. Now, he watched as she began to disrobe.

She glanced over her shoulder at him. "You must take off your clothes. I can't do this alone."

"Yes," he stammered back at her smile. "We must make children."

"What we must do now, is make love."

• • •

Chin Yao-wu took Ling An-yee to bed for the first time. On his wedding night, like many men before him, he suspected that his bride was not a virgin. Inside, the notion outraged him. It made him furious. But he contained it within. Afterward, he sat on the bedside, quaffing one glass of Scotch after another.

As he drank, he recalled a statement Red had made, quite inadvertent, relating to the time Crayle had spent in Hong Kong formulating Chin's strategy of conquest. The Blackstone, as it was referenced, garnered his total focus during that period. Red had just noted that Black had been required to spend an inordinate amount of time with the American. Had he touched her? Had he …

His frame of thought was interrupted when his new bride reached for him. For the second and final time, they finished, and Ling fell asleep. He stepped away and poured another drink.

She moaned.

He turned to look at her. A bad dream? He readied to awaken her, but she moaned again. It sounded like a word. He moved closer. Her beautiful rounded lips repeated the word.

Chin jerked away. Enraged.

Again. "Magus," she moaned.

For the first time, he saw the look of love. He stormed to the side table, yanking the bottle to his lips, and drank it dry.

• • •

"Father! Father! Wake up!"

Chin could barely discern the sounds entering his ears.

"Father!"

He opened his eyes. She sat on her haunches before him, her hands holding his. He swung his head to the left, noticing the empty bottle a few feet away. Then back to Ling.

"You must not use that word."

"But—"

"Never again. We are lovers. You are An-yee. I am Yao-wu."

She realized what had just transpired. He had set aside his self-preservation defenses for the first time. Her chest heaved at having been accepted into his heart. She moved close, placing her head against his chest, closing her eyes.

Chin noticed that she had fallen asleep. He leaned his head back, against the wall. His eyes stared at the ceiling, unseeing—what a military man would call the thousand-yard stare. The relatively simple life to which he had grown accustomed as stock market mogul was changed forever. What had been knowable and predictable was no longer so. He yearned for the council of one man—the man, Crayle.

• • •

After Ling drifted off to sleep, her mind entered the nether region where reality and fantasy blend. She saw Chin serially with each of his mature daughters, committing the sexual act she remembered well. She saw the older girls graduate, one-by-one, to be led away to freedom by the two eunuchs. They must have found peace and harmony out in the world, because they were never seen or heard from again.

She saw in her vision a young woman commit the ultimate act of violence against the man she'd called Father for seven years. Lastly, she envisaged the young woman of her dream becoming the sole ruler—Empress of China.

CHAPTER 36

The meeting had become standard operating procedure at the pope's official offices in the Vatican. He would receive a variety of people, Swiss guards in attendance to assure that nothing amiss came to pass. For two very special officers, Cardinals Fratze and Alighieri, the guards moved outside and closed the heavy doors.

The German took a chair next to the pope so he could point out the figures and explain away any questions the Illuminé's pontiff might conjure.

"The sales are going well, Zoran," the financial wizard of convenience, Cardinal Fratze, reported.

"I am no longer Zoran of Dalmatia. I am Innocent the … what was the number?" He grinned.

"It doesn't matter. Your use of the Sistine Chapel for the private auctions of treasures was inspirational."

"Ass-kissing has no place in our Vatican, my dear friend."

Fratze was surprised. The new pope calling him a dear friend. Things would go well, he was sure.

The pope resumed the business at hand. He glanced at Alighieri, wanting to assure himself that both cardinals were up to speed on the project.

"The world's wealthiest assemble here daily. Our premier Botticelli just sold at auction for 37.5 million Euros. Over 45 million in U.S. dollars. You will certainly be able to feed the poor with the proceeds."

"I'm afraid we shall find the poor very difficult to feed."

"But—" said Fratze, turning his gaze to the Italian for support.

"You have been most loyal to the Illuminé over the years, but I wonder if you are *with the program*, as the Americans say."

Cardinal Fratze's jaw dropped. He turned to the pope, not believing what he was hearing.

Pfft.

A perfect shot to the heart. What one would expect. Especially, from a man who'd assassinated heads of state in his pre-papal incarnation.

The cardinal collapsed, the red blood absorbed by his woolen vestments—the colors a match.

The body moved a little here and there for a few minutes, then lay still.

The pope addressed the corpse. "I'm afraid your debit side has exceeded your credit side, my financial friend. You have become an accounting casualty."

The special weapon had fired a needle-like projectile that produced a small explosion the instant it touched blood.

The pontiff depressed the gold-encrusted housekeeping button on his desk. That accomplished, he turned to the other man.

"Cardinal Alighieri. You will accompany the cleaners to an appropriate location. There, you will see to it that the proper death certificates—diagnosing heart failure as cause of death—are prepared, and suitable burial plans and honors bestowed."

It had been less than a minute before those assigned to clean up such messes arrived. After all in attendance had made signs of the cross, the cleaners boxed up the German cardinal and carted him away to be prepared for his stately funeral.

As the door closed, the phone rang. The special phone. Good. Things had gone as planned, meaning he was prepared to present positive news. He lifted the ornate handset of the ancient and elaborate communication device, knowing that encryption and decryption of all calls was built in. Safe.

"Yes, Elder?"

"A situation report, Zoran."

The pope provided his report of sales and percentage completion, plus the total amount transferred to Kobler's Swiss bank in Zurich. The Elder, in turn, informed him that poor Kobler—murdered by the Elder's daughter, Pattie—had been replaced. One of Sylvain Lalumière's daughters who'd been living and studying in Switzerland. Alice.

Pope Innocent finished just as Alighieri returned.

"Everything is prepared. I have set the wheels in motion. The bells of Saint Peter's shall chime for our dearly departed colleague."

"As it should be, Cardinal. Here." He pushed a tray of *petit fours* across his desk.

The cardinal, having just witnessed the cold-blooded murder of his fellow cardinal and co-conspirator, declined. It wasn't his appetite. It was that he worried more than normal for his own longevity.

"Is there anything else you wish from me today, Your Eminence?"

The pope smiled. He retrieved the dish and took a confection for himself. "These are very good. Are you sure?"

"Thank you, Your Eminence. I'll pass just this once."

"I had hoped you would relieve me of some of these latent calories. The holidays, I mean, the Holy Days, have not been kind to my waistline. I find that popes sit a great deal. I also find that they get very little exercise since there are so many assistants here for this and that. Oh, before you leave. We have just lost our financial expert with respect to the auctions. I would like for you to pick up where he left off. I'm sure you are aware that your vaunted ancestor, Dante, suffered exile for financial misdeeds. See that you do not get caught."

The pope slid the former Cardinal Fratze's papers across his desk. "Please. Take a look. We'll discuss these numbers again tomorrow."

"As you say, Your Eminence."

Cardinal Alighieri exited the room, papers in hand. He did not at all like the notion of acquiring the position vacated by a colleague who'd been murdered. It also pained him that he could not submit a prayer for his own salvation and deliverance. Like the others, he, too, was Illuminé. He, too, was without God.

CHAPTER 37

Sylvain Lalumière sat at the Mount Royal's Table One sipping through his fifth pot of English Breakfast Tea. He had reserved the alcove seat two days earlier. The sun had risen in slow motion, backlighting the curve of bay and centering behind the Saint Michael's Mount. Now, the mid-morning sun produced a glare and caused him to wear sunglasses. He'd wondered for a second whether France's former kings had worn sunglasses. The picture that notion summoned caused him to smile, but only slightly. His reality was that Pattie had left him for *other work* sixteen days earlier. "Don't go anywhere," she'd said. "I'll be back soon." Sixteen days.

"Would you care for another pot … King Louis?"

Though he was worn to a nub, Lalumière's head spun in the direction of the sound. A welcome, familiar sound. "Jean-Marc. Finally. At least someone has returned." The father noticed something about his son's countenance. It showed what he read as contentment, even happiness.

"That's right. You can see it. My days and nights with the Swedish queen were fabulous. Like the original James Bond, I have won her to our side by using my masculine wiles."

"Have you heard from her?"

"I just left early this morning."

"Not her. Pattie. I've not seen nor heard from her for more than two weeks. Have you seen or talked to her?"

He shook his head. "She'd call you long before she'd call me. That is strange, though."

"We are stuck in this place. The food is wonderful. The staff is wonderful. But I cannot move forward. All I am able to do is watch the news. I see our people suffer. The entirety of the French government is in hiding, probably in a cave in Pakistan. The people are fending for themselves, and the police and other government service people are doing their best, but their own families are suffering."

"I get that. You know you can help and are frustrated because you aren't able—as things stand."

"At least you understand. You are a good son, Jean-Marc." He didn't rise, but held out his arms for a hug.

"There's something I've needed to tell you for some time. I have no excuses. I was just afraid."

"Afraid? But why? You can tell me anything. Was it about getting to France and ascending the throne?"

"Uh, no."

"What then? What could be so important."

"She confided to me, Father." Jean-Marc averted his glance to the sea-mount in the distance. "And I'm truly sorry for this part. It happened while we were making love."

Sylvain Lalumière couldn't believe his ears. "Making love?" He laid his head onto folded arms. Wanting to sob, he hadn't the energy. "Betrayed. By both of you. I am lost. Completely."

"It wasn't me. I knew she would betray you. Coming in second is not in her makeup. Perhaps it is good to know this now."

"Good?" Lalumière grieved.

"Yes, good. Our country has been led down the socialist heaven pathway, which has delivered exactly as we expected. Chaos. Lawlessness. Punitive taxes. The poor getting poorer. Add to that the flight of our business leaders and their fortunes, and there is no one left to tax." He leaned down to look into his father's eyes. "Father. We can still take the throne."

"*C'est impossible.* We sit here in this Penzance, the land of pirates, with a boat that is barely seaworthy ..."

"But, it's the people. Can't you see? She's kept you out of touch in these hideouts, providing only what she wanted you to hear. She controlled the news. The people of *La Belle France* ... they still cry for a return to monarchy. For Mitim, their superhero. For you, Father."

Sylvain Lalumière, barely able to lift his head from the table, gazed dejectedly into his son's eyes. "Can you operate the boat?"

Jean-Marc knew he'd won the battle. "Yes! I can operate the boat. I have the instructions. They are written in both English and French."

"I have listened to you and you have served me well. As my son and as the new Crown Prince. *Dauphin*, as we say. We will clean up, and then we will find our way to the boat. It is full of fuel by now."

"But—"

"Then we will sail *La Manche* under cover of darkness."

"Oh, no, that is too difficult."

"And then we will sail up the Seine at Le Havre, and not stop until we have reached Paris."

His son stood and began to pace the room. It seemed he'd won a Pyrrhic victory. His father had grabbed the reins and taken control. Now, what?

"Prior to our arrival at the City of Light, we will make portage near Versailles. Do you see the possibilities, my Son?"

Jean-Marc realized that his fears were misguided. His father definitely had the mind of a head of state. "It is the perfect solution." Prepared for a high-five, he turned to his father with a smile. "Versailles?"

"Versailles."

• • •

Lalumière and his son had forgotten a critical point in plotting their next tactical move. The Pattie they schemed against happened to be the biological daughter of the man known as the Elder. At the same moment during which they resolved their next move, he was disturbed at his Monaco palace by an operative he'd tasked to oversee the Lalumière operation. That he was always in control was becoming a notion stretched thin by the man's report.

Although he'd met with his spy many times over the years, it always surprised and disturbed him that the lanky man was so thin he could hide behind the classic light poles of Paris.

"You've disturbed me only twice in the past twenty years. I am sure your information has great value and requires prompt action. Your report?"

The man, disheveled to say the least, bowed in brief. The annoyed nature of his handler caused him to report in the most succinct manner possible. "Your primary operative is working the Aryans in southern Germany. She has left the Frenchman in southwest England."

"I know that. What else?"

"As of two hours ago, the Frenchman and his son … they left port."

"No. You are mistaken. She ordered him to stay put until she came for him. I am confident that he is still there."

"I have checked and double checked. Monsieur Lalumière checked out of his room, leaving a generous tip. A guest at a next-door residence noticed the two quite tall men leave. I further checked at the dock and found the boat had left fifteen minutes after he checked out. Everything fits."

The Elder pushed an eighteenth century pill box toward his man, who tossed the pills down in a single gulp.

"You are to contact operative Gretje and provide to me a situation report *toute de suite*. I have a state function to attend, or I would do it myself." He glanced left and right at his formal dress in the royal mirror. "Tell her we have spoken and that she is ordered back to

Penzance. You will accompany her. The two of you can pick up the trail. Tell her this is Priority One. Understood?"

The operative acknowledged in the affirmative. He had worked with the prince's daughter before and, in his own mind, referred to her as a volatile explosive device. Even if he were quite careful, she could get him killed.

The Prince of Monaco—the Elder's other incarnation—terminated the conversation and, for the first time in a long time, felt *Opération Française* to be in danger.

• • •

The message had come in the middle of the night. Fortunately, Pattie's cell was on vibrate and her bedmate, sound asleep, had not felt the vibration. The private message indicate a mandatory meet in one hour in the observation tower near the BMW factory. She arrived at the base of the 1972 Olympics relic to find a man holding open the sole elevator door. With her hand in her purse grasping the deadly compact, she entered. In seconds they were high above Munich with a superb view. As she peered out at the vista, she realized that darkness punctuated by light seemed to define her.

Operative Gretje spoke to the wisp of a man's reflection in the glass viewing panel. "You are saying that my father sent you rather than just calling me on the phone. He'd never do that."

"I only know what he told me. He said he could not reach you."

"I was deep inside with the Aryans. They're smart people. They would've found my cell and that would have been that. Okay, what'd he want?"

The Elder's operative decided not to insert himself as the one who discovered the Lalumière exodus from Penzance. "The one calling himself Louis and his son have departed from Penzance."

"Hold on. My father knows this? How?"

The operative shook his head. "He just knows. I am to tell you that we, you and I, are tasked to Penzance, there to pick up their trail and track them down."

"Anything else? Extreme prejudice?"

"No. Just find them. We must leave immediately."

"Hell. I think I know where they're going. It's easy. We'll take a short cut."

"No again. My orders are that we, you and I, track them from the English town. Please don't make this difficult. Your father can forgive you. Me ..."

"Compromise. We'll fly to a little airport I know just outside Paris. I'll check my little Vestige chip tracker and, if they've been where I think they have, we'll have them. If not, we'll hop over to Cornwall, England and go from there. *Capisce*?"

"*Capisco*."

The private flight took a couple of hours from their departure in Munich until the Falcon 7X settled into Toussus-le-Noble airport just southwest of Paris. More important, it was even closer to Versailles.

• • •

Across La Manche in Penzance, the cruise in the *African Queen* started well. Mid-channel, however, a storm blew in from the west, churning the waves into fourteen foot swells. The wind that had created the heavy seas blew across the tiny vessel and drenched the occupants. As a matter of self-preservation, the tall men wedged themselves into the leeward side of the boiler to keep the wind, water, and cold at bay.

As they sailed to within sight of the Normandy Coast, Lalumière had to speak if only to stop his teeth from chattering.

"This is what it was like, my Son."

"What was like?"

"The attack by the British and the Americans. And the others. They approached in small boats while the Germans pounded them with artillery from the heights."

"This makes it more real than the textbooks in school."

"They were very brave. And though we have our differences with the English, they lost a lot of lives returning us to freedom. From the Nazis."

"Speaking of whom. Pattie has gone off to them for some purpose, and she has our bomb. What could she be up to? She wouldn't sell it. They might use it against us."

"That's right. And she wouldn't go over to them. They murdered many of her countrymen in the war."

"Perhaps she plans to blow them up. Listen to my thoughts on this. She was born too late to have experienced the Second World War, but she can still seek revenge. A five megaton nuclear bomb would do nicely."

"Yes, Jean-Marc. But she would need something like Monsieur Crayle's Blackstone Strategy to gather them all together in order to eliminate them with our only bomb."

"You're right. It was a silly thought."

The squall passed a short time later. They soon entered the mouth of the Seine River at France's famous northern seaport, Le Havre.

A few miles upriver, nightfall overtook them as they enjoyed the splendid lights of Rouen, where French heroine Joan of Arc had been burned at the stake, and Giverny, where Monet had worked his magic in his walled garden. What a grand difference a few kilometers could make.

Another hour in the direction of Paris and Lalumière guided the boat to a dock on the starboard side. He'd been seeking his destiny for far too long and yet the fabled Versailles and its monumental palace were a short distance away. He felt so close.

His son had been thoughtful enough to purchase a wagon in Penzance. The young man pulled it along with their two suitcases and the three Scotch crates. The roads and pathways varied from cobblestones to dirt, making the trip arduous. But the abundance of trees and bushes provided coverage for their trek.

"Breathe the air, Jean-Marc. It is always special in this place, but it is more special at this moment. We march, much as did Napoléon, on Paris."

Jean-Marc had studied well the former French emperor's return from exile, albeit with a small force. He decided not to let the fact that they were just two in number spoil his father's triumph. "While some may comment in a negative fashion regarding the large size of the aristocratic French nose, it is perfectly suited to inhale the aromas you mention."

"She is gone to us, my Son. Off with the Germans and their quest for a new land. Aryan purity, they cite as the required end-game to return their country to its prominence. With Pattie's help, I wouldn't be surprised if they managed to take power and expel the immigrants."

"It would suit them. They have demonized those peoples in the manner that Hitler demonized the Jews back in the 1930's."

"But the new Germany cannot exist as if it were an island. They must deal with interdependence to other nations and peoples. These people will take a dim view of the notion of a master race. They won't need Germany as much as Germany will need them. They will fail again."

"For our new regime to succeed, Father, we must ensure that the Aryan onslaught does not once again spill over our borders. By your leave, I shall take it upon myself to ensure no such possibility is afforded them."

"Well spoken. But I request that—when we talk alone—that you drop the early eighteenth century impressionism. You are to be formally crowned Prince soon … of modern France. You must become, not play, that part."

They both knew the lay of the land at Versailles. Each had walked every inch of its 37,000 acre expanse from the palace entry, to the famous fountains and grand canal behind, and to the grounds with hunting cottages for King Louis XIV's guests.

When they had trudged for what seemed like several hours, Lalumière grasped Jean-Marc's sleeve and halted.

"A few steps, and we are there. On the grounds. My heart. It pounds for myself, for you, and for France itself."

They took the few more steps.

Perhaps the greatest fright and the greatest surprise came next. A full brass band began to play the Marsellaise. The song, written in 1792 to evince patriotism against a Prussian and Austrian coalition, was later selected for the post-monarch republic in 1879. It couldn't have been more inappropriate. They turned to each other.

"How?" asked the prospective king. "Who?"

"It's a surprise, Father. For you. The Swedish queen helped me set it up. Come on. We're a short walk away from the palace. Our palace."

Sylvain Lalumière was beside himself. For once, he was without words. But like the politicians he was replacing, that didn't last for long.

"In my heart, I wish Pattie could see this. Why did she leave us just before our grandest moment?"

"Our grandest moment is in a few days—also with the queen's help. The coronation. Pattie abandoned you. And since her father and the pope proclaimed her queen in the ceremony at the Roman Colosseum, it is essential that she be exiled."

"Exiled?"

"Yes. I cannot do that because I am technically third in line. You must say the words."

"She made all this happen. She broke me out of the Bastille and carried me to safety. She eliminated that evil CIA man, Neil Wohlford, probably saving my life."

"Mr. Wohlford was an Illuminé plant. She did it for her own benefit."

"She led me to Paris and to our grandest day … setting the bomb at the top of the Tower."

"She failed there, too. I think she wanted to spare Versailles so much, she engineered the catastrophe that occurred. With all the French government gathered beneath, the explosion would have destroyed them all. Perfect for our needs."

"I don't think so. She asked me personally to have you fly over Paris at midnight. To see the spectacle of lights."

"And when was the bomb to go off?"

The realization of Pattie's side plot to blow Jean-Marc out of the sky and remove a future political thorn hit Lalumière like a sledge hammer. "She wanted you dead." His eyes slammed shut like sprung mouse traps as his hands pounded his cheeks red. "Oh, my God. I've been a fool. She will try again, if she can. And she knows how important you are to me. Very well. She is in exile."

"I knew you would draw that conclusion on your own." He pulled a document from a man bag strapped diagonally across his chest. "I've had this drawn up in appropriate calligraphic text." He withdrew a replica quill pen and handed it to his father. "Sign her exile as Louis XIX, King of France. It will be your first official declaration."

The extreme bitterness he felt clashed with the love he had gained for his young partner-in-crime. "Turn your back." Feeling as if he actually was the new king of France, Sylvain Lalumière scrawled an ornate signature for the first time.

Jean-Marc retrieved it, rolled it, and slid it into a waterproof tube, which he placed back in his bag.

They marched up the pathway toward the palace with the band into its third rendition of the anthem. The musicians were relieved as the royal pair disappeared into the rear entrance. None of them had known who the two tall men were, but the pay, in the new Swedish royal currency—something other than the Euro—was very, very good.

• • •

Since they'd both been to Versailles many times, it took them just a few minutes to find the throne room. Lalumière found the King

Louis XIV chair a little small, but not lacking for comfort. His son stood before him as if sizing it up for himself. "It's perfect as we knew it would be. But I must excuse myself and seek the royal bathroom."

"One second. I hereby officially confirm that Pattie has been exiled by France's new king while in Barbados with her Aryan accomplice and Chin's general, Li. By that act, I have assured that my son shall be safe, as well as our new monarchy. I expect that she will deal her bomb to someone else, and we shall be done with her forever. Paris has been spared, and we shall reside and govern here at Versailles. There, how was that?"

"Swell, Dad. Now, by your leave, I really need to go."

"One more item, then you are dismissed. In order for us to appeal to French emotions, I have a second order. Due to the Muslim bombing of Marseille, I hereby decree that all Muslim populations of France shall be labeled "not French" and shall be repatriated to live happily among their own. And one more thing. Taxes shall be lowered due in part to diminished government and politicians. Business shall be unleashed as in China."

"Father …"

"Finally, I am charging you to find the infamous Black diamond, which shall legitimize my reign. Now, you may go."

As Jean-Marc scampered off, he wondered to what extent Pattie's insanity had infected his father. Thoughts for another day.

• • •

France's new king sprang out of his throne, his countenance ashen. He commanded to anyone within earshot, "Find Jean-Marc! See that he is safe!"

Pattie half-walked, half staggered before him. She held a serving tray. Covered. "I told you I would serve in Versailles. That I'd serve the people."

"Guards!" the king yelled, his voice breaking.

No one responded.

"Oh. The other dish I prepared contained nerve gas. Inhalable only. I left the ugly mask I wore outside, so you could see these." She smiled.

Overwhelmed, Lalumière could only gasp. "Dimples."

"Do you remember seeing them up close. Each time we made love?"

Lalumière collapsed back onto his throne. "How did you find me?"

"My father sent an operative to assist me with the Aryans. The silly man thought we should fly to Penzance in order to track you down. I told him that was unnecessary. I knew where you'd go. I flew into Toussus-le-Noble."

"Where we flew previously in order to attack Paris."

"*Ce ça*."

It took him a minute to digest that she knew him through and through. A moment later, Lalumière pointed. "You serve the people. You are beyond demented. In that tray, is there one of my guard's heads?"

"Or Jean-Marc's?"

His mouth fell open. His hand went to his heart.

"Come see. I'll let you do the honors."

Shaking, he rose. He stepped forward.

"Don't be shy. Only you could appreciate what's under the cover."

He reached for the handle. Abruptly, he stopped. His hand retreated as though it had touched a burning flame. "*No!*"

A quick laugh, she continued, "It's not Jean-Marc's head. I was kidding." She gushed a real laugh.

"You are beyond insane! I knew it!"

"Go ahead, Sylvain. It won't bite. I promise."

With care, with trepidation, he grasped the handle. And lifted.

"*Oh la la! Sacré bleu! Merde!*" Lalumière stared. Thankful that it wasn't his son's most useful body part, he felt he needed to accede to her cleverness. "I lost this at the Colosseum in Rome. In the flood devised by Magus Crayle." He looked into her eyes. "You had it all along."

"I'm returning it. It belongs here with you."

She placed the tray on the floor.

"I … you …"

From her coat, she withdrew her French gem-encrusted version of the CIA's universal remote control. As she moved it, its gems cast sparkles of light streaking across all surfaces like a 1970's disco ball, rather than the hundreds of years old, crystal-adorned chandeliers above.

Sweat drenched the Frenchman's face. It overwhelmed his royal handkerchief. He looked at her. She'd always known what to do.

She read the quandary in his eyes. She answered.

"*Run, Sylvain! Run!*"

Near hyperventilation, he spun away. His crown clanked on the throne as it toppled.

He ran.

Her laughter echoed off the hard, flat surfaces of the throne chamber.

He glanced back once to see her—the lunatic that he loved.

In that instant, a young man strode into the hall.

"Hey. What's going—"

When he saw her, he stopped cold.

The woman born with the Dutch name Geertruida, and nicknamed Gretje, who'd adopted many pseudonyms, pointed her device at the football on the platter. Her laughter subsided.

With Jean-Marc to her right and Sylvain halfway across the room, she deployed her dimples once more.

"Queen!" she yelled.

She moved her thumb to the button she wanted.

"I am Queen!"

Sweet Pattie, as she thought of herself, pressed *Play*.

She hadn't mentioned that the bomb was on a timer and that she was the only one with motorized transportation to get them all away. She dropped the remote on a table and ran after her husband. She would save the day. She would spirit them to safety. "No one shall call me crazy!" she yelled as she exited the throne room. "I am Queen!"

• • •

His trip halfway around the world for a high-level meet with the Elder provided Magus Crayle plenty of time to think. His mind had settled on expectations and reservations. That accomplished, he'd slept for most of the journey. Upon arrival, he was up, refreshed, and prepared for everything to play out in slow motion at the Elder's intellectual pace.

Structural damage from the Marseille nuclear bombing to France's *Côte d'Azur* airports caused Crayle's flight to Monaco via Nice to be diverted to the Italian airport at Genoa. So the pilot had been told. No sooner had the passenger arrived and deplaned than he heard someone yelling his name over a bullhorn.

A hundred feet away and leaning out the doorway of their own Falcon 7X, Micmac bellowed and waved. Crayle ran across the tarmac and found not only the former UDT sailor, but Phoebe, Lenny, and Hekka inside. Before he could properly greet his new wife, and apologize profusely, they were aloft and being read in by Jack on the big screen. In ninety minutes they touched down at Paris Orly and were westbound in a hardened SUV.

As Crayle and the team raced along the Autoroute, he felt the car start to jump the road. It seemed as if the suspension had come undone on all four wheels. He fought for control, as he observed a sight for which he was unprepared.

Ahead, like an endless ribbon of licorice someone had violently shaken up and down at one end, the road rippled toward them. In the distance, a cylinder of dust and debris lifted the landscape.

"My God!" he yelled to the others. "It's Versailles!"

He heard gasps from his team.

Without further words, he swerved left over the second lane. He screeched to a stop.

'Out!" he screamed. "Into the drainage culvert!"

They gathered their wits and jumped from the vehicle as Crayle pulled it over the bank, angling it into the ditch. The angle caused his door to jam.

He pounded the window with his elbow. It withstood his assault.

Furiously, the team beat and kicked the door.

As the ground beneath shook, he enacted the sunroof and pulled himself through the opening.

The three on the ground grabbed arms and legs and settled him next to them.

Ever the one to monitor his surroundings, Crayle directed the team. "I saw a pipe. Under the road. Quick. This way."

He ran ahead, stumbling over the standard fare of flotsam and jetsam of culverts. Weary, he fell, then regained his footing.

They reached a cement abutment. Crayle stood at the pipe's opening, pulling each one of them inside. Hekka … Phoebe … Micmac … Lenny.

The cement pipe was very old and in disrepair.

Without allowing time for them to rest, the first shock wave from the explosion at Versailles struck.

The thick cement, above and behind, cracked like thunder. A large chunk fell, just missing Hekka.

Crayle glanced at Micmac.

His long-term team member and now friend nodded.

The men knew what to do. Thousands of years of survival had been baked into their souls. They covered their women. They each pulled their loved ones to the pipe's floor. They protected them with their bodies.

The nuclear wind blasted past both openings, creating a horrific screech as it did.

• • •

After a mere ten minutes, the shaking subsided. Crayle and Micmac peered out both ends of the drainage pipe. Looking back at the two women, they considered their options.

"Ahem!" came from the perpetual third wheel, Lenny.

"Okay, folks. Micmac and I will check out things topside. See if it's safe. We'll be back for you if it is."

"I'm not letting you out of my sight, Mr. Crayle," Hekka informed her husband.

"It's just as well. I'll stand protective duty down here while you two are gone." Micmac didn't push the genderist jibe, but Phoebe's scowl proved it unnecessary.

As the Crayles climbed over debris and stepped outside into the ditch, they observed that their vehicle hadn't moved an inch. It was still stuck. They struggled up the steep, wet grass banking to the highway only to hit the deck as a chunk of marble crashed nearby. Careful, they stood and glanced into the distance, grateful they hadn't gotten closer.

"That mushroom cloud in the distance looks a bit small. It seems Chin may have a quality control issue," Crayle observed.

"I think he wanted to fulfill his obligation to Lalumière …"

"… but hoped we'd take them all down before this dud was discovered."

Crayle pulled his phone from his pocket and checked its display. "The French government, wherever they are, just tweeted that there's been a gas explosion at the Versailles Palace. They've put it off limits for safety reasons. Even to the press."

Before he could comment further, Hekka grabbed his arm, pointing into the distance. A vehicle was headed their way from the direction of the destruction. Surprised at first, they stood like statues.

"Let's not get the team's hopes up. We'll do a quiet but frantic wave."

They mastered the frantic wave in short order as the car neared.

"That's no ordinary … I'll be damned … it's a …"

"Hearse," said Hekka. "It's strange that they got there so fast."

The driver screeched to a halt abreast of them. The front and middle passenger side windows, emitting no sounds, slid down.

"*Pattie!*"

"*Jean-Marc!*"

Like the windows, the tranquilizer guns made no noises. They also didn't render the Crayles unconscious—just immobile and silent.

"Quick. Get them in the back."

Jean-Marc scratched his head. He didn't like taking orders from Pattie. There was a logistical problem, as well. "There's only enough room back there for the coffin."

Pattie provided her dimpled smile. "It's a double-wide."

• • •

Those still in the pipe heard the screech of tires. They hustled out just as the hearse peeled out.

"Catch the license plate, Phoebs! Your eyes are better than mine!"

Shielding her eyes, she read the plate. "Monaco Royal Palace."

CHAPTER 38

A normal day at the Palace of Monaco saw one or more hordes of tourists formed in an arc in front, anticipating the changing of the guard. Each time the process concluded, they'd either be marched back to their buses or would walk the short distance to the world-famous aquarium. The paparazzi would be left behind, drooling for that one-in-a-million shot. They not only covered the front of the palace, but sides and back, as well.

When workers had placed a run of sawhorses from the palace loading dock down both sides of the service road, they found that uninteresting. Until plumes of smoke billowed from each one. The smokescreen created a corridor that no camera could penetrate. Wild shouts of protest in Italian, French, and other continental languages disappeared into the fog.

The tactic concealed the arrival of a long black hearse, an event that would've sparked both shutter and speculation madness to last for weeks. Good for the tabloids, bad for the monarch.

Lalumière, Pattie, and Jean-Marc jumped from the car as Elder acolytes spirited the coffin into the palace rear entry. A fortuitous photo would have shown the Prince and his daughter attempting to kiss each other's cheeks while wearing gas masks.

The hearse, its coffin emptied in the Yellow Room and reloaded, escaped before the induced fog dissipated.

A breeze whipped through the Fontvielle Harbor just west of the principality, carrying the smoke with it and affording the throng of photo journalists a chance to see what they missed. Nothing. As the relief shift arrived, no one took note of the workers calmly removing the sawhorses.

Inside the palace, the Elder had given orders that the Crayles be provided the opportunity for an attended bathroom break. When finished, they were led away separately. Five of the ten armed guards led Crayle into the Elder's location of choice for ultimate privacy.

It was atypical for the Elder to be late for a rendezvous, but this was no ordinary day. The Monaco Formula 1 Grand Prix would begin officially the next day—Thursday—with morning and afternoon practice sessions, followed on Saturday with qualifying, and Sunday with the two hour race. It was his alter ego's duty to participate in the starting ceremonies, which preparation he had just attended. It was the same every year. All was in order, as expected.

Normally accompanied by staff of all sorts, he paced down the hallway alone stopping at a very special door. He checked visually all around before stepping inside. He entered a special code on a wall pad. His guest today was exceptional—he was not to be disturbed.

The ornate trappings of royalty surrounded one in the Yellow Room, the place he always used for clandestine meetings. There were no hidden microphones or cameras, and no spyglass apertures hidden in the priceless paintings that adorned the walls.

The man affixed to one of the ornate chairs appeared to require a lecture about the necessities of control.

"I am aware of the incident at Versailles. I expected that, if you survived, you would finally come for me. In that way, it was quite easy to gain custody of you."

"It's about your narcissism. You want something for yourself and don't give a damn who gets killed."

"No, Mr. Crayle. It's not about that at all. It's about ideologies and their effect on populations. You see, governments, especially democracies, are doomed to failure. So the miserable peoples will always seek an ideology to worship. It doesn't matter which one."

"So the Nazis stepped in where democracy failed—but murdered millions."

"But their elite were gods on Earth. They were worshiped. They could do no wrong."

"Then Stalin and his communists brought in their ideology."

"Correct. He used the *Workers of the World Unite* tenet to justify land acquisition around Russia. To use your characterization, he murdered far more people than did the Nazis."

"Yes, but Hitler and the Nazis justified grabbing land around Germany while declaring a need for additional living space, *Lebensraum*, as their excuse."

"You are indeed a knowledgeable and insightful man, Mr. Crayle. In World War II, the communist elite and the Nazi elite hated each other, not for ideology, but because one ideology must stand above all others for the scheme to bear fruit."

"I see what you mean. There can only be one absolute authority." He pondered a moment. "And that's why religion had to be destroyed. It presented a competing authority."

"Of course."

"I understand the principle, but where's your elite?"

"My Illuminé has leaders around the globe. And one component of my trinity, the monarchic resurgence, provides the elite requisite of absolute power."

"It's the absolute power you crave. You're just another megalomaniac like Chin and Lalumière."

"It's a matter of scale."

"I'll fight you, if I can. You know that."

"No, no, Mr. Crayle. When Herr Doktor Rorschach presses that button." He motioned to the white-frocked doctor nearby whom the intended victim knew only too well. "You will refer back to a former incarnation of yourself."

"What … what are you talking about?" He struggled against the leather straps.

"I might as well tell you. In ten minutes, you will remember none of this. But, in fairness, I will let you in—temporarily—on a little secret. There were three distinct Magus Crayles. Using *Dante's Inferno* as a frame of reference, your current self is equivalent to *Heaven*. You are a good man, an honorable man. You wish to do what is best for mankind. Laudable. Your previous version we'll call *Purgatory*. You were the man manipulated—your brilliant strategic mind couched between good and evil. The strategist, convinced he was doing the right thing, but only a pawn."

"And when your need for me ended, you caused my amnesia—to protect your insane game."

"Insane? No. Peoples must be led. That's been proven for millennia. Absolute leadership is all that can succeed. But we digress." The Elder rose from his throne. "Your third self is the earlier one. In your days with the CIA before the strategic methodology training."

"I don't recall. You know that."

"But I know." He motioned to the others in the room. "Frau Doctor Rikki and Herr Doktor Rorschach. They know.

Crayle found the strapping to be impregnable. He settled into the chair, resolved. "Then tell me. Before you destroy my memories. You owe me that much."

"Oh, no, no, Mr. Crayle. That won't be necessary. When the good doctor presses *Play*, your early memories will be your only memories. Vivid, but your only ones."

"No! Hekka! The others! No!" His eyes fluttered, then closed. His head fell to one side.

The Elder smiled. "The original Crayle matches up with Dante's *Hell.* He was an in-the-cold operative and assassin, par excellence. He's the man I need at this juncture. You won't appreciate this, but his first task will be to eradicate his entire team."

"No!"

The Elder turned. He nodded at Rorschach.

CHAPTER 39

The session with Magus Crayle had concluded with Rorschach pressing the red button on his computer. Crayle's head had bounced from side to side, while his body seemed to vibrate as if being electrocuted. In mere minutes, the act had been completed. Doctor Rikki checked the spy's vital signs and signaled thumbs up.

"Finally," the Elder said. "Make him comfortable. I shall give him two days for recovery—at your recommendation, Monika—and then Pirmin …" He nodded at Rorschach. "… shall commence programming him for our grand finale." Content, he left the room.

The Elder was unused to violence in his presence, but had to attend for assurance that his dictum—returning Crayle to his original CIA self—had been carried out.

The session had worn out the Elder. He retired early only to be awakened an hour later by someone shaking him. Someone with small, excited hands.

"Wake up, my prince of a father!"

The Elder, and Prince of Monaco, struggled to cover his head with the nearest available pillow. His annoyance was heightened by the gold fleur-de-lis woven into the blue Egyptian cotton. Due to Pattie's persistence, he surrendered. "Alright, my daughter. I will listen. But you must make this brief. I've had an excruciating day."

"I'll be quick. You used Chin to our purpose, right?"

"I used Chin to perfection. His lust for power caused him to procure six nuclear bombs. Three for himself. Three for us. Nearly a year ago."

"I would say that he used *his* bombs to perfection. Everyone in China and the world blamed fanatical Muslims."

"Chin has what he wanted. There will be no more bombs available to us."

"Pity. I believe the new pope, Innocent, can be of assistance. And the mind researcher, Dr. Rikki. I close my eyes, and I can see her genuflecting before him. But not in a religious manner."

The Elder spoke not a word. His relationship with Monika Rikki had ranged from the deeply intellectual to the fiery physical. That she might pleasure another man struck a nerve. He changed the subject. "You didn't realize it until that night, did you? Inside the Roman Colosseum."

"That I would be able to rescue the sixth and final bomb? After the place flooded?"

"No. That the bomb you rescued could have been pivotal in the Illuminé quest."

"There's more to your reference to the Colosseum affair, isn't there?"

"Forget about that place. What I refer to is the fact that you are my daughter. As such, you are the Crown Princess of Monaco. Right behind your half-brother."

She glittered. Her dimples underscored her delight. "It is fantastic. If something were to happen to brother …"

The Elder realized his mistake. His daughter had mutated into a sickened state. As intensely useful as she had been, strategic assassinations had become as facile as crossing a *t* or dotting an *i*. He made a mental note to leave orders: the Crown Prince was to be guarded whenever Pattie resided at the palace.

CHAPTER 40

Following his treatment by Doctor Rorschach, Crayle recovered in a sumptuous bedroom in the rear portion of the Monaco Palace. He wiped his eyes as if they'd been coated with Vaseline. He could not seem to erase the blur of natural light streaming into an open window.

They must have made a mistake. He checked his arms. They moved freely. He hopped off the bed and made a beeline toward freedom.

Snap!

His freedom extended ten feet and no farther. At cable's end, he slammed hard onto the centuries old floor planks. The noise brought a knock at the door, then entry.

Thoughts flashed through his mind. He had to play the game.

"Mr. Crayle. You are awake."

He instantly recognized the white-bermed head that peered around the door's edge. "Rorschach!"

The doctor smiled a broad smile, as if the game Crayle had considered earlier weren't deadly serious—just deadly.

After Rorschach had checked behind and ensured that no one could see him enter, he stepped in and helped Crayle back onto the bed.

"You must be careful. You should require two days of complete, uninterrupted rest given what you went through."

"What did you put in me? While everyone watched your finger on the red button, you jabbed my hip with your other hand."

"Just a little something left over from World War II. Quite unpleasant, but certain to create the effect we required."

Crayle saw that the doctor, probably the furthest from an operative he'd ever seen, was pleased with his solution to this particular problem. "I haven't lost my memories. I remember everything that happened last night."

Rorschach, not one to seek external gratification, began to speak.

Crayle held up a hand. "I would've lost everything. The strategic planning for Lalumière and Chin, all that's happened in the past four years. The team. Even you."

"And ..." the doctor smiled again.

"Hekka. She's my whole world, Doctor, and I owe you more than I can ever repay on that one."

"We will figure out the repayment another time. First, we must help you escape."

CHAPTER 41

It was a signature style that distinguished him from his predecessor in the short time he'd been in office. The president, Kimbel Stones, had come in strong. He'd responded to an appeal from Jack Sommers on behalf of Magus Crayle to start the ball rolling.

Fresh from the Heesen shipyard in Holland, the 230-foot cabin cruiser, painted a gloss black with gunmetal gray highlights, looked serious and fast. It was both. It also had a former Navy UDT man at its helm, and a team consisting of Phoebe, Mandy, Marli, and Lenny dressed for the mission ahead and trying to keep their nerves under control.

The men manning the port authority facility of the Principality of Monaco had seen some over-sized private craft before, but this one pushed the limit. It sat docile outside the jetty, demanding a slip. The lead man, Antoine, had responded that they had none available due to the impending Formula 1 race. "It never fails," he advised his subordinate. "When the rich can't get what they want, they pick up field glasses, and stare at you."

At that point they were advised by the vessel's radio operator that the craft carried the American Secretary of State, called away from her vacation, for a matter of greatest import with the Prince. They would be in Monaco for no more than two hours.

"The Secretary of State," repeated the heavier of the two.

The other laughed so hard he nearly spit out his gum. The other man, his supervisor, joined in.

At that moment, their archaic fax machine came to life, spewing forth a single page of paper.

The bigger man nodded to the other to check it out. It might be something worthwhile.

Three seconds later, the skinny one glanced over the text, and turned pale. "It is verification. Not from them."

"Then, from where?"

"From the palace."

Antoine's heart jumped a beat. "We have only one slip big enough. It holds the Sheikh's yacht."

They both began to sweat. "I've got it. The Sheikh and his crew are in Nice at the casino. No one is aboard. We'll pull it out. We'll anchor it. This Secretary, whoever she is, can have it for two hours."

The man-in-charge didn't like it, but had no alternative. "Communicate that to them."

"How much time?"

"Three hours," squeaked the big man, who appeared as if he was losing weight through his pores. He turned. "See to it. Quickly. Do not damage the Sheikh's boat."

His second-in-command rushed from the office. He turned back to view the yacht, but didn't like what he saw. A sizeable helicopter on the aft deck was spinning up its rotors. He noted side pods suitable for extra fuel. Their scheme seemed reasonable. But that didn't help the nausea he felt insinuating itself in his abdomen. "They're not waiting," he said to himself.

In short order, the chopper lifted off and headed for the palace. The port officer expected gunfire or something. Instead, he watched the aircraft land at the royal heliport without incident. The power of the American diplomat to get approach and landing clearance in seconds was too much. He crashed to the floor in a dead faint.

• • •

As the helicopter bearing the rescue team hovered ten feet above the landing pad, the palace guards snapped to attention. They expected dignitaries at this site, and the dignitaries expected pomp and circumstance. Since their automatic rifles were loaded with blanks, lest something untoward happen, they didn't expect what was about to happen.

Their first surprise came as the craft touched down. A blonde woman sporting a black pant suit, trailed by a redhead carrying a clipboard, jumped down. The Sergeant of the Guard recognized the appearance of an American Secretary of State, and stood tall.

Their second surprise came when a heavier-than-air white fog began streaming from the ends of the spinning rotors. It evoked several quizzical looks. "Stand firm," came the order from the sergeant.

The side doors sprung open and out jumped the team, fully armed and in black tactical gear. The two women turned, and dove back into the chopper. Micmac and his team fired first.

A quick order put the guards onto one knee, a synchronized demonstration move they had practiced many times. They returned fire. Blanks.

Though Micmac had supplied his team with rubber bullets for this part of the mission, those being struck by them felt serious pain. The men who were knocked off balance appeared to have being hit by live fire, adding realism and panic.

The faux Secretary of State and her assistant rejoined the battle, adding their own firepower to the mix.

The last thing the guards noticed was that the team of five insurgents had donned gas masks. As the fog drifted across the ground to them, one-by-one, the men keeled over.

The team moved carefully, but quickly, to the rear entrance. Micmac, armed with detailed plans of the place, had already advised the team that an elite personal guard would be found inside. Not some of life's rejects like Lalumière's Jacquard brothers. These were from the French Foreign Legion Monaco Unit.

Micmac had pulled with him a hose hooked to a cutoff pump on one of the fake gas pods. As they made their way inside, he handed off team leadership to hostage rescue expert Mandy. Hose in hand, he headed down a set of stairs to the palace HVAC room.

Intel fed to him by Jack indicated that the room contained controls for eight separate ventilation systems. The genius of that arrangement was that, if a system or two went down, the rest would operate while the errant one or ones could be repaired.

He connected his hose and selected the seven not expected to contain target Crayle. The downside was that the remaining system kept the Prince and any personal guards fog free, as well.

Since he'd equipped his helo with infrared sensors pre-flight, Micmac had observed the non-movement of those live souls outside the Prince's chambers and the nearby bedroom holding Crayle. He owed Doctor Rorschach for the intel, but parked that away for a later thank you. He pulled the seven levers to pump the fogged gas.

Above, the team's special masks not only kept them gas free, but allowed them to see through this particular fog of war. Mandy was tasked with using her Delta Force expertise to find and separate Crayle from any threats, and then to lead him out along the preplanned exfiltration route.

They deliberately moved through fogged rooms. They encountered no resistance. Mandy reached a door leading into the main hallway. She knew it would be free of the chemical. Those guarding Crayle, and down the hall guarding the Prince, would have live ammunition. Once she opened the door, they were in the danger zone.

She turned to the team. "I'll take off my mask and breathe in a little of this soup. Then I'll step out into the hall and realistically collapse at the guard's feet. It will look real because it will be real. He'll become vulnerable."

"Do it naked," Lenny advised.

She'd been read in. *Ignore most of what Lenny says.* She did. She turned to Phoebe. "Okay, Sis?"

Phoebe loved working missions with her sister. They'd separated after college, Mandy going to Delta Force and Phoebe to the FBI. But this just wasn't her fight. She ripped off her own mask and took a long pull of the befouled air.

Mandy was overwhelmed. Seeing her sister's *now's when it matters* attitude in action first hand made her proud.

The guard snapped to attention the minute the door across the hall opened. That Phoebe had left the door ajar didn't catch his eye. She staggered a few feet closer, then collapsed. For real.

With his rifle's strap strung tight for appearance sake, the guard set it aside and rushed to the fallen women. That his pulse had doubled in the past few seconds caused him to breathe enough of the seeping gas to become incapacitated, then unconscious.

The team moved on the second body thud. Lenny handcuffed the guard and taped his mouth, then stood ready with the others outside Crayle's room. Before they could enter, the door burst open.

There stood Doctor Rorschach, his white-bermed pate glistening in the humidity, supporting Crayle's weight with the operative's arm slung around his own neck. Lenny placed gas masks retrieved from his side pouch over both heads.

The team snapped around upon hearing a gasp from behind. Micmac had made his way up from the HVAC control room and had crouched beside his fallen wife.

He fitted an oxygen module into her mouth.

A couple of breaths, and she tried to stand.

He leaned in, trying to hear the few words she uttered.

"It's just the fog, Sailor."

"The guards will come around soon, we've got to get out." Micmac pulled her onto his back in a fireman's carry, and followed Mandy, on point, along with Lenny. The trailing Rorschach had his subject almost to the end door, when someone spoke to them from behind.

Crayle turned his head.

Standing at the other end of the hall, his hands on his hips, stood the man everyone knew as the Elder. Whatever he said, got lost on its way down the long hallway. Another day, thought Crayle.

They'd been distracted. Two men jumped from a side alcove ahead.

Now on one knee, Mandy had them.

Pop, pop.

Chest, chest.

Pop, pop.

Forehead, forehead.

Down, down.

Lenny checked out the headshots as he passed. Dead center. "It's genetic."

Just before the door leading outside, Rorschach pulled Crayle over to a code-protected doorway and punched in the cipher. Before he could explain, the door pulled open and Hekka emerged. The drugs had worn off, and she'd pulled her Bowie from under her blouse.

Outside, the team passed a still unconscious ceremonial guard unit. "We have to depart Monaco's sovereignty. Beyond the reach of the Elder's official resources. Let's get loaded up." At that instant, everyone knew that Crayle had his game back.

Before they could reach the helicopter, a whooshing sound came from the door they'd just exited. Instinctively, the team hit the deck.

Only thirty yards away, their Plan A exfiltration vehicle, the chopper, exploded into a fireball.

They glanced behind to see the Elder, having fired the single shot weapon, retreat inside, possibly for another weapon.

Micmac jumped to his feet. "Plan B." He engaged the exfil app on his special smartphone, and in less than a minute a vehicle pulled up. The Range Rover had been extended and hardened. Two German shepherds jumped from an open door, sprinting to the former Delta Force operative's side.

Mandy crouched low and whispered to them as if laying out a conspiratory plot.

The palace door opened once again. Out stepped the Elder. He moved his second light antitank weapon to his shoulder. Mandy pointed at the man, and yelled, "Hit!"

The dogs looked like super-heroes with four legs. They sprinted toward the hapless and frightened Prince cum Elder, who dropped his weapon and stepped back inside just as they arrived. For extra measure, the two dogs flew through the air slamming against the door. An apparent message: *don't come out again.*

Mandy whistled them back. Unharmed, they returned at full gait. The Land Rover and team vacated the grounds in sixty seconds.

• • •

"We have a ride out," Micmac informed. "The French town to the west, Nice, is the closest. That's the good news. The airport there is still bunged up big time from the blast in Marseille. They've cleaned up the surface crap, but the underground shock waves of a five-megaton nuclear bump had the effect of a severe earthquake. Even as we speak, all runways near the Mediterranean coast of France are being re-stabilized."

Crayle looked at him. "Where are we now? I don't even know that."

"I'm sorry. We had to keep you away from the windows. We're blowing through a berg east of Monaco called Menton. As you might have guessed, the Elder has major pull in this area of France. But a little further and we hit the Italian border. We'll motor out of harms way to a little runway in San Remo."

"Then?"

"Refuel in the Azores just like before. Back to Big Bear from there."

"How long?"

"Twelve hours max."

"We need to hurry this up," Lenny interrupted. "Jack just messaged me. The eastern Riviera is starting to buzz. Lotsa comm traffic. Something about a terrorist attack in Monaco. Uh, oh. They're having to postpone the Grand Prix. They're talking September."

Micmac drew curtains closing off the aft portion of the stretch SUV. "Listen up. Phoebe and I are going into the bedroom and fix each other up."

"Uh, I'm not sure we have time for that," Lenny chimed.

"No. Not for that. Disguises. We'll be right back."

True to his word, the two emerged fifteen minutes later. Phoebe, with mousy dishwater blonde hair and 60's hippie garb, next to a classic rock, tattoo-adorned version of Micmac.

Crayle aired a new concern. "What about us?"

"Into the back of the vehicle. Weapons ready. We'll have some assistance if we need it. I've spent some time on this vehicle—it's not normal."

"It's probably the only van with mini-guns, am I right?"

"You're stealing my secrets."

Crayle shrugged his shoulders. "I'm a spy."

• • •

Back in Big Bear, the team could see that Crayle was depressed by all that had occurred. Each of them had spent sufficient time with him to have a slightly different perspective. It was no longer like a special operations team thrown together for a one-timer. Now, it was personal.

And he knew them as individuals. He could read their concern. It was time to just talk. Of that he was certain. Just let it flow. Stream of consciousness.

"I think of Hekka and what Pattie did to her. And to the two of us. I get furious, and then comes an intense numbness. I don't know which will explode first, my mind or my heart. And if the mention of heart seems strange for a man like me, listen to this. The Elder informed me that I was, due to his handiwork, now three people. Patriotic spy. Evil strategist. And now a man trying to put pieces—shards rather—together without getting sliced to ribbons. Physically or emotionally."

When she was sure that he'd let everything out, Phoebe spoke. "We had classes in psychology when I took my criminology degree. This is sounding like a bit of depression here. We need to get you to someone who is qualified in this shit."

Crayle looked at her. "I can't just walk into a clinic and tell them I'm nuts, can I? Who knows who might show up to shoot me or blow me up? It seems I attract danger everywhere I go."

She understood the signs. From the manner of her father's death. And the time it had come in her life couldn't have been worse. "I understand. I truly do. And with the classified stuff and all … we can ask Jack to get someone at Langley."

"I appreciate your help. But with the mindset I now have, Langley represents more danger to me than its help would be worth. Not the way to bet, I'm afraid."

"Then, there is one alternative."

He twisted around, and read her expression. "You can't be serious."

"He's the only card in the deck, Magus."

"I want a new deck. Or better yet, a new game."

She placed her hand on his shoulder. "No new game, no new deck. C'mon. I'll drive."

• • •

It took them the better part of forty minutes to exit the Big Bear Valley and arrive at the Quarry's multi-purpose garage. A quick ride into the depths to the covert hospital and the two stood before the psychiatric man-in-white.

"*Aaaah!*" cried Permin Rorschach. "It is you. I did not expect you back, Mr. Crayle. I have my subject once again. *Alles ist in ordnung!*"

"All is not in order, Doctor. I need counsel this time, not memories restored. Do you have one of those couches?"

CHAPTER 42

Following the kidnap and delivery of Magus and Hekka Crayle from Versailles into her father's clutches in Monaco, Pattie had led the trio of she, Lalumière, and Jean-Marc back to the region west of the Île de France. Not wanting to spend the hours driving the hearse, she'd directed Jean-Marc to an abandoned Italian airbase in the foothills just over the Italian border. Pattie ordered the awaiting jet's pilot to land near Le Mans.

"Every year in June, hundreds of thousands of people come here to witness the race. Hey, there's our driver."

The man with the sign FAMILLE ANTOINETTE tapped his foot, as if he wished to be otherwise occupied. Under orders to treat the guests with utmost deference, his demeanor changed dramatically when they displayed their recognition and headed his way.

The trip south on the E502, leading them to the outskirts of Tours, took less than forty-five minutes. The three stepped out into a fresh spring breeze and total sunshine. Pattie led them to a wide river's edge, and she waited for Lalumière and his son to react.

"*N'est pas possible.* It is not possible," said the elder man. "Jean-Marc and I parked it on the Seine. We never saw it again. Now it is here on the Loire." He turned to the faux nun, who replied with her signature dimpled smile. She said nothing. She didn't have to. She merely held aloft one of the infamous CIA remote controls.

"Get her fired up, boys. I promised our chauffeur a generous tip." She made the return trip back to the car, and reached in through the window. The two men watched as she stepped back, said thank you in French, and then crossed herself.

Jean-Marc frowned. "Does it count when a fake nun blesses you?"

Lalumière said nothing. He knew what it meant. Although their driver had attended the famous nearby Le Mans race every year since the age of twelve, he would not experience it this year. Nor ever again.

Once Pattie returned and stepped aboard, the *African Queen* headed east. The trip took them to the south of their destination, and they walked the rest of the way.

Their first indication of the mayhem Pattie had caused manifested itself in trees either flattened to the ground or uprooted completely. The second was the plethora of sawhorses holding bright yellow plastic tape and signs warning those who might stray farther with dire consequences. There were even radiation hazard warnings that the three knew to be false, but they did manage to keep the curious and the thieves away. In fact, there was no one in sight.

"Follow me, gentlemen." Pattie led the way past the long, narrow waterless pond and past the 17th Century, world-famous—but empty—fountain. "I wonder where the chariot and horses went. And Apollo. Oh, well. C'mon, let's sit on the steps." They did.

Jean-Marc no sooner hit the stoneware, than he rose. "I'm still cramped from the car and the boat. I will walk through the destruction. Your destruction, Miss Pattie. Perhaps there is something left of value." He walked the short distance, grumbling to himself as he carefully inspected the flattened palace.

When he was beyond earshot, Pattie turned to her new husband. "It got to me, Sylvain. I've finally realized the truth."

Lalumière recalled those words from an intimate conversation they'd had at Penzance. He worried for her mental health. Like a practiced actor—the one France knew as Mitim—he played along.

"First, I am no longer Sylvain. I am Louis Nineteen—"

"You must say *We are Louis Nineteen.* It's the royal plural."

"Of course, you are correct. Now, what do you mean by truth?"

"The biggest truth of all. The God truth."

"My little one. We shall have the finest doctors of the mind make the necessary repairs. You have been under excessive strain for too long." He smiled knowingly.

"It was this nun's habit. It's as if some manner of holiness is contained inside the fabric." She began to write in a special notebook. "Isn't this cool? Check out the leather cover. It's the one I picked up on Montserrat. On Mother Superior's desk the day she was summoned to heaven."

Lalumière peered over. "What do you write?"

"I will accept Jesus and salvation. It will make me the perfect Queen of France. I shall list all of the people."

"Those you've killed?"

"Yes. An inventory of sorts."

"And when do you present this inventory, and to whom?"

"I'm not quite sure. St. Peter? The pope?"

"This is wonderful news, my dear. It means you've finished with the killing."

"Yes. Well, almost. There's one left." She smiled, embarrassed.

"You are right. Once you have removed Mr. Crayle, we shall be secure in our new status."

She nodded. But, in truth, she'd forgotten Mr. Crayle.

Just then, Prince Jean-Marc returned. Her final target.

"There is nothing for me here. Not even a *urinoir* for the weary, which, at this royal moment, *Le Dauphin* Jean-Marc requires."

Clearly, Pattie had enjoyed the time until now that the young man had remained silent. She pointed behind him. "Look. Over there. There's still a tree standing. Let it symbolize the strength of France's new Crown Prince."

Having no repartee, he shrugged and trotted off.

With Jean-Marc once again beyond earshot, Pattie returned her attention to his father.

"There's one slight problem with Louis XIX."

"No. There can't be. I am Louis. The Elder and the pope—they said it."

"Technically, you're correct. But we require our Versailles and … *c'est finis*! I'm afraid we're forced back to Plan B."

Having pursued his dream for most of his life and through several life-threatening hardships, Lalumière was stunned by the reality of what she'd just said.

She pulled a metal flask from her purse and offered it to him.

"There."

"What's this?"

"Plan B. Just in case. Take a swig. It's brandy."

"Napoléon?"

"*Oui.*"

He shook his head as his eyes traversed from hers to the flask and back. She always managed to amaze him. They could never be separated again, of that he was certain. "*Adieu* to Marie Antoinette. To my Josephine then," he toasted.

A long pull later he handed her the flask.

As they imbibed more and more of the intoxicant, Pattie felt she needed to finally open up on her most private personal items. She was discovering that spies develop a nasty habit of keeping secrets. Everything held inside for years and decades. The time had come, and there was no one better with which to share.

"You know, Sylvain, I can screw 'til the cows come home, but I've never in my life had love. Not 'til now."

"What's this *'til the cows come home*?"

"It kinda means forever. It a phrase from the American Midwest."

"But why the cows?"

"Oh. All of their sayings in that part of the country involve farm animals."

"I see."

Clearly, he didn't, but she let it slide. There was something serious she had to relate to him.

"As I was saying, I've never been able to love—"

"Before you continue, what about this Crayle? I feel that, at some point, you knew him. Did you love him?"

The question caught her by surprise. She shifted back and forth in her discomfort with it.

"I am sorry. I can see that there were strong feelings."

"It's okay. I have to get it all out and, if you catch me clamming up, say something. Okay?"

He nodded. He knew he might finally cross the bridge to what this enigmatic young woman he's journeyed with so far was about.

"In Holland, I'd tried for relationships, but it never got past the sex. I found I could seduce any man, which gave me power. I relished it, not realizing that power is not and cannot be love."

"You are correct, my little one. We French learn at a young age that, in order to love, one must make himself—or herself—vulnerable. Totally vulnerable."

She turned her face up to him and searched his eyes.

"What of those you couldn't seduce?"

"There were only a few. They didn't end well."

"So it was with those men that you developed your skills."

"For killing? Yes. For loving, no."

"But back to Magus Crayle. What of him?"

"Interpol initiated a task force to track down the killer of these men. The deaths all fit a similar M.O., they determined. A single killer. Female. When I learned that, I managed my way to Washington, D.C. under an American sponsor."

"You must have attained American citizenship to join the CIA. How was that accomplished?"

"My sponsor was a widower. He adopted me."

"I see. Tell me about meeting and working with Crayle."

Before he could obtain a response, a twig snapped, announcing Jean-Marc's return. "I leaned against that tree while doing my business. I didn't notice that a fissure from the bomb crater had reached that far. The tree fell and I with it." He brushed at his soiled clothing for effect.

Trying in vain to quaff a smile, Pattie unwound the boat's tie down line from its cleat, and turned to Jean-Marc. "Here. Hang on to this. We'll pull you along until your clothes clean up."

The young man climbed into the *Queen* and assisted his father aboard. "They're going to rebuild Versailles. The government said so on social media. After the explosion, French morale dipped to an all time low. I think we can swing a deal with them."

"What sort of deal?"

Pattie jumped in and headed the boat west toward the Atlantic coast.

"The government has screwed up so badly that lies and other deceptions no longer work. They all want out with their heads affixed, so they're trying to pander. That's actually good news. We want the power they'll be vacating."

"So?"

Jean-Marc pulled in close to disclose his scheme. He glanced at Pattie. Her eyes sprung wide.

"Watch out for those rocks!" she yelled. She pushed an autopilot override button under the tiller and yanked the arm to her side.

When they'd skirted the danger posed by the Versailles Apollo fountain centerpiece, and the adrenaline had passed through their systems, Pattie stopped the boat. Carefully, she backed it to within inches of the green-with-age work of art. "We can't leave that here. Salvagers will find it and haul it out for scrap. Besides, the Sun god was supposed to rise from the water and light up the sky. Looks like he needs a little help."

Jean-Marc tied a line to it, and they resumed their voyage. The *African Queen*, at its best, struggled under its own weight. The drag of the new attachment strained it to its limit.

Lalumière spoke. "I am sorry about the near accident, my darling Queen. We French must look at the person with whom we are speaking. It becomes a flaw when piloting a boat."

"No, my darling King. It is just French. Look, we can talk about our nemesis, Mr. Crayle, another time … I have found love." She pulled his head to hers and planted a sensuous kiss. When she pulled away, she gave him a smile.

It was different this time, he noticed. The dimples were still there, but it was sincere and warm.

"*Je t'aime, Sylvain. Je t'aime.*"

Jean-Marc had just the tool to disrupt her magic. He resumed regarding his plot. "We'll work together with them to rebuild Versailles. We'll upgrade to the new building codes and to a new grandeur. One of our design." He pointed behind their watercraft. "We'll supply the old fountain. France will love it. They get rid of the socialists, get their Louis XIV palace back, and get Mitim as successor, Louis XIX. It doesn't get better than that."

Sylvain Lalumière's head swam with the possibilities.

Pattie's fretted. The Crown Prince had diffused her spell and incanted one of his own. He definitely had to go.

CHAPTER 43

The Battle of Monaco, the long flight back from Italy, and a round trip from Big Bear to Washington, D.C. caused the team to be so tired they could have slept standing up. But their minds wouldn't allow it. The job remained undone. Where they stood in the scheme of things played as a quandary, over and over, through each mind. Still, they were back home. For the moment, that seemed right.

Crayle led them all into the living room of his cabin. He knew he had to set minds at rest, so that their bodies could follow. "Lenny. Give us an enumeration by name of all who've died. Since day 1."

"Yeah. I've been keeping track. Here goes. Sammy, Wolfie, Neil, Chantal, Randy Norbrunn, Hamid, etc. Add to that all the unknown victims from the nuclear stuff at Fasd, Marseille, Ürümqi, Beijing, and New York from the Queen Mary 2 mishap. Oh, and Versailles."

Lenny broke the next ten minutes of silence by marching over to what had become the Vulgarity Cabinet and retrieved the current biscotti jar. "A little more, and we can have a righteous party. Phoebe?"

The FBI Agent considered the prospect. “No. I don’t want to waste it.” She glanced at the near-stuffed receptacle. “New Year’s Resolution: stop swearing?”

“That’s an easy one. How about make Micmac unattractive to other women?”

“Who says he’s attractive to other women?”

Micmac joined the game. “Admit it, Phoebs. When you first saw me onstage at the Sugerloafer with my guitar …”

“No comment. And don’t be gettin’ full of yourself.”

“Ah, you liked the cut of my jib. That’s an old nautical expression.” He produced an attitudinal wink.

“No. I liked the shape of your bulge. And that’s an old FBI Agent Comma Female expression.”

“Whew!” Micmac feigned wiping sweat from his forehead. “When you talk dirty …”

“Hmmm.”

“My resolution? Spend all my time with Phoebe.”

“I just might keep you.” She thought a moment. “I am keeping you.”

Magus Crayle couldn’t follow the light-hearted mood. “Resolved: Stop the plots. Stop the schemes. Stop the killing.”

Silence.

Hekka spoke last. “My resolution? Lock Magus in a safe place.” She gave him a quick glance with an uptilt of her chin.

That said, she stood and reached for his hand. They excused themselves and strolled toward the master bedroom, there to turn, toss a kiss to the on-looking team, and disappear behind the closing door.

In one of their few private moments, Hekka knew what she needed to do. It was time to listen. She sat on the bed’s edge, still holding his hand, and waited.

“I’m not sure what resolutions to have made. I find myself yanked from the reality I want into other worlds that seem surreal.

To Europe. To Hong Kong. I fight physical battles when I'm not engaged in mental battles … and mind skirmishes when not engaged in fire fights. I find myself divided into three complete, yet different individuals. It has to stop here. It has to stop now."

She lifted his face from where it was buried in his hands. She worked her head to one side and pressed her lips heavy against his. Then, she pulled back. "I understand all that you've said. More than that, I feel what you feel. It must end at this time."

Her kiss, slow and deliberate, had spoken volumes. They were two sides of a single coin. An entity. Indelible.

Without further words, the two lovers, who a mere five months before had become newlyweds, disrobed and moved onto the bed. They didn't make love this time, they just pulled each other close, flesh against flesh, and fell asleep.

Seconds later, the phone chimed. Crayle grabbed a pillow. Before he could heave it, the phone answered itself and went to speaker.

"Magus. I know you're there. Trust me on this, you need to take this call. Now."

"How …" Crayle picked the handset from its cradle, stopping a moment before pressing it to his ear.

Seconds later he re-entered the living room, breathless like a man who'd just completed a marathon wearing only a towel. "Break up the love fest. We've got a tango. Grab your gear! Rock and roll!"

Micmac looked puzzled as he tossed his boogie-bag over his shoulder with a shrug.

Phoebe's heart knew the drill. It jumped a beat. She turned to Micmac and nodded at Crayle. "He's channeling Jack. Let's do it!"

Single file, they exited through the kitchen and down into the garage tunnel. Now more suitably attired, the Crayles trailed close behind.

CHAPTER 44

The flight had been blind. A non-descript business jet met them at Jack's old airstrip on the north side of the Big Bear plateau. With all windows blacked out, they had no idea of their destination even as they touched down five hours later. Lenny's attempts at using GPS locater services had all been blocked. It all smelled to Crayle like black ops even when they exited through a jetway directly into a visually impaired SUV.

After a number of stops and starts, and many lefts and rights, they finally halted. The driver cut the engine. The doors opened. They stepped out of the vehicle, mouths agape with shock. Lenny made the first sound.

"Holy Excrement, Batman. The frikkin' White House."

"That's five bucks, P.I. Legal tender." Phoebe held out her hand.

He pointed at his crotch. "Put it down here so I can piss in it."

"Zip it, guys," admonished Crayle. "This has me worried."

Men and women looking precisely like Secret Service led him away. Others tended to the remainder of the team.

• • •

"Welcome to the Oval Office," said President Kimbel Stones. "Sorry about the drama. I'll get to the point. We just broke the DCI."

"The Director of Central Intelligence?"

"That is correct. Turns out he was one of the Elder's Illuminé plants. At this moment I believe he's meeting with his legal counsel. He doesn't know it yet, but his attorney is also a prisoner at the Colorado Supermax. Cutting right to the chase, I need you, Magus. You're the only one I've ever met with the intellectual wherewithal to remake Central Intelligence after those radical ideologue bastards fucked it up."

Crayle worked at catching his breath. He could tell by Kimbel Stones' expression that DCI was the job in question.

"What could possibly need remaking. The head is defined by the nature of things to be a political appointee whose sole job is to insure the president's hands stay relatively clean. They have a term for it: *plausible deniability*. That assures that the top tiers of the Agency are going to be, likewise, political."

"Precisely. The overarching problem is this. Politicians and politics don't solve problems. It's get into power, stay in power, end of story. They no longer even *try* to solve problems, lest they fail. So they craft stories of how nothing is their fault—or caused by them—and take credit for work they didn't do."

"Look at the flip side. If all of the CIA were operative types, there would be no plausible deniability for a president such as yourself. You'd have to take the heat whenever something went badly. Unless . . ."

"Precisely. Unless we return Central Intelligence to the uber-secretive entity it was meant to be. No former operatives on TV. No Agency t-shirts or coffee cups. And when they're asked *Where do you work? I work—or worked—for the government* is the sole response."

"That's the dilemma."

"So, what do you say?"

"I'll do this for you, Kimbel. I'll find a quiet place, and analyze the situation. When I'm ready, I'll return right here and use my education, experience, and skills to provide a master strategy, with workable options, for the major remake our country needs with respect to intel."

"What of your Asian activities?"

"Not complete. I'll have to contact Chin with a sitrep, less the DCI component."

"You know, setting up his master strategy could work very well for us."

"He's already made that observation."

That Chin was a cagey and perceptive adversary was quite clear. "If I read between the lines correctly, you are not committing to take the position, if offered again, at a later date, but not rejecting it either."

"Color me noncommittal. I need down time. Peaceful down time."

"And your team?"

"You mean the four sets of newlyweds? The ones you and the pope married this past New Year's Day?"

The president chuckled.

"We need a vacation from nuclear bombs that look like footballs, and other forms of mayhem. Peace. Love."

"And understanding."

"That, too. We need a place where the welcome wagon doesn't shoot at you."

"I'll tell you what. I can put this job on hold for now. I'll see that you get the requisite space and time for your peace, love, and understanding. Money?"

"We're good."

• • •

The team, nervous systems on high alert, waited for Crayle in the White House lobby. Not their choice. Several Secret Service operatives escorted them there, while others whisked their vehicle away to a staging area.

"What is it, Mag?" asked an exhausted Micmac. "Another op? Why were we dragged here like lemmings at a moment's notice?"

"I guess that's how presidents roll. I'd love to tell you, but I can't. What I can say is that we're taking one helluva long spring break. I have some things to think about, but not until later. Much later."

"Ooh, where are we going?" asked Hekka.

"It's Top Secret—Sensitive Information." He glanced around. And then in a whisper, "Follow me. I'll fill you in on the way."

CHAPTER 45

Sitting alone in the Yellow Room, the Elder reviewed recent events. The master escape of Crayle from inside his palace grounds and in spite of his own special guards did not sit well. He would simply track down the French government-in-hiding and spirit them, surreptitiously, back to Paris. He would place them in a holding cell, of sorts, to await his next move. And while his operatives enacted his latest scheme, he would order the rescheduling of the Grand Prix to an open calendar slot in September. In a week's time, the Elder's latest scheme was concluded. He had the French buffoons precisely where he wanted them.

• • •

The darkness completed the dark mood and dank odor of the encasement. The man, smelling of his own encrusted sweat, awakened. He examined his head for the source of the pain. Stumbling to his feet, his first step took him into a wall. His own asthmatic breathing obscured any other sounds—he could not hold his breath to listen.

He stepped in the other direction, hands before him to eliminate another head-first battering.

"*Bof!*" he cried out.

Another person.

"*Merde!*" came the reply.

The two grasped and twisted—danger unknown. A third joined the panicked, violent fray. They tumbled to the floor.

Hungry, thirsty, exhausted.

The man who rose first spoke. "Who are you? Where am I?"

"Ah, you speak to me in the language of our barbarian neighbors to the north. The English. Very well. Pierre is my name. Your President." He felt the face of the man who stood less than two feet distant. "It is my prime minister, Gustave, *n'est pas*?"

Pierre Bouchard recognized the voice of his Prime Minister, but was not one for succinct verbiage. "Who else?"

"René. *C'est moi*," came the garbled voice of the only one with a sense of humor. "President of the *Assemblée Nationale*."

Slowly, Pierre backed into the nearest wall. With his fingertips, he sampled its texture. "These blocks have been naturally hewn." He moved sideways, feeling, sensing. "Where are we?"

A loud crash startled them all. A small door opened, allowing a beam of kerosene-fueled light to pour into the room. It highlighted a metal hash pattern in the opening. Unmistakable.

"Our political careers seem to be at an end, gentlemen," René observed.

The former French president's head wagged up and down. "Yes. The symbolism is inspired."

"Our new king?" Gustave mused.

"If my guess is correct, we are being kept in a very special place."

"I'm afraid so. In the very same one where we kept our nemesis, Mitim."

"A prison cell? I am outraged!"

Pierre ignored his former political colleague. He smiled at the appropriate irony of Lalumière's revenge. "The Bastille."

• • •

The French royal trio had taken to the Atlantic skies in one of the Illuminé's private jets. They'd stashed the *African Queen* and Versailles fountain at a very special fishing village along the Loire, and had boarded the aircraft at the Nantes airport in south Brittany. After Lalumière completed a four-hour cat nap and felt fully refreshed, he turned the bedroom over to his son, and took a seat next to Pattie in the main cabin.

Lalumière—now known throughout France as Louis XIX—and Pattie—known everywhere as Marie Antoinette's second coming—listened to the recording again.

"That's the fourth time, Sylvain. How about something more exiting?" She started unfastening her buttons.

He reached over and gently grasped her wrist. "We shall engage in mutual pleasure in a short while. But I have a request that has festered in my mind since our transit from Scotland."

"I'm not certain what you mean."

"About Crayle. You mentioned your relocation to America, your adoption, your entry into the Central Intelligence. Who brought you in? I believe I know, but tell me the rest of your story, including Crayle. It may help us with our next move."

"First, I'm impressed once again. You're starting to think like an operative, but at the tactical level."

He knew her well enough to know that she was not ready for this discussion. He also knew that these circumstances would produce his best chance at getting to the truth. With a wave of his hand, he put the ball back in her court. "Please, continue."

"Very well, Sylvain. As I said, I was in Washington, D.C. with my adoptive father, but I knew that the Interpol task force, with the aid of their colleagues in the FBI, could still track me down. That's when I seduced Neil."

"You managed to locate the man who'd solicited your mother as a prostitute after somehow learning that he was CIA?"

"Uh-huh. Remember that, on that night in Amsterdam, he paid extra to have me enter the activities with he and my mother. You can guess that I discovered who his employer was. Loose lips may sink ships, but they also can leave a person's calling card. Oddly enough, he wanted to make it exciting for her, bedding a spy."

"And for you, her daughter."

She paused at his cynicism, but she'd resolved long ago never again to permit that night to bring anger to her lips, or tears to her eyes. "When we met in Washington, I'd grown up. He didn't even recognize me. Anyways, it was he who pulled me in. He also assured that I passed the polygraph test."

"And Monsieur Crayle?"

"Don't be getting ahead of me. Mr. Crayle came later. First I had to survive The Farm. It was tougher than I anticipated. I managed to kill two of the instructors."

"After bedding them, am I correct?"

"Only one."

"And …"

"Well, the other it was just bad timing on his part. I overheard him talking with Interpol. He was one who repeated everything he heard so the caller would know he understood what had been said. It's a great idea when two people have different base languages."

"I can see that. Please continue."

"Well, I was really impressed when Neil got me past that. He also managed to get Interpol to drop the hunt for me. Some DGSE man code-named Charleroi. I owe him sex if I ever run into him."

"And then you will kill him?"

She shrugged in the affirmative. "Back to Magus. It was my very first gig. Neil read me in. The mission was not the usual black ops kind of thing. It wasn't becoming a case officer out of some foreign diplomatic unit. And it wasn't an out-in-the-cold infiltration into an intel resource overseas."

"But that is what spies do, is it not?"

"Spies do whatever is necessary in the moment. Because of my fluency in French, I was to assist him linguistically in that country on what was called an intellectual mission."

Lalumière sat back. The profundity of her remarks hit him square between the eyes. "It was you on the phone. When he arrived to work up my segment of the Blackstone Strategy, it was you on the phone. My God!"

"Once again, *mon frère*, there is no God. So says the Illuminé."

"Please do not refer to me as your brother. We do not do incest in France."

"Duly noted. So, yes, I was there in the background and, since I was a newbie, I was never *in situ*, as we say, always a safe distance. Magus the strategist would return from your château in the Vosges to our safe house across the Rhine River in Kehl, Germany. He'd always have his recordings of things you or others said in French, and I would translate."

"I don't think I wish to know how you amused yourself when he was absent. I can only imagine the uncharacteristic depletion of the German male population in the immediate area."

"I'll take that as a compliment."

"And what did your handler—I believe that's the term—Neil Wohlford think about this operation when it was complete?"

"He rewarded me. But I don't think it was just for the operation. While his wife was away visiting relatives in her native Montreal, he and I did some stuff. You know. I think he felt like he was entering a beyond-his-control danger zone. Shortly thereafter, he transferred me to our embassy in Paris with cover as the staff travel agent. It allowed me to venture out on research trips. Neil would come over several times a year, and we'd screw a lot. He said it relaxed him."

Lalumière tried to put the likely images out of his mind, but he knew too well from his own experiences just how effective she could be.

"But with respect to my formal duties, I ran ops out of there. It turned out I was a natural. I had legends for every region, and I performed in my home country, Holland, as well."

"And that was all with Crayle?"

"Yeah," she lied. "Say, this talking has made me horny. It's time for a royal screwing, king and queen. What do you say?"

He smiled at her even as he shook his head. Quite special, this one.

CHAPTER 46

On the Caribbean island of Saint Lucia, the empress Josephine's bed chambers at Soufrière village had been maintained to perfection over the centuries. It wasn't that anyone expected her to return, but rather that the property brought direct income from international tourists, as well as the French who wished to examine their heritage. The latter was important, the former necessary.

The near iridescent golds and creamy whites were further embellished by ceiling art and bas-relief plaster figures. The master bed was size-appropriate for the earlier times, but not adequate for modern, taller Frenchmen like the man stretched diagonally across it. Staring up at the bed canopy, he spoke.

"Father is away gathering his coronation team. He had to go into town to use his relic cell phone. Couldn't get service in this house or nearby. I showed him how, but I still can't believe he's using social media."

"He must remember to check the pope's calendar. The man-in-white must lead the ceremony. That is, if he still insists on being a king."

Jean-Marc held up his Smartphone. "I have it here. I'll locate a span of three days in the pope's calendar. That should be enough."

"Yes. He arrives in the rebuilt Versailles one day. Then, the ceremony. We all party. He's out the third day."

"Since he is Illuminé and not a believer, must we supply him with courtesans? You know—"

"Bedmates? Hookers?"

"Because of your CIA cover in Amsterdam—as Angel—you would know how to procure them. That will be your responsibility."

"Prince, dear. You shall not assign tasks to your queen."

He reached behind her and pulled a ribbon. The tight-fitting dress fell loose.

"Not here, Jean-Marc. I will service you in grand style, but only in *your* chambers. You will retreat there via the same secret passage that brought you to me. Prepare the royal raincoats and set up some mood lighting. Candles. Scented candles. I'll take my Moment Before pill, and be along shortly."

He smiled and produced a shallow bow. "As you wish, my Queen." He disappeared through the opening behind the armoire.

Pleased with her handling of the situation, she searched her bag for a special item. "Ah," she said. She gave her compact a twist. Unfortunately, the dried blood of her former husband, caused it to stick. Not a problem, she broke up the congealed masses with a nail file from her vanity, then whisked the offending particles away with an eyelash brush.

There. Operational.

She placed the item in a clutch that had been carried by the prostitute Angel—as she'd plied her cover trade—and followed Jean-Marc's path. She entered the secret passageway, pulling the armoire closed behind her.

As she hurried along, her mind switched to Magus Crayle. She realized for the first time that she couldn't kill her fellow spy. He possessed exactly the mind she would need to rule France. Other than the fact that he was not French like her Sylvain, she felt certain he would make a perfect king.

She shook her head at the epiphany. Now she realized what Chin must've gone through. Crayle represented, at once, his greatest potential threat, and his greatest potential ally going forward. What a dilemma. To kill or not to kill.

As she neared Jean-Marc's bedchamber, she experienced a second epiphany. Since she had to stay close to home for security purposes, she would lure Crayle to her. She'd lay out a proposition. If he accepted, fine. If not, she'd remove him.

She heaved open a centuries-old bookcase, and stepped into the room.

Jean-Marc stood with his back to her. He removed four straps from a drawer.

In seconds, he lay on the bed, attached to the four posts and looking like Da Vinci's spread-eagle man.

Pattie might as well have been the queen of Velcro. She stripped herself naked in under five seconds and climbed on top.

First, she shoved her hands under his pillow as she bent down for a very French kiss. She moved down.

His heart gained momentum as he observed.

She smiled as she engaged him.

"I've seen your dimples before. Under a similar circumstance." His breathing accelerated, inflecting his speech. "Amsterdam."

"I was your Angel. I took you to heaven," she said. "Now I am Josephine in the very house where Napoléon's woman grew up, but heaven is not far away."

"Take me there, Josephine … oh! My God!"

She moved atop him, seated on his belly.

"No! Don't stop!"

She pulled the compact from under the pillow where she'd stashed it earlier.

Once again, a knowing smile.

He yanked with both arms. Then both legs. The bonds held fast.

"*No!*"

Slowly, deliberately, she twisted the sides in opposite directions.

The razor-sharp blade protruded.

With his body writhing side-to-side, and up-and-down, her experience with electronic bulls kept her on top.

She bent down onto his chest, and placed her cheek over his heart. She heard as well as felt the pounding.

She pressed the side of the compact against his neck at a not-yet-lethal angle.

The pounding increased.

"No, Pattie, no!" he gasped. His heart approached its upper limit.

She reached down, pulling them together. She began to writhe on him.

Setting the compact aside, she pinched the nipples of his pectorals.

She pounded.

He writhed.

"Ah!" he cried out. And again and again.

As they both reached climax, they barely heard something new. The noise outside repeated, this time louder. And clear.

"Jean-Marc. My son, I have fabulous news. Are you here?"

CHAPTER 47

The two, Jean-Marc and Pattie, had managed to dress before Lalumière could make it upstairs. There on the landing she stood with his son on his knees searching as his father entered.

"My son. What in the world?"

"Looking for her contact lens." He pretended to inspect the sumptuous carpet strip.

"I didn't even know." He glanced at her. "Something new every day."

Jean-Marc, exhausted from his physical interaction with Pattie only moments ago, rolled onto the floor on his back. Still a Frenchman, he was able to shrug as if to say, "What did you find out?"

"I have great news. With my new app, I checked the pope's calendar and reserved the earliest open date. We shall have the pope present in two weeks if we can find a French palace for the ceremony. He would prefer a cathedral, but my choice, Notre Dame in Paris, was damaged from the blast at Versailles. His office will make all the arrangements, invite all the proper people, and provide decorations and security. One of his cardinals is apparently the equivalent of a wedding planner."

"There's still the decision on whether to become king or emperor. But you know that."

"I'll think about it. I still like king. For me to consider the possibilities, I will need total quiet. Would you do me a huge favor and take Pattie somewhere? Entertain her."

Jean-Marc and Pattie neatly kept their recent entertainment to themselves. "I can do that."

In short order, they walked into the hills. Pattie seemed to know her way around the island, he merely followed her lead. After a good hour, they arrived at a rope bridge. It appeared to him to be at least 100 feet long, but was only eighty-five. It swung pendulum-like as they walked. In short order, it was clear who intended to accomplish the entertaining. Within the next minute, she had the young man stark naked.

She knelt before him, using her fingernails to push the blood from his thighs to his sexual center.

"It intensifies the experience," she whispered.

His head rocked back, his focus lost.

In an instant, she twisted her hands under and outward. Using her sprinter's legs, she thrust upward.

The young prince's eyes gaped as he flipped over the hand rope railing.

As much as she wanted to, she didn't step forward to watch.

She screamed. Face in hands, she ran from the bridge.

At full gate, it took her far less time to return to the house of Josephine. She ran through the front entry, her face red, eyes streaming.

"There's been a tragedy!" she cried.

CHAPTER 48

Jack Sommers should have been tired of the whole operation. The costs in wear and tear alone of his resources chasing crazies around the globe were hard for him to justify in his mind. Although a person in his position might be concerned with the millions of dollars expended with respect to minimal results, Jack was not. Spies did not even think about operational costs unless they effected assets. Deep underground at Manassas, he played with some of the French artifacts his former boss, Neil Wohlford, had on his desk.

Cloisonné thimbles and the like—who needed these things. But he knew the answer. That Neil had been a mole for years was known by few. That he'd been born in France and had been Illuminé—even fewer. Spy agencies always tried to keep such discoveries away from prying eyes. In Neil, they'd unearthed a spy in their midst, and he was now dead. Even Jack would like to crow about it, but you just couldn't expose your weaknesses: personnel who'd allowed Neil into the Agency in the first place.

A humming sound caught his attention. He glanced everywhere, trying to detect the source. It continued. He started extracting desk drawers. Nothing. He walked around the room, checking a buffet, an armoire, and then the wet bar.

He leaned down to a floor-standing ice bucket and pressed the back of his hand against it. It vibrated along with the humming sound. Carefully, he lifted the lid. No response. He peeked over the edge.

He popped upright with a half sneer, half smile. The cell phone, once removed from its hiding place and with its speaker function enabled, spoke.

"Hello, Jack. You look like shit. Do you recognize the voice?"

Jack placed his thumb over the back-facing camera lens.

"That's right. We supplied this phone so you and I could communicate in private. You never know what the CIA can do with its own phones. And it's set up so that we can see with both front- and rear-facing cameras even when its not turned on. That's how I knew it was you."

"So I figured. Well, it's good to speak with you, Mr. President. What can I do for you this fine day."

"It's pouring over here in D.C., so I'm not sure about the fine part. As I'm still settling into my new job, I realize that you are doing the same. We have a severe risk out there named Crayle. That's the bad news. It's also the good news. Have I confused you yet?"

"Not yet, Sir."

"I'm about to fix that. Here goes."

"Shoot, Sir. I mean …"

"Here's some backstory on your Hekka Poppi Crayle. I had my former associates back at the NSA do a little digging. It turns out that she's not just a Serrano Indian, she's got royal blood. A princess."

"Oh, my. She never said a thing."

"Jack, she doesn't even know."

"Oh, crap. Are you asking me to break the news?"

"No, I'll do that at the proper time. Perhaps we'll have drinks when this is all over."

Jack's head jerked back. "All over" the president had just said. "Is there something I need to know?"

"Jack, this is a tough one. Probably the toughest decision I've ever had to make. But I don't have a choice. I'm tasking you to assure for me personally that they stay safe, do you understand?"

"Ack."

"Thank you for the acknowledgment. Here's what I need you to do."

"How about you stop by. Better in person." Jack laughed in silence.

"See you in thirty."

• • •

For the president of the United States to come to him, Jack realized that it had to be very, very special. Not merely a sitrep, something more. He reasoned that the leader of the free world had something earth-shattering to say. He tried to imagine a man of his status, along with his Secret Service protective squad, trying to enter the facility through the porta potty ingress. He decided to put that visual aside.

The thirty passed in a blink. Jack remembered why he preferred to be out in the field. Chain-of-command authority—as in Top Dog—really made him nervous.

The security door, supposedly with specific high-level need-to-enter proximity access, clicked and the president stepped inside. The well-built man wore soiled gray sweats with a hood. He took the seat opposite Jack. His guards had to be out in the chartreuse hallway, trying not to go blind.

"Make your sitrep chop-chop: fast and succinct. You're talking directly to me, because Neil Wohlford's boss, the DDCI, and her boss, the DCI, are both out of service. They're being interrogated as we speak. I suspect one or both are of the same secret organization as Wohlford."

"Yes, Sir. I know you have other resources, Mr. President, so I don't know what you know or don't. Here's the post New Year's Day synopsis.

"One. After just four months of marital bliss, Crayle and Hekka kidnapped in Helsinki. Taken by Aryans to Southern Germany. Escaped captors. Brought home.

"Two. Chin has taken charge in China. Carrying out threat to disputed islands.

"Three. Crayle off to China. Chin wants Blackstone 2.

"Four. Pattie Norbrunn had Lalumière hidden away. All made it to Versailles, ready for coup.

"Five. Team on way to get them. *Boom!* Up goes Versailles. Last bomb gone. Crayle and Hekka grabbed off to Monaco. Et cetera.

"Six. Upshot: I'm sending the three team couples on separate R and R. It's chill time."

Kimbel rose to his feet and walked to the wet bar. He poured a glass of X.O. and returned to Jack's desk. "Here."

Jack peered into a pair of laser-focused eyes.

"Down the hatch."

Knowing that now was not the time to ask why, the Other Specialized Staffs manager pro-tem took a gulp.

Kimbel shook his head ever so slightly. "The rest of it."

Jack followed orders. The brandy burned a good burn.

"Did I ever tell you that Magus saved my life? In a place and circumstance where Hell actually did freeze over. For me. I owe him for that."

"Then this is personal. Way up there personal."

The president plucked Jack's glass and took it back for a refill, changed his mind, took a swig from the crystal bottle, and brought it back to the other man.

"Magus deserves more than I can ever give him—do you understand what I'm saying?"

"Yes, Sir." Jack took a hard pull of brandy.

"I want you personally to look out for him and his wife when all this special vacationing is done."

"No problem. I've got plans for them to relax their bodies and souls."

The president drew in a deep breath, then blew it out.

"There's been a slight change of plans."

CHAPTER 49

"You can both thank me now," said Jack.

"A cruise for the two of us as compensation—read that, partial compensation—for all we've accomplished? All expenses paid? By you?"

Crayle and Hekka glanced at each other for an approximate two seconds when both heads bobbed up and down. "That would be yes on both accounts. So, what haven't you told us?"

"I don't know what you mean."

Crayle sensed the smile on Jack's lips. "Say the following: there is no op."

"There's no op, Magus. You need and deserve a vacation."

"D'ya think?" Hekka had moved closer to the phone. Her impression of a Lenny-ism caused the other two to laugh. She slapped her hand over her mouth to suppress most of her own laugh. "First there was …"

"Alright. Alright. I don't need the laundry list. You've earned this a dozen times over."

Crayle returned quickly to the practical issues. "What's the ship and where do we pick it up?"

"Your 7X is waiting for you. It's ready to go and the pilot has her orders. The ship's already left home port, so you'll have to sneak aboard at one of its stops."

"Did I hear you mention *pilot* and *her* in the same sentence? I didn't realize you ball-scratchers would allow that?"

Crayle glancedover at Hekka. His eyes looked like they'd been pried open.

"Oh. I'm sorry. I don't talk like that."

Jack read between the lines. "You've been hanging out with that Fibbee woman again—what was her name?"

"Phoebe doesn't even talk like that. Well, not a lot," added a red-faced Hekka.

Crayle leaned over and kissed her cheek. "We need to pack. I'll finish up with Jack."

She looked up at him, knowing that he was feigning chauvinism. She knew him that well. She didn't move.

Her husband remembered that he still held a phone in his hand, and that it was silent. "The ship?"

"I was waiting for that one. The name's a natural. With all the ops involving emperors and empresses and kings and queens, and for the lovely and charming lady standing beside you, it's called the Royal Princess."

"It sounds perfect." They glanced approvingly at each other. "Where do we pick it up?"

"That's the best part. You're going to the Caribbean. Place called … wait for it … Barbados."

• • •

Two hours later, Crayle, Hekka, Micmac, and Phoebe stood ready to board their jet in a special section of Washington's Reagan National airport. The ramp was already down and the excited members hurried aboard. Hekka stopped first and glanced around. Perplexed, she turned to Crayle.

"Magus? Where's our flight attendant? Has there been some kind of budget cutback?" Hekka asked as she looked left and right.

He put his finger to his lips. His pistol came easily into his grip from under his jacket.

Hekka slid her Bowie from her carry-on.

They proceeded to the bedroom door, taking positions to either side. She turned the knob as he pushed it open with his foot.

No one.

Back toward the flight deck.

They noticed that the flight deck door was not fully closed. This time Hekka pushed it open, Crayle ready to fire.

The word they heard was familiar. "*Oi!*" Hello in Brazilian Portuguese.

"What are you doing there?" said the exasperated pair.

The young woman beamed. "I'm a pilot now. I passed my test."

"Flori, when did you learn to fly? And where's your co-pilot? And why didn't Jack tell us about this?"

"He wanted it to be a surprise." Her joy at her accomplishment couldn't mask her ever-sexual voice.

"I'll kill him," said Crayle. "I'll kill him."

"There will be no killing of my new husband. You must check the closets in the bedroom for some appropriate attire, and then you must take your seats. I will not be back there to provide the statutory pre-flight safety lecture, but you've done this before. So, go! Go! I cannot skip pre-flight and my co-pilot—the soon-to-return ex-Navy man—will be here in a few seconds, and then we will take off."

"I'll kill him," was still emanating from Crayle's mouth as Hekka pulled him by the arm to the rear of the craft.

"Jack. I'll kill him."

• • •

Fifteen minutes passed before the Navy pilot ducked inside the bedroom portal, said hello, and disappeared forward into the cockpit. “You can examine the items Jack provided once we are aloft,” came Flori’s voice across the intercom. “But right now, buckle up!”

The flight commenced in an abbreviated ten minutes with a liftoff that was as smooth as Flori’s demeanor. As soon as the seatbelts OFF sign dinged, the Crayles popped their seatbelts, and darted into the bedroom to examine the wardrobe Jack had provided. Flori entered with a pitcher of drinks—her signature Brazilian Caipirinhas.

“Look at this, Hekka. A new set of suitcases already packed for us.”

“I’d look inside but I don’t have the energy right now. And the contents are packed so tightly we’d never get them back in.”

“I agree. We’ll have to wear and toss some of them when we’re finished with the cruise and ready to return home.”

“I’m taking a positive attitude about this vacation, and I’m not sure when or if I want to return home to the cabin.”

“Well said. I may have misspoken … about killing Jack. Maybe he’s redeemed himself this time. What’s your take?”

“Redeemed? Perhaps a partial redemption. But, I’ll take it.”

Crayle clinked glassed. “I’ll propose a toast. Here’s to Jack.”

They drank … and then drank some more. Each time they reached the bottom of the pitcher, Flori magically reappeared with a fresh one. Forty-five minutes after takeoff, they were out over the Caribbean Sea and fast asleep.

• • •

Made from cachaça sugar cane juice, white sugar, and quartered limes and lemons, their Caipirinhas shouldn’t have been so effective. The next thing Magus and Hekka Crayle knew, Flori was shaking them awake.

“We are arriving at our destination soon. You will have to return to the cabin and buckle up one last time.”

"After what we've been through, one last time seems like a meaningless phrase."

Hekka agreed. "He's right. It's been like riding round and round in a clothes dryer, stepping out for a moment, then climbing right back in."

Flori's hyper sexual voice provided an assessment. "That, my dear Mr. and Mrs. Crayle, is the world of intelligence."

With that, she returned to the flight deck. The Dassault Falcon 7X was hers to land.

"Hekka, we forgot to ask what we're supposed to do on these beautiful and peaceful islands. I guess it's one of Jack's signature surprises." He regretted that observation. "I take it back. We're only going to think positive thoughts from here on out."

"I do love you, Mr. Crayle."

"I love you right back, Mrs. Crayle."

• • •

The landing was butter smooth. Suitcases in hand, the jet's passengers exited through the door and descended to the tarmac. They paused to get their bearings. On the side of what they presumed was the main building, one of their answers was provided.

"Barbados," they said in unison.

"We're in the Caribbean, Magus. I'm moving past a new liking for Jack to a bit of love."

"I'm jealous."

"No, you're not jealous. He doesn't get *this*." She pulled him down by his shirt collar and planted a sensuous kiss.

"We definitely need to get a room. But we'll have to wait until we board our cruise ship." He pointed behind them. "I believe that's it over there."

She turned to see a giant ship in the distance. White against a clear blue sky.

"Look at all those balconies, Magus. I hope we have one."

"Jack's really taking care of us. I'm sure we do."

A driver pulled up in a steel gray Range Rover, tossed their new luggage in the back, and promised to have them dockside in anxious minutes.

"How much time before she sails?" Hekka asked.

"About three hours," the driver replied.

"Show us your island a bit then. Okay?"

With a bright smile that exuded deep pride, the driver whisked them on a three hour tour.

"Magus, look at the bright colors of these houses. Green and yellow and blue. Even the bank." She pointed out a Scotiabank sign—white on an orange background.

"And there's more green here than even at Big Bear. Palm trees, and bushes with long, narrow leaves. I'm feeling the vacation already."

In twenty minutes, they had traveled from the airport at the south tip of the island to an old church. The driver let them out and only said, "Ten minutes." Again the warm smile.

"It's St. John Parish Church," Hekka said. "1645."

"Check out how the light springs the stained glass in the windows to life." Crayle stepped to a wall to read a plaque embedded there. Hekka saw him place the palm of his hand against it, and bow his head.

"There are four there. Honored by their family. A hundred years ago." She knew what he was thinking. The tens of thousands killed by the Blackstone Strategy bombs had been individuals, not the statistics reported by the press. Just like these. They deserved to be honored as well.

They exited the church of beige stone both feeling humbled. Hand-in-hand, they returned to the car. He stopped and gave her a long hug. "Do good people always have to suffer from the bad ones?"

On their way to the port capital, Bridgetown, the Crayles turned less somber. They gawked at the Bajan scenery as if they'd never been outside of their home towns.

"See that place, Magus? Some day, I want to stay at The Sandpiper. Can we come back?"

He didn't answer. He kissed her instead.

A few more minutes and they had not only reached the port, but were dockside. The fact that there was no one else boarding the ship along with them didn't even register. They were finally here.

CHAPTER 50

Their driver passed the Crayles' luggage to a lanky porter clad in white, who loaded it onto a cart. He then tipped the brim of his hat, re-entered the car, and drove away without waiting for a tip.

"Here," said the porter. "Just climb the gangway and you will be directed further. Normally, you would undergo security, but I understand that's been waived. The elevators are just inside and here is your deck map to the ship."

The dark blue credit card size packet contained a fold-out, color-coded layout of the ship. Their previous experience on the Queen Mary 2 revealed the complexities of a large ship and the necessity for such a guide. He noticed the words under the PRINCESS CRUISES logo in lower case type: *escape completely*. Indeed.

Crayle reached for his wallet. The porter waved him off. "I've been seen to, thank you." He handed them each a stateroom key card, then pushed away with his cart.

They did as instructed and everything went as the porter had advised. It took a mere five minutes to ascend the gangway and enter the large ship.

"This stateroom key card indicates that we're on the Riviera deck. But this elevator only has numbers."

Crayle unfolded the map, and checked. "Here it is. Press 14."

The elevator lifted them to their floor in a couple of minutes. They stepped out to a large brass wall plaque—a lateral view of the ship's deck structure with the word *Starboard* engraved.

"It says that even numbered staterooms are on the port side and odd on the starboard. Just like the Queen Mary 2."

"That's right. I almost forgot. This is our second cruise together." He passed over the less-than-vacation-like encounter with Lalumière and his gang. The latter had spirited a mini-nuke aboard, intending to detonate it in New York City.

"This time, no bomb."

"And this is our side."

They high-fived and followed stateroom directions down a passageway until they stood outside their room. There below the number on their mail drop was a card. *Mr. and Mrs. Crayle.*

"That makes it official." He smiled.

Inside, they found their suitcases staged on the bed. But when they opened them, they were empty. Their first reaction was to check for intruders. Finding none, they checked the closet and drawers. There, they found everything Jack had promised perfectly stowed.

Crayle scratched his head. "How …" Then, for an unknown reason, the weight of all that had gone before hit him.

"These guys are good," Hekka observed. She turned, expecting to find a smile. "We are on a cruise in the Caribbean, Magus. Why do you look so sad?"

"It's the pain I've brought into your life. I just can't shake the facts."

"But you've taken me from my little ranch existence in a mountain valley to places that only challenged my imagination before."

"I'm afraid it was the E-ticket."

"I've learned so much from you. You need to let those feelings rest, as does my father."

"You've taught me, and continue to teach me, a great deal given the differences in both of our lives and our cultures."

She took his hand. "Here. Come with me." She led him from the bedroom past a sitting area and through a floor-to-ceiling sliding door. Outside on the balcony, they plopped down onto two chaise lounges, positioned side by side.

"I want you to remember our special times like our—shall we say—encounter at the waterfall in my back yard."

"Encounter?"

"Mmm. And my bed, warmed by each other, and the blankets made of the scalps of your ancestors." She cocked her head, smiling into his eyes.

"Those comments about the blankets … they were the first sign of a sense of humor from you." He sat up on the edge of his chaise. "Move over just a bit."

She did.

He moved next to her as she shifted onto her side to accommodate him. He wrapped his arm and pulled her tight. Her warmth, and that of the Caribbean sun, caused him to relax, to bury once more the sight they'd experienced—upon entering her ranch house—of her father, sitting in his favorite chair, with a red semicircle around his neck and a blood-drenched shirt.

"We still have our share of the diamonds. We can travel for awhile."

"Would you like to revisit any of our past locales in—what would you call it—peacetime?"

"Without the bullets and the bombs, I've heard Paris and Rome are quite romantic." She planted a kiss on his cheek. He turned and, touching her cheek, planted a durable kiss on her lips.

"Alright, break it up. Get a room. Yada yada." Traditional destroyer of the wet dream, Lenny approached from inside. Trying for a view over her husband's shoulder, Alona moved forward on tiptoes.

"What are you … why …" Crayle couldn't get his bearings.

"No need to worry. Jack got me a master key, and he got Alona and me aboard at the last minute."

"And us," came from behind.

Both Crayles sat up in concert. They knew the voices. Phoebe and Micmac.

"What've we had, twelve minutes of peace and quiet?" Hekka joined her husband at the word *minutes*.

"No, Magus," Phoebe corrected. She glanced at her bare wrist. "Thirteen."

Micmac intervened. "Come on, gang. We need to let these other newlyweds have some space. The dance band's about to start topside by the main pool. For the Sail Away Party. I want to see what they've got."

"Then, I shall join with my guitar-playing sailor …" She took Micmac by one arm and Lenny by the other. "… and see who is the best dancer."

"Bet on Micmac." Alona shook her head.

"Hey!" said Lenny as the foursome filed out the cabin door.

Dumbfounded, Crayle watched them leave. "I'm thinking evil thoughts toward Jack right now."

Hekka stood and tugged on his arm. "I know how to push those thoughts away. Cabin time."

The Crayles, having had their blissful moment terminated, stepped inside, sliding closed the door behind.

"Wait a minute. This is *our* room. Let's start over." As if for the first time, Hekka observed the queen-sized bed, as well as the motel painting above the headboard. Stepping through the sitting area, she drew the drapes. "Look, Magus. Jack was so thoughtful. A balcony. With two lounge chairs and a table for our drinks." She turned to see why there was no response. "Oh no!"

No Crayle.

She ran to the short hallway between the bedroom and the cabin door. She peered left, expecting to see him playing hide and seek in the seven-foot long, open closet.

Still, no Crayle.

To her right, she pulled open the bathroom door. A step up took her inside. What she saw stopped her in her tracks.

To her left, inside the tub, under the shower spray, stood her lost husband. Stark naked.

"I thought we'd freshen up," was all he had time to say.

She hopped over the edge of the tub. "You scared me." She pulled off her partially wet clothes. "You did it on purpose."

In the style of the French, he shrugged.

"And I'm going to teach you how we Serrano women exact revenge … in a hot shower."

• • •

As soon as Hekka finished her shower, she dried, dressed, and threw a "I'll be back shortly" over her shoulder. Before Crayle could respond, he heard the cabin door clunk shut. He decided to relax on the bed until she returned.

After forty-five minutes, Crayle turned into a worry wart. To no avail. He propped up on the bed when he heard the door reopen, reaching under his pillow just in case.

"You'll love my intel, Magus." She pressed through the heavily sprung door with a handful of papers. "I went down to the Captain's Circle desk and asked the helpful young woman about our Platinum status. Just four more cruises, and we'll be Elite. It takes everyone else fifteen."

"This is only our first cruise with Princess. Our man Jack has some pull."

"I love it already. We must take more cruises."

"Ditto on that idea." His interrogative nature took over. "So, what was she like, the one who helped you so much?"

"What? Are you planning to write a book?"

"You never can tell."

"The person there was like a little doll—red hair, red freckles. She put her palms to her cheeks every time she went to smile. Like this."

Hekka demonstrated. “It was cute. I asked about excursions and she said passengers usually book them in advance, but that one was still available. So, I took it.” She held two paper tickets aloft.

He squinted. “They say 7:30 A.M.”

“I’ll set the alarm for 5:30. Plenty of time for our morning exercise.”

He caught the look in her eye and knew she didn’t mean treadmills. “Yeah, the Love Boat stuff.”

“Then to a buffet breakfast at the Horizon Court, and then down to the pier. I already have stickers with our bus number on them. We’re to put them on our tee shirts.”

“Terrific. We finally get a vacation and we’re getting up at oh-dark-thirty.”

“She said you’d say that. All husbands say that. But only the first time.”

“To which wondrous places does this excursion take us?”

“She’s so smart. She knew you’d say that, too. She said I should make it a surprise.”

He laid back on the bed. “As long as I’m with you, it’ll be fabulous.”

She turned to reply, but too late. He’d fallen asleep.

• • •

The next morning, Crayle awoke to noises he didn’t recognize. It wasn’t his cruise enthusiast wife laying out clothes for their visit to the new port of call, Saint Lucia. Something else.

He rolled from the bed, brushed the floor-to-ceiling curtains aside, and stepped through the open sliding door onto the balcony to join Hekka. He appreciated that there were no shots fired or laser dots painted. The trade wind breeze blew fresh in their faces. Their first port, Castries, and the surrounding verdant hills with gingerbread dwellings pasted here and there, exceeded postcard beautiful.

In a quick seventy-five minutes, they showered, dressed, filled their stomachs, and, along with hundreds of other passengers, descended the railed metal gangway.

Hekka pointed to the number on their newly affixed labels. "We're in bus five." She scanned for a second. "There!"

As Crayle attempted to rub his eyes, she grabbed his hand and pulled him along. "They must've had a guide get sick. Ours is the Captain's Circle woman I told you about."

"I don't see her."

"She stepped out of sight. Probably answering questions for someone. She's really dedicated."

Their bus was smaller—better for the narrow two-lane roads—and only held twenty passengers. After a forty minute ride, they arrived at a summit where all were invited to step outside for the view.

Over the communication system, the tour guide pronounced the French name of the red-roofed town wedged into a valley below. *Soufrière*. She added that Napoleon's empress, Josephine, spent her early years there. Beyond the village, the tourists were treated to a view of Saint Lucia's two famous cone-shaped mountains, *Gros Piton* and *Petit Piton*. Notable to all, no soil showed. Every square inch of structure-free landscape bore shrubs and trees.

Seated last in the back of the bus, the Crayles took in the scenery until their turn. Just as they reached the doorway, it slammed shut. They spun toward their driver, shocked to see him wearing a gas mask.

What appeared to be thick smoke poured in through the air conditioning system. Crayle's last view was of the guide outside, handing out sealed envelopes to the other passengers.

• • •

They woke to a gentle shaking. When their eyes cleared, something else cleared as well. Standing before them was the Captain's Circle woman, the tour guide, and—when she smiled and revealed her dimples—Pattie Norbrunn.

"Hi, guys. Welcome to Saint Lucia. No need to stand, we're going to play a little game. Okay?"

Bound hand and foot to chairs, standing was not an option. As for a response to her question, gags prevented that.

"Sylvain will return in twenty minutes. He'll cut you free. What I'm going to do is take my little football ..." She picked up what was disguised as a large pineapple from a centerpiece on the table. "... and head out on the path outside. Left. If you can catch me, you can wrest it from my arms. Not much of a chance since I'm taking a head start. You don't have a lot of choices, do you?"

With that, the freckled redhead darted out the door whistling a tune titled *Catch Me If You Can*.

When Lalumière returned from his grocery shopping, the sight caught him by surprise. Magus Crayle and his wife bound to chairs. It took him a moment to spot a note stuck to the dining table via a butcher knife. He extracted the knife and read the message aloud.

"Don't kill them, darling. Cut them free so they can join my game. Oh, don't worry ... I have the bomb."

Before he could process further, Lalumière dropped the knife, fainted dead away, and crashed to the floor.

Blade down, the potential instrument of death missed the board flooring, wedging itself three inches deep in a crack.

Hekka attempted to rock her chair, but it was stuck between Crayle and a loveseat. He had better luck and landed between the Frenchman and the knife. Scooting sideways by sidewinder-like shifts of his body, he thrust his ropes against the embedded blade.

He freed himself within five minutes, withdrew the butcher knife, and stood over his immobile nemesis. He leaned down, grasping the weapon tighter.

"*Magus! She's got the bomb! Forget him!*"

No sooner had they left the cabin, Lenny and Alona arrived, wedged into an aged Suzuki Samurai. The P.I. had tracked them via Crayle's phone GPS.

"Where are Micmac and Phoebe?"

Lenny shook his head. "Don't know. All the fancy little trips—like the one you took—were booked. I think they went out on their own."

"How do you know they left the ship?"

"As you are aware, all stateroom cards are scanned when you board and leave. Jack gave me an app."

Alona jerked his phone away. "Give me a second, I'm still learning this spy shit. There. They left right after we docked."

"Your vehicle is too wide for Pattie's pathway. You two stay behind as a rear guard and provide the wherewithal for exfiltration. And while you're waiting, Lenny, call Jack. Give him a sitrep."

Lenny nodded acknowledgment. "Stay safe, you two."

Alona gave a deep sigh, wondering whether they'd see them again.

The Crayle's set out after Pattie. They knew they had the correct path since the diminutive spy's footprints showed in detail due to an early morning rain.

Hekka pulled her Smartphone from her cargo pants. "I have an app for trails. Let's see, Saint Lucia. Oh, I have to enable GPS. There." She showed him the high resolution display.

"The path splits just ahead. I see where she's going. Damn! If we approach her on her chosen path, she can escape the other way." He looked into her eyes. "Let's just go back. Let's not play. I don't want to split up, but that's what needs to be done."

Hekka withdrew her ten-inch blade. "Be careful." She took the left fork and headed downhill toward a beach.

CHAPTER 51

With all shore excursions sold out, Micmac and Phoebe had decided to try the island on their own. While she was in the shower, he'd received a message on his encrypted CIA link. He couldn't believe what he was reading. The credible threat to her life forced him to leave her in order to protect her.

The two processed ashore, strolling into the colorful and cheerful downtown aspect of Saint Lucia. There seemed to be enough smiles to go around for every tourist and local that happened by. It was as if the lives of these people never touched those of the uniformed military or the less visible ones who lived in the darkness. Micmac concluded that it was for the better. His mind snapped back to what he must do.

He left her at a Saint Lucia gift shop, promising that he'd be right back. After boarding transport by ultra-light as arranged by the sender, he climbed the treacherous dirt path that'd been loaded onto his phone's GPS. The former SEAL specialist, in excellent shape, found himself breathing hard.

"It's safe." A young pregnant-appearing woman wrapped in a charcoal coat stepped out of the shadows of a stand of banana trees.

He turned, ready to defend. A little of his wife's expertise had rubbed off. The woman wearing thick-soled boots not ten feet distant, measured an inch or so short of Phoebe. Her eyes—the same blue. Her hair—the same blonde. The southern accent was different.

"I don't believe we've been formally introduced, Mr. Micmac. At least, not that night at the Eiffel Tower. We were all a bit occupied at the time. My name is Pattie. And I brought what I promised. First, we take a walk."

At first, he was nearly struck down by the fact that he stood mere feet from the one person in the world that everyone on his side wanted dead. But Phoebe for Pattie wasn't even a remote consideration.

She smiled an inquisitive smile. "Y'all like my little note?"

He guessed how she'd gotten through the CIA's secure network. Beneath her cover in the Paris embassy, she'd set up travel for operatives. That linked her back to Langley and its communications systems. Easy enough for her to message an operative like himself via official covert channels, which she'd compromised.

The dirt path passed through a small clearing of wild grasses near, but not too near, cliffs. He heard the crashing sounds of a high waterfall and a surging river below.

"Did you tell anyone?"

"No. No one. Let's get this done." He pulled an envelope from inside his leather jacket. "It's the amount you specified."

She smiled. Wiping her forefinger across her lips, she pressed the lip gloss between his. He stepped back.

She turned and continued along the pathway. He caught up.

"What was that about?"

"I know about your wife. Strong. Loyal. Honorable. A tough nut to crack, as one might say." She withdrew a water bottle from a large khaki shoulder bag.

"May I have some?" he asked. "My mouth is dry."

"It's amazing, isn't it? We're on a Caribbean island, a bazillion gallons of water all around it …" She motioned. "… and the air is bone dry.

"It happens when the trade winds luff. It confines the warm air."

"Here." She handed the bottle to him. "It's brand new." She turned and walked out on a seldom-travelled rope-and-wood bridge that could have been constructed 100 years before.

As he followed, Micmac inspected the plastic bottle carefully, then violated the security seal and took several swigs.

She glanced around. "I chose this place because no one comes here even during the day. The cliffs are unstable and a number of people have fallen to their deaths, and so on."

He returned the bottle. "Your turn."

"Actually, no. My mouth is fine."

In the distance behind, he heard the ultra-light take off. He stumbled, falling to his knees. He reached for her, but his arms fell limply to his sides. He toppled onto the half-rotted boards.

"There, there, Mr. Micmac." Her accent gone, she removed her boots and knelt next to him. She stretched him out, but a safe distance away from the edge.

"You are unable to move, but can see, hear, and feel. You see, the water was tainted. A hypodermic. Listen to this. After I injected the drug, some leaked when I withdrew the needle. I tasted it." She pushed her finger through her pursed lips, then withdrew it. "Just that little bit, and for twenty minutes, I was where you are now. So I can sympathize with you."

She unfastened his trousers and pushed them to his ankles. Then his SEAL skivvies. "This will feel good. Hamid the Iranian general felt good, rest his soul. Did you know him? No?"

He couldn't speak.

"I hear the ultra-light on its way back here. Damn. I'd planned to go to work on you. I knew you'd feel my magic. It wouldn't have been personal. Just business," she said. "Your Phoebe is very dangerous. I need her gone so I devised this plan. I was going to dump your body in a convenient place. When you were found, the authorities would discover that you'd recently had sex. Phoebe would already be distraught, you know, from your death. Then they'd tell her you had sex just prior to expiring, and she'd know it wasn't her. At her moment of greatest weakness and distraction, I'd strike. So much for plans. I'm out of time, so I'm improvising. She's been told you're the one who needs saving. Well, I ran out of time for anything that fancy, so she's coming in on the same ultra-light."

Micmac was still, his head to the side, eyes on her.

"She'll still be vulnerable. But I promise you here and now, she won't suffer when she goes. There, that's my revised plan. What do you think? Oh, you can't answer. I told it to my significant other, and Sylvain said I'm crazy. But he always says that."

Pattie didn't linger to view her handiwork. She packed the bottle and envelope to prepare for next the scene. Careful not to dislodge the football attached at her waist, she'd removed the blonde wig and blue contacts. After sliding a pair of flats onto her feet, she looked her normal 5'3" with short brown hair and a beret.

She was already considering an encounter with a weakened Phoebe. Sex and dead. Or just dead. She smiled her dimpled smile.

She sat back, her arms extended behind for balance and leverage. Utilizing her sprinter's legs, she pushed him toward the edge. "I'd love to chat some more, but I have another appointment." Scooting forward, she gave him a final nudge.

There was no scream, no yell, just a long silence punctuated with a splash.

CHAPTER 52

A mere twenty minutes after Micmac had left Phoebe, she received a very different message than had he. He'd made arrangements for a fabulous—and private—picnic getaway. "Let's have some fun … and a little mystery. You'll be given provisions and further directions by your pilot, so just bring them along. See you soon. Love, Micmac."

Over an encrypted CIA link, no less. She carried her broad smile all the way to the lift-off pad. "Let's go," she hollered over the engine noise as she buckled herself in.

Flown to the same remote clearing, Phoebe whistled along the path, carrying lunch in a ballistic nylon bag and feeling good. Rather than claustrophobic, the lush foliage that pushed in on each side comforted her. Pressing her pocket to feel Micmac's electronic note safely tucked away, she smiled at his notion of a romantic rendezvous.

As she neared the rope and wood slat bridge, she heard a scuffle.

She dropped the food and ran, arming herself as she did. Just as she cleared the greenery, she saw Pattie halfway across, thrusting something over the side. Micmac.

In a last glance, he spotted Phoebe. Unable to speak, he couldn't warn her.

Due to her effort with the taller, heftier man, the bomb Pattie'd secured around her waist to appear pregnant fell and bounced along the half-rotted slats to a stop five feet away.

Phoebe ran to the edge of the bridge's landing. Through the intrusions of the jungle into her sight-line, she saw him splash into the roil of water at the base of the falls. He disappeared.

"Oh!" she cried out. "No!" Her lips pursed out to their maximum, sucking in a quantum of humid jungle air. She turned to the perpetrator. "You!"

Pattie started after the football, lodged between broken cross boards.

Phoebe screamed at her. "Don't move!"

Pattie froze.

"Don't shoot her!" came a cry from the opposite end. Crayle had just arrived on the scene. "Her fall could dislodge the bomb!"

Phoebe glanced back and forth. At Pattie. At the aquatic tumult below.

Crayle seized the moment. He half-ran toward Pattie.

Spinning toward the Agent, Pattie seized the football, pulling it up to her forehead. "I know you," she yelled to Phoebe over the waterfall din. "Annie Oakley, the FBI calls you. It has to be one shot between the eyes, doesn't it? It's even in your profile."

Phoebe, who'd just lost her husband and lover for life, stood dazed, grasping for meaning.

"To get to me, you have to shoot through the bomb." She laughed like the crazed winner of a chess match.

Phoebe stepped onto the bridge. Crayle stepped onto the other end.

Their motion induced a wobble.

The constructors of the antiquated bridge had utilized the materials of the time, rope and wood, to fabricate a hand rail and foot path across the 100-foot chasm. The boards had splintered and rotted with age. One had to grab the rope railings on either side and watch every step. No allowances had been made for operatives trying to manage handguns and bombs.

"I can set this off," Pattie teased. "Ha, ha."

"You killed him," Phoebe said. She glanced past the little psychopath to Crayle. "She killed him, Magus."

"Ha, ha, ha." Pattie grinned. "You don't want to live …" She jerked her head toward Crayle. "… but he does. Have you been to bed with Mr. Crayle?" She paused, turning her head to one side. "You have. Dear me. Ha, ha, ha."

Phoebe raised her Glock. As soon as she acquired a sightline, her team's nemesis ducked back behind the football.

Surprising everyone, Pattie spun. She tucked the ball under her arm like a running back, and ran directly at Crayle.

The move caught him by surprise. His CIA operative self re-established. It suppressed any analysis. *He* ran at *her*.

The bridge began to swing wildly, buck like a bull, and creak like an over-employed wedding bed.

Her element of surprise having disappeared, a confused Pattie reversed toward the Agent.

Phoebe's line-of-sight placed Crayle in line with her target. She might risk taking both of them out. Still, she aimed.

By instinct, Pattie ducked to the side, hoping Phoebe would fire and hit Crayle. She misjudged.

Phoebe threw herself left into the rope. Her feet slipped from the foot boards.

Pattie saw her enemy hook her left arm over the rope. It was all that saved her from the same fate as Micmac.

Her free gun hand was all that Phoebe required.

The .45 caliber Glock boomed.

Crayle launched, full tilt.

Pattie hit the safety rope. Old and tattered, and nicked by the Glock round, it snapped.

The diminutive spy grasped a flailing end with her hand. Under her other arm, the ball.

As Crayle reached her, she looked up. “Here,” she smiled. She tossed it.

He stumbled on the rocking bridge, but retained his footing. Like a receiver in a national championship game, he snatched the five megaton device with one hand and tucked it in.

He had it. The final bomb. Something caused him to want to thank her. He turned.

She smiled, dimples deployed. “Hell is warm this time of year.” She laughed as a tear escaped her eye.

Crayle grabbed for her as she released the rope.

Phoebe had collected herself back onto the bridge. She arrived just as Pattie Norbrunn, along with all of her personalities, took the long fall.

“Bye, Magus!” echoed from the granite surrounds.

CHAPTER 53

Even though the bridge was in tatters, the oscillations stabilized. It took Crayle a moment to gather some calm. He made his way to Phoebe very slowly, very carefully. When he reached her, she was close to catatonic. He knew he had to take the lead and get her to a safe place. Micmac would have wanted that. He knelt next to her and placed his arm on hers.

"C'mon, Phoebe. We have to go that way." He nodded toward the far end of the bridge.

"Our car … is back that way." She pointed in the opposite direction, as she continued to stare down into the foaming, deadly liquid.

Crayle placed his hand on her shoulder. "C'mon. The river runs from the falls that way. Right now, it's best if you trust me."

"Yes, Magus. His body—" She broke into tears. Not her usual controlled effluence. Body-wracking tears.

Clutching the football under his left arm, he wrapped the other around her, drawing her close.

A minute passed before she pulled from him, and wiped away the wetness on her cheeks with her thumbs. “We need to go.” She still held her Glock and waved it to emphasize her words.

“I will take point. Any danger will come from behind.”

“I’ll cover our six. That’s my dad’s Air Force speak for—”

“I know.”

Gingerly, he stepped forward.

Ever scanning, she watched both front and rear, as well as the treacherous footing.

They approached the end of the bridge as Hekka stepped out from a stand of trees and bushes.

“I don’t want to take a chance dropping this or falling through with it. Hekka, catch.”

His wife, who had been covering the hill’s ascent side, received his throw. Even without the ball, it was still a struggle for Crayle and Phoebe to get off of the bridge.

He retrieved the football. “The news is bad. We lost Micmac.”

Hekka glanced at Phoebe’s grief-stricken countenance. “Oh, my God!”

“Pattie, too. C’mon. It’s best we leave this place.”

Additional words were unnecessary and inappropriate. He’d save the full sitrep for later.

With his trailblazer wife leading the way, the three proceeded along a brief path through trees and dense foliage, and then downhill, retracing Hekka’s ascent. They merged with the waterfall’s stream as it exited its rock-strewn bed and smoothed out toward the wide sand beach.

“We’ll take a break here, then follow it down.”

“When we find him, then what?”

“If I can find a satellite, I’ll call in an exfil to Jack. An extraction. We’ll take him home.”

Although her face was blank, tears meandered their way down her cheeks. “Never leave a man behind. He always said that.”

• • •

Two children, ages four and seven, ran along the beach. They waved with glee as they passed a lone lifeguard, replete in a bright red Speedo. With access only possible at low tide, their mother never missed an opportunity to let them stretch out a bit. Whenever they'd extend approximately fifty feet distant, she'd break into a run. They'd spot her, giggle, and take off again, knowing she'd catch them every time.

They were close to the limit now. She smiled and started after them. She stopped.

They'd stopped, too. They stood over what appeared at a distance to be a beached seal. It wasn't. She broke into a sprint. As she drew closer, she recognized the body of a man.

"Mommy!" her daughter screamed. Her younger brother began to cry.

The woman reached them seconds later. When not on vacation, she worked at a large hospital complex in eastern Ohio. For seven years now, she'd served as an ER nurse. She'd seen trauma before. The man's head bore a nasty gash. The waves had pushed his blood-spattered pants, still unbuckled, up to his waist.

She reached inside a black neoprene collar and tested his neck. "Kids!" She pointed down the beach. "Run to the lifeguard!" She began CPR. "Tell him! *He's alive!*"

• • •

A short time later, Phoebe stood with the Crayle's, the three still staring over the jungle foliage and out to sea. What to do with a crumbled world was just one of many questions. Finally, she felt she could utter a couple of sentences without breaking down. "You know what? Certainty is long gone right now, but I'm certain of one thing. I will love him forever."

"Hey!" came from behind. "You talking about me?"

Phoebe jumped. She spun toward the sound.

There, fifteen feet away, he stood, looking like the cat that swallowed the canary. "Aren't you going to say hi?"

Crayle couldn't believe his eyes. His lips could only form one word. "Micmac."

The man looked like a train wreck. Blood and gashes everywhere.

Though the landscape was rocky and uneven, Phoebe ran to him.

"It was my new device." He tugged at the neoprene material hanging around his neck. "It inflates when it touches water." He grinned.

Phoebe arrived and delivered a left hook into his right shoulder.

"Ow!" he grimaced. "I whacked that shoulder on a boulder."

She took one step sideways. Her right hook caught the other shoulder flush. "You … you …"

As she took a step back to her left, Crayle set the nuclear football on level ground and ran to them. Before Phoebe could deliver another blow, he grabbed her jacket, just below her neck. He grabbed the back of Micmac's flotation invention, and shoved their mouths together.

Their lips met with a force like that of the waterfall thundering in the background.

Crayle smiled at his intervention. He turned to speak.

Hekka was inches from him. She replicated the other two. Instead of extreme prejudice—the spy-warrior credo—they embraced with extreme passion. They couldn't hear Phoebe's words behind them.

"Why didn't you tell me you had this?"

Thump.

"Ow!"

An alarm sounded. Hekka pulled away and checked her wrist phone. "Everyone! Our excursion is nearly over! Back to the ship!"

CHAPTER 54

With all the violence apparently complete, Jack arrived in Saint Lucia. It was no less than the ship's captain who greeted him as he boarded the Royal Princess. It seemed the parent company of Princess Cruises was the same as that of Cunard, owner of the Queen Mary 2. Jack, the titular leader of the team that had saved the QM2, regretfully declined the royal treatment planned as a thank you.

He located two of the three couples and wished the MacKays and Lipschitzes an *enjoy the cruise*. That accomplished, he extricated Crayle and Hekka and transported them to the local airport where he packed them into his new Falcon 8X. His "Next stop, Helsinki" was all they needed to hear. He skipped his normal "Rock and Roll!" expletive—this was not going to be an operation. Just a reuniting of Hekka with her mother followed by a coming home.

After an uneventful and sleep-filled flight, the Crayle's deplaned at the Finnish capital's airport and waved back at Jack and Flori as they headed for their pre-arranged transfer vehicle. The unseasonal fifty degree weather felt good. Minutes later, their driver dropped them off at the harbor. Near the same outdoor restaurant where they'd both been kidnapped thirty days before.

"It looks the same as I remember it."

"There will be no kidnaps this time."

"Do we risk taking the same seats?"

"My two memory restores from Rorschach didn't include superstitions."

"Same seats, then."

Crayle considered their last time in these seats. "Just in case … I love you, Hekka Crayle."

"I love you back, MC."

"How about we leave Lenny-isms like first and last initials back in Big Bear?"

Her smile was not relaxed. "You were the one who discussed this with Jack. When does our contact arrive, and how will we know her?"

"Look for a blonde, he said."

"Without dimples?"

"Definitely without dimples."

"Magus, I see perhaps one hundred people from our position. Most of them are blonde."

"Not to worry. Jack said she's 5'10". When she comes close, my Vestige chip monitor ear buds will chirp."

"Micmac?"

Crayle nodded.

"By now, Lenny and Alona are home. Jack and Flori are home. Micmac and Phoebe, too. Do you think I'm being selfish?"

Before Crayle could answer, his ear pieces generated the sound of a crow. "Some chirp."

A woman sporting the requisite hair coaxed her wheelchair next to him.

"Are you five-foot-ten?" Hekka asked.

"I am 1.78 meters. So, yes to your question. I know you are anxious. I won't waste your time. I have located a woman fitting the photograph supplied to me."

Hekka leaned in. "I must be sure."

The blonde extracted a Q-tip from her pocket. "Provide a sample of your DNA, please."

"I can't wait a week or two for a DNA match. I just can't," Hekka pleaded.

"Here. Open your mouth. I'll do it."

Crayle took the item from the woman and handed it to his wife. "It's best if you do it."

After Hekka completed the swabbing of her inner cheek, her eyes, like her mind, defocused.

The blonde retrieved the sample and pushed it into a tube. She surprised them by reversing the tube to reveal a second Q-tip, already inserted.

Hekka caught her breath. "That's from the woman you located? My mother?" She fought back the tears. She fought the possibility there would be no match. She fought the other possibility, that there would. She summoned the strength of her deceased father.

Time appeared to stop as the blonde held up the tube and shook the clear liquid inside. Chemically, it subtracted one DNA from the other. "Green is good," she advised.

They waited

Nothing.

There was no change.

"No!"

"It takes two minutes." The blonde started a timer on her watch. She held it out, drawing their focus.

Two of the three held their breaths.

"Green!" yelled Hekka. Quickly, she covered her mouth. When she removed her hand, she said in a whisper, "Green." She squeezed Crayle's hand. "It's green."

Crayle turned to the blonde. "Where do we find her?"

"Not far. On an island." The blonde stood.

Hekka rose from her seat. "We must leave now."

"I can't advise that. It's their rest period."

Hekka appeared stupefied. "Rest? They?"

The blonde reconsidered. "If we have to wait, it will be best to wait there. We go. You will see. Come. We go by boat."

She led them to a quay and to a mahogany runabout. While passersby were captivated by Hekka's beauty, they noticed that her emotions strained their limits. Her appearance and demeanor were so unlike that of the Finns. And the woman Crayle felt he knew so well.

The blonde stood from the wheelchair. "Here. Fold my chair and bring it with you as you step aboard."

The non-plussed Crayles folded the chair and boarded.

Without any explanation of the deception, the blonde untied the lines, hopped in, and powered the boat away from the dock.

The two passengers, nearly thrown to the deck, scooted themselves into bucket seats.

Clearing the Helsinki breakwater, the blonde accelerated to full power.

Hekka took her mind elsewhere. "The thrust of this boat. It's as if Micmac …" Her attempt failed. She leaned forward, as if to find her lost mother through the mist ahead.

Five minutes later, the blonde tied their boat to an aluminum dock. There was but a single structure on the small island. The remainder consisted of trees, grassy yards separated by wooden walkways, and a rocky surround.

A lone gravel path led the trio to an iron-studded and hinged door.

Hekka balked.

A small security aperture opened and an eye peered out.

"For Häkkinen," said the blonde.

The door creaked open. They stepped inside.

Hekka scanned the large room before them. There were women her mother's age throughout. On couches, chairs, wheelchairs, standing—a kaleidoscope of aged femininity. She felt weak. Light-headed.

"Close your eyes," Crayle said.

She did. She could only hear them now. Her dizziness abated.

Slowly, she opened her eyes once more. "Which one is she? I don't recognize any of them. I don't see her."

Anxiety enveloped the most steadfast woman in Crayle's memory. He stepped behind her, grasping her shoulders. He shared with her his own strength.

He cares deeply, she thought. Now, he's *my* rock. A smile found a way to her lips.

"She's outside," said the blonde. "She takes in the same view every day at this time." She whispered to the matron who'd admitted them. She nodded in response.

"That is good news. Please, follow me."

In less than a minute, they'd crossed the room and transited through French doors to an outdoor lawn, defined on three sides by a short, stone wall. Sitting there, under a hundred-year-old shade tree, was the woman in question. She faced away from them, staring across the edge of the Gulf of Finland at a small village.

Hekka turned to the blonde. "What is the name of that village?" she whispered.

"Oh. She always does this, I'm told." She pronounced a town's name.

It sounded to Hekka like the one that was printed on her own birth certificate, after her mother's name. She dropped Crayle's hand, and ran, nearly stumbled, over the uneven ground. She reached the wall. She stopped short.

Her courage was still intact. She knew it. Somewhere.

"Mother?"

She waited.

The blonde had moved close behind. "They found this woman in a street. There had been an accident. A taxi had hit her. Very hard. At the airport. A thief had grabbed her purse. She gave chase. That's when she was struck. They saved her, but her memory was lost. And without identification, they brought her here."

Hekka took a step closer. She turned and sat next to the lady.

The woman showed no acknowledgment of her presence. She only stared across the bay.

"Mother. It's me. It's Hekka." She started to cry. "Your daughter." A trickle became a torrent.

Crayle sat beside her. "We'll take her back with us. If the government here hassles us, Jack will help. Beyond that, we've got the president."

Hekka looked up at him. "Yes, Magus. Thank you."

"We won't quit there. We'll get her back for you. I know just who is going to help, too."

"Mother?" Hekka repeated. She wrapped an arm around the woman's shoulder, pulling her close. She waited … and watched.

Crayle whispered. "Try her given name."

"*Vilhelmiina?*"

There was no response.

Hekka turned to him with the most saddened look he'd ever seen. Then, a spark of light shone in her eyes.

"Wait! Father called her by her short name." She turned back to her mother, pressing closer. "*Helmi?*"

The response from the woman, more than before, was still very Finnish. Minimal. A single tear.

EPILOGUE

In Southern California's mountainous Big Bear Valley, the sun had moved past its apex several hours earlier. With the advent of daylight savings time in March, plenty of time remained before the darkness would only be disrupted by a wolf moon. The eastern Santa Ana breezes had left a haze west of the ranch that those experienced in such things knew would produce a remarkable sunset. And just before that, the sparkling water diamonds on the lake.

Hekka's mother had been taken to the Quarry hospital. Doctor Rorschach would see to her medical needs. Based on the doctor's experiences with Crayle, special attention would be given to the restoration of her memory.

"At last, we have our own home," Hekka announced. She set the hot meal on the rough timber dining table in front of her husband.

He smiled at both the aroma and the sight of one of his favorites—mashed potatoes, gravy, meat loaf. "You are so right. Living at Jack's safe house felt temporary. When will you teach me to train quarter horses so I can be useful?"

"As soon as you master a woman's touch."

He took a bite of the meatloaf and produced a transported-to-heaven expression.

"Now that your Chin has his empire and you will be providing his new strategic plan, there will be no more bombs, no more deaths, and no need for us to go anywhere but our beautiful valley."

"And Lalumière, without Pattie or Jean-Marc or bombs, is done."

"Roger that."

Playfully, he frowned at her use of a Micmac sailor-ism. "What about those cruises you wanted to take?"

"Yes, but with the following exceptions. No Patties as guides. Deal?"

"Deal."

"Amen to that. When we next see Phoebe and Micmac, Lenny and Alona, and Flori and Jack, it will be for barbeque. No more ops."

"I'm not sure I want to see him again."

She started to look down at her food. To be silent during a man's emotional moment. But that was Hekka before she'd met Crayle. "Jack?"

"Yes."

"I understand. There's healing to accomplish. Fortunately, as Serrano, I'm an expert on healing. For all of us."

They finished the entrée, and she stepped back into the kitchen. The sound of her old-fashioned coffee pot drowned out the buzz of Crayle's phone. He checked the display. "I'll be back in a second," he shouted.

She smiled, fishing homemade cheesecake from the fridge. She poured coffee and served the dessert. She sat. She watched. She jumped to her feet and was through the door in a flash.

His car. Gone.

"*No!*"

Her eyes swept the area. The father-made waterfall where they'd first consummated their unity. Unexplained silence.

"*No!*"

"Boo!" He stood behind her.

She turned, ready to enact Serrano justice. He pulled her tight to him. As if to draw her inside—to make them one.

• • •

And it all would have ended peacefully if just three days before, a body hadn't washed up on a stone-bedded river bank of the Caribbean island, Saint Lucia. Not far from a high, wood and rope bridge. And if a dedicated physician, keeping his promise to protect the Crayle team, hadn't followed a beacon from a device embedded in that body. A device called Vestige. And if the doctor's companion, a tall, strong man with a Gallic nose, hadn't rescued the young woman. And if they hadn't saved her life.

• • •

In two days, Doctor Rorschach pronounced the patient out of danger, excused himself, and departed back to his realm beneath the landscape of Southern California. He'd left instructions for her to rest for at least six weeks, but no sooner has he left than she popped out of bed, grabbed Lalumière by the hand, and led him to an open space embedded in the dense jungle. He stared at the apparatus before him in disbelief.

"Would you like to go to Montserrat?"

"To once again sit in a one-room shack atop those pillars of sandstone … pretending to be a religious hermit … waiting to be discovered?"

"No one was going to discover you there. I heard that the Spanish authorities use that place for witness relocation. You know, when the witness doesn't come through."

"It would be perfect for that purpose, but not for me."

"Not a problem. I was referring to a different Montserrat. It's a deserted island of the same name just west of here. We would be at peace to rest and to scheme."

"Deserted? In the Caribbean? Why does no one live there?"

"There's just one minor problem."

"With you, problems are never minor."

A few moments of silence passed.

Sylvain Lalumière grew frustrated. "What *is* the problem?"

"Well, it seems there's this volcano. But they don't expect it to erupt again …" She glanced at her watch.

"Sometimes I am afraid. I fear that your mind is beyond rescue."

She turned up the burner on the hot air balloon. "The breeze is coming from the west. We will rise up into its stream. I have made up our minds. We are going home … to France."

Lalumière, desperate to save his own life, jumped up to stop her from releasing the ground tethers.

She spun into him, thrusting a hypodermic into his arm.

The fluid inside was fast. He fell back into the basket.

"By the time you awaken, we'll be setting down in our country. This time, we won't leave until we have our rightful crowns and have restored the monarchy. How's that?"

Before his eyes closed, he wondered if she could pull it off. From the Caribbean. Across the Atlantic. To France.

"No one would suspect a balloon."

The End

ABOUT THE AUTHOR

Committed to international affairs, political intrigue and espionage, novelist Dennis Bowen has researched his stories in more than 60 countries. That Bowen engenders realism and spice in his thrillers due to his wartime service, and his defense and intelligence community background, led one reader to remark, "Bowen knows his stuff." *The Redrock Quarantine* follows *The Water Diamonds*, T*he Blackstone Perfection*, and *The Crystal Seduction* as Book 4 in his International Thriller Series. When not traveling the globe to research his next book, he resides on the Southern California coast.

Twitter: http://www.twitter.com/DBowenThrillers/
Facebook: http://www.facebook.com/DennisBowenThrillers
Website: http://www.dennisbowen.com/

THE
FINAL MASQUERADE

BOOK 5:
INTERNATIONAL THRILLER SERIES

Available: Summer 2016

CHAPTER 1

There was no doubt whatsoever in Magus Crayle's mind that the man standing across the bedroom from him was the Roman Catholic pope. Though the man's white vestments appeared soiled and tattered, he recognized Zoran on sight. Next to him, another man he knew only too well. The Elder, known outside his Illuminé secret society frame of reference as the Prince of Monaco, spoke.

"Remember my words to you, Mr. Crayle? You are, in actuality, three men. The first, a cold-blooded CIA assassin." He handed a device to the pope. "Here, Zoran. You do the honors."

Before Crayle could react, the pope pressed '1' and allowed a sneer to replace his normally pleasant, holy countenance.

With a snap of his head, the man with three lives rose from his bed, extracting a SIG-Sauer .40 caliber from under his pillow as he did.

"Give him his orders, Zoran."

The pope produced one mere sentence, which he followed with a sign of the cross.

Crayle walked from the bedroom toward the kitchen. A beautiful woman stood at a stove preparing what smelled like eggs, ham, and hash browns. She turned just in time to see her husband point the weapon.

The two reports rebounded off the ranch house's flat surfaces like the mini-explosives that they were.

Boom!

Boom!

The impact on her chest flung her back against the frying pan handle splattering food across adjacent walls.

Red fluid spurted from the wounds, decorating his clothing and his face in a deathly pattern.

One glimpse of her vacant eyes was all he received as her lifeless corpse fell forward onto the hundred-year-old floor.

For a moment, Crayle the assassin couldn't process what he'd done. What he'd been caused to do. He dropped the weapon, and scooped up the woman he'd declared the love of his life more than once.

It was dark and cold as he carried her into the back yard, laying her next to the waterfall built by her father. Next to his grave.

The Elder and the pope watched with interest.

Crayle prepared a new grave in the fashion of her Serrano Indian traditions, and laid her to rest.

"You can see now, Zoran, that his programming is complete. We can choose the assassin, the genius strategist, or the third Crayle. However, should we choose number three, he would come after us for a final time. Final for us. For obvious reasons, we must take care not to press the three on this device.

The original Crayle had been reprogrammed to remove compassion and caring by a crew of devious psychiatric researchers at Central Intelligence. That had facilitated Crayle Two to develop strategies utilizing minimized, tactical nuclear weapons that had killed tens of thousands of innocent victims in Marseille, Ürümqi, Beijing, and in Central Iran.

The two men re-entered the ranch house and exited by the front door.

Crayle could hardly hear their vehicle depart as he squatted on his shins, hands on thighs, staring at the fresh gravesite. The one they'd caused him to create.

• • •

The devastating tranquility of the moment was not to last.

"Okay! Alright! Lock and load!" The voice of Lenny Lipschitz caused sweat-drenched Crayle to sit bolt upright in his bed. Prepared to defend.

Seeing there was no need, he rubbed the muck from his eyes, as if in preparation to fire laser-like death ray beams through the private investigator's head.

"Breakfast is on! Follow me!" Lenny spun on his heel and marched himself outside to a waiting table.

As the beleaguered spy stumbled from under the covers and through the living room, he caught a glimpse that caused his heart to skip. Stepping from the kitchen with two plates full of eggs, ham, and hash browns, was the woman he'd just slaughtered.

No red holes on her chest. Nothing but her butterscotch-hued skin and minimal Serrano smile.

"Have a good sleep, Magus?" she asked as she passed before him. "Better close that gaping mouth. It's early September, but there are still flying insects about."

He realized his mouth hung full open and shut it.

"Might want to put on some clothes, too."

Summer 2016

THE FINAL MASQUERADE

From International Thriller Writer
DENNIS BOWEN

www.ingramcontent.com/pod-product-compliance
Lightning Source LLC
Chambersburg PA
CBHW020258030826
48979CB00026B/1394/J

* 9 7 8 0 9 9 6 0 4 1 2 5 6 *